MEDLAR LUCAN & DURIAN GRAY

4   811
HALF
PRICE BOOKS

D0104115

THE
DECADENT
GARDENER

Edited by Alex Martin & Jerome Fletcher
with
Engravings and drawings by François Houtin

DEDALUS

*Dedalus would like to thank the Eastern Arts Board
for its assistance in producing this book.*

Published by Dedalus Ltd., Langford Lodge, Sawtry, Cambs, PE17 5XE.

ISBN 1 873982 82 8

Distributed in Australia & New Zealand by Peribo Pty Ltd,
58 Beaumont Road, Mount Kuring-gai, N.S.W. 2080.

Distributed in Canada by Marginal Distribution,
Unit 102, 277 George Street North, Peterborough, Ontario KJ9 3G9.

Distributed in the U.S. by Subterranean,
PO Box 160, 265 South Fifth Street, Monroe, Oregon 97456.

First published by Dedalus in 1996.
Copyright © Alex Martin and Jerome Fletcher 1996.

The right of Alex Martin & Jerome Fletcher to be identified as the authors of this work has been
asserted by them in accordance with the Copyright, Designs and Patent Act, 1988.

The book has been designed and typeset by David Bird.
Printed in Finland by Wsoy.

This book is sold subject to the condition that it shall not, by way of trade or otherwise, be lent,
resold, hired out, or otherwise circulated without the publisher's prior consent in any form of
binding or cover other than that in which it is published and without a similar condition
including this condition being imposed on the subsequent purchaser.

A C.I.P. listing for this title is available on request.

TABLE OF CONTENTS

INTRODUCTION

In October 1995, we were approached by Dedalus and offered the chance to edit more of the writings of Durian Gray and Medlar Lucan. We were not only delighted by the offer, but also curious to know what Gray and Lucan had been up to since the closure of their infamous restaurant in January '94. After their sudden departure from Edinburgh, they had completely vanished. Of course, rumours of their whereabouts abounded - they had been spotted in Samarkand, in Fez, in Cartagena - each location mentioned more exotic than the last. So it came as something of a surprise when a confirmed sighting of the two fugitives was made on the south west coast of Ireland. It seemed a most unlikely destination for such inveterate urbanites and there was general concern as to whether their delicate health would survive exposure to all that clean air and the rigours of country living.

These fears were allayed by the news that Gray and Lucan were guests of Mrs Conchita Gordon at her country seat, Mountcullen. This splendid woman had been a regular and welcome guest at the Edinburgh restaurant. On one occasion, she hired a *cabinet particulier* to entertain a down-and-out who had stopped her in the street and asked for the price of a cup of tea. It was an act of generosity from which the poor man never recovered. Gray and Lucan were clearly in good hands and a stay at Mountcullen might allow them to rest and recuperate.

By what proved to be a happy coincidence, they arrived at a time when Mrs Gordon was thinking of redesigning the gardens which surrounded her house. Whether in a moment of madness or inspiration it is difficult to say, but she made up her mind that her two guests would be ideally suited to this task. A project like this would help them put their recent disappointments behind them, and " After all," Mrs Gordon argued,"if one can design a menu, one can design a garden".

Mountcullen, which had recently been acquired by Conchita Gordon, is a well-proportioned Georgian house in Co. Cork. It stands squarely in eighteen acres of gardens and woods. From the front of the house, one looks out across a broad expanse of parkland and mature trees towards the waters of Lough Doon in the distance. Offshore lies a small island which forms part of the estate. The back of the house is protected by a ring of thickly-wooded hills at the foot of which flows the river Cull. It describes a graceful curve through the grounds before debouching into the lake about a mile to the south-east of the house.

The climate in this part of the country is very mild - mild enough to support certain varieties of exotic plants - and the soil is rich and fertile, ideally suited to creating gardens. Immediately around the house were a series of formal gardens, orchards, walled kitchen gardens and greenhouses. Beyond these a sort of park had been laid out. All had been neglected for many years and one of the great attractions of the estate for Mrs Gordon was its air of romantic melancholy. Lucan and Gray's ambitions for the grounds would soon change all that.

It took very little to persuade them to undertake the task of redesigning the gardens. Unencumbered by doubts or experience, they set about the project with their usual *élan*. Many hours were spent in the library at Mountcullen and in Dublin, immersing themselves in the history of garden design, poring over vast horticultural tomes, poking around in the rich compost of garden history. Conchita Gordon saw little of her guests during this period. They became secretive and obsessed, and began communicating with their patroness by pushing notes under the locked door of the library. After six months or so without tangible results, however, the gracious hostess was becoming impatient. She wanted a full progress report at once.

The two designers began by explaining their overall conception for the new gardens. According to Mrs Gordon, they had become intrigued by the figure of Bernard Palissy, a 16th century French ceramicist and staunch Protestant. Monsieur Palissy was a man at odds with his times. He saw himself living in a world ruled by folly. He played the role of a second John the Baptist, railing against decadence, greed and corruption. His aim was to use whatever weapons were at his disposal in the fight against depravity, and one project he considered was the building of a garden - a garden which would be entirely devoted to the

Durian Gray and Medlar Lucan photographed in the Library at Mountcullen, posing as James Joyce and Augustus John.

celebration of wisdom.

Palissy's Garden of Wisdom was to be made up of eight different areas. In each of these areas, the visitor would find tranquillity and repose. Edifying texts from Proverbs or Ecclesiastes would be carved into stone tablets or formed from cut branches. At the very heart of the garden a pavilion would stand, bearing the words of warning: 'Cursed be those who reject Wisdom.' At the four corners of the garden would stand rustic cabinets. These would be constructed on a brick frame over which would be placed 'large pieces of rock uncut and unpolished so that the exterior of the said cabinet would in no way have the appearance of a building.' Herbs and shrubs would be planted on top and water made to trickle down the outside as if springing from the rock itself. Inside the cabinet was a furnace in which would be smelted the enamels used to line the walls. Hence, like a shell, the cabinets would be rough on the outside and smooth and multi-coloured on the inside.

Unfortunately, only verbal descriptions of the garden are available. No exact plans exist. This was deliberate on Palissy's part. Only the initiated few would be allowed access, so to speak, to his garden of Wisdom

Mrs Gordon was not at all sure what the connection was between this pious, Protestant craftsman and the former proprietors of *The Decadent* restaurant. So Lucan and Gray went on to explain that here was a clear case of the attraction of opposites. Their intention was to take Palissy's idea of the Garden of Wisdom and turn it on its head. Their Grand Design was to remodel the estate at Mountcullen as a celebration of Decadence and Folly. Where Monsieur Palissy had engaged in an intimate and respectful dialogue with Nature, they would be roundly abusing her. They saw her as the enemy. The goddess had to be vanquished, enslaved, placed in bondage. The Artificial is what they venerated. Whereas Palissy's style would countenance no antique statues, grotesque sculptures, low reliefs of satirical or pastoral subjects from pagan fables, Gray and Lucan's style consisted of little else. Palissy laid great stress on reason and order in his garden. In their designs, Gray and Lucan sought to represent the excessive and the irrational. The 'land-lady' whole-heartedly approved of the conception thus far, but she wanted a little more flesh on the bones.

Having described the historical model for the Mountcullen garden, Gray and Lucan now specified the different areas into which the Decadent garden would be divided. They had come up with the following:

- The Sacred, or 'Blasphemous', Garden
- The Garden of Venus
- The Cruel Garden

- The Water Garden
- The Garden of Histrion
- The *Paradis artificel*
- The Synthetic Garden
- The Garden of Oblivion
- The Fatal Garden
- Gardens of the Mind

At this point, Mrs Gordon announced that she was both very excited by the whole scheme and that she was off to Kashmir for the summer. She looked forward to seeing some significant developments on her return.

During her absence, Gray and Lucan set about realising their ideas. Not that this entailed them actually getting their hands dirty. Perish the thought! At Mountcullen, there was a small army of gardeners, estate workers, and contractors to do that - all of them supervised by Mrs Gordon's factotum, Ryan, who worked closely with the two designers.

When it comes to defining Gray and Lucan's approach to gardening, one word which immediately springs to mind is 'Robertsonian'. This adjective was coined by Medlar Lucan in honour of the Irish garden designer, Daniel Robertson. In 1843 he was commissioned by Lord Powerscourt to remodel the terraces at Powerscourt, Co. Wicklow. He took his inspiration from the Villa Butera in Sicily - among other things. This is what his employer wrote of Daniel Robertson's style of gardening:

He was much given to the drink and was never able to design or draw so well as when his brain was excited by sherry. He suffered from gout and used to be wheeled out onto the terrace in a wheel-barrow, with a bottle of sherry, and as long as that lasted he was able to design and direct the workmen, but when the sherry was finished he collapsed and was incapable of working till the drunken fit evaporated.

Another gardener upon whom Gray and Lucan modelled themselves was William Beckford. An insight into his approach was provided by one H. Bennett, Esq. in the following passage:

It appears that Mr Beckford pursued the objects of his wishes, whatever they were, not coolly, but with all the enthusiasm of passion. No sooner did he decide upon any point than he had it carried into immediate execution, whatever might be the cost.

In confirmation of our idea that Mr Beckford's enjoyments consisted of a succession of violent impulses, we may mention that, when he wished a new walk to be cut in the woods, or any work of that kind to be done, he used to say nothing about it in the way of preparation, but merely gave orders, perhaps late in the afternoon, that it should be cleared out and in a perfect state by the following morning at the time he came out to take his morning ride. The whole strength of the village (of Hindon) was then put into requisition, and employed during the night; and the next day, when Mr Beckford came to inspect what was done, he used to give a £5 or a £10 note to the men who had been employed to drink, besides, of course, paying their wages, which were always liberal.

... We admire in Mr Beckford his vivid imagination and cultivated mind, and that good taste in landscape gardening which produced the perfect unity of character which pervades the grounds of Fonthill. ... We must, however, enter our protest against the recklessness with which he employed his wealth to gratify his wishes, without regard to its demoralising effects on the labouring population of his neighbourhood, effects so serious that it will take a generation to remove them.

The words 'pusillanimous claptrap', written in Medlar Lucan's hand, appear in the margin of this passage.

There was only one area of the practical side of gardening which appealed to them - 'clearing the ground', i.e. the wholesale destruction of what had been there before. In this they took their lead from two well-known figures. Firstly, the Italian poet, D'Annunzio, who always began redecorating a house by removing anything that carried the taint of the bourgeois. He referred to this process as 'aesthetic disinfection'. Secondly, from Humphrey Repton. Of Repton, Durian Gray wrote:

His greatness lay not in his ability to create acres of tedious English parkland, but in his ruthlessness. As a gardener he was without mercy. At (?), he was quite prepared to flatten an entire mining village because it spoilt a particular sight line.

The great artist is concerned with destruction as much as with creation. Perhaps more so. Certainly one of the attractions of the garden for the Decadent is that it is ephemeral. It does not last. It should not last.

In the garden, the Decadent seeks to create a moment of beauty, which should then be allowed to fall into decay and ruin.

For Gray and Lucan, there was only one acceptable way of destroying the old garden at Mountcullen - with fire. They saw this as the time-honoured way of clearing a garden. Durian Gray again:

Take the Yuan Ming Yuan, the 'Garden of Perfect Brightness', a huge complex of lakes, gardens and palaces, 70 miles in circumference, 60,000 acres, quite simply the most spectacular pleasure garden on the face of this earth. It was the talk of Europe, designed 'with so much Art that you would take it to be the Work of Nature.' Then on October 18th, 1860, British and French soldiers moved into the Garden of Perfect Brightness and set fire to it, in retaliation for the torture of British prisoners. By the end of two days of burning most of the garden lay in ruins. But then the downfall of Chinese dynasties has always been signalled by two things - the sound of women screaming and the smell of Imperial gardens burning. Then the next emperor comes along and builds something even more elaborate. So that is what we are doing. The old gardens will be put to the torch and the new one will rise from the ashes.

Whether Gray and Lucan wore 19th century military uniforms to torch the old garden at Mountcullen is not known. Given their propensity for dressing up, it seems probable.

When Mrs Gordon arrived home in the autumn, she was immediately aware of the changes that had taken place in her absence. Around the house, particularly on the south, west and east sides, there was evidence of a great deal of work. The shape of the terrain had undergone various transformations. New beds had been created, new planting had been carried out, strange constructions had appeared here and there. Among these were what looked like three crucifixes which had been raised against the skyline. Mrs Gordon was eager to know how far Gray and Lucan had progressed.

However, of the decadent designers there was no sign. When Mrs Gordon asked Ryan, her factotum, where they were, a sorry story emerged. A week previously, Fr O'Malley, the local priest, and a number of parishioners had turned up unannounced at Mountcullen to put forward their objections to the Sacred, or

'Blasphemous' garden, as it had become known. Unfortunately they caught Gray, Lucan, *et al.* in the middle of rehearsing an outdoor play. The play in question was the Earl of Rochester's pornographic farce, *Sodom, or the Quintessence of Debauchery* which was to be performed in the Garden of Histrion to celebrate Mrs Gordon's return from India. The priest and his flock were outraged by the scenes which they witnessed and were soon locked in furious debate with 'King Bolloximian' and 'Queen Cuntigratia'. Tempers became frayed, voices were raised and blows may have been exchanged. (The full text of the play and a fuller account of the confrontation can be found on page 95) The upshot was that by the next morning Lucan and Gray had packed their bags and gone.

So, what was Mrs Gordon left with? Just one area of the project had been completed (i.e. the Sacred garden, to which Gray and Lucan had also written the guide, reproduced below). Otherwise, it seemed, little else was to be found, one or two features of the remaining gardens, plus a library strewn with files, discarded costumes, and a great many dirty plates and bottles. The files, on examination, proved to be very full and intriguing. Out of the chaos of papers they contained - sketches, design notes, photographs, quotations, historical jottings, and unpaid contractors' bills - a remarkably coherent vision of a garden emerged. It was bold, grotesque, and utterly uncompromising in its commitment to extend, and more often pervert, the accepted norms of horticulture. Artifice, theatrical effect, and a kind of 'terrible beauty' were paramount. Here, albeit only on paper, was a Decadent garden with a vengeance, a true anti-garden; a reflection, as Lucan and Gray saw it, of the madness and corruption not only of our age, but all preceeding ages as well. It is these papers which form the bulk of this book.

What is perhaps sad about the whole Mountcullen project is that so little of it was built, although most grandiose garden schemes, as it turns out, remain incomplete. This is indeed part of their fascination. Visitors to such unfinished gardens find themselves imagining what might have been, or how they might have completed them with the benefit of a team of gardeners and a couple of million pounds. Perhaps, in reading this book, somebody may feel inspired to pick up the torch that Gray and Lucan have lit. At least some of the groundwork has already been done and Gray and Lucan, although they have once again disappeared, have not suffered the same fate as Monsieur Palissy. He died, impoverished and imprisoned, his Garden of Wisdom flourishing nowhere except in the landscape of his mind.

A.M. and J.F.

A Guide to the Sacred Garden at Mountcullen House

" ... within the garden all is deceit and fantasy;
Nothing subsists.
Decay triumphs over everything;
Both the dancer and the dance
Will cease to be."

Le Roman de la Rose

The Sacred Garden at Mountcullen consists of not one, but five different spaces linked by a walk. This walk begins at the front of Mountcullen House. It takes the visitor in a one mile circuit around the house and returns to the point of departure.

The garden is a celebration of Decadence. Since the whole notion of Decadence implies a 'fall', it makes absolute sense to start with the formal garden in front of the house and to re-design it as a representation of the Garden of Eden.

The Garden of Eden is completely enclosed by the south facade of the house on one side and by wrought-iron railings on the other three sides. We divided this large square area into four, with water-channels which run north-south and east-west. These were covered with thick glass, the water is heated and teems with multi-coloured angel fish. As in a monastery garden, these channels symbolise the four rivers that ran out of Eden. This is also the basic shape of the Persian paradise garden. Within the four quarters, we have planted only wild and primitive flowers, and in great profusion. As far as possible we wish to represent the entire vegetable world within these spaces. The effect is a madhouse of colour and form, but constrained within strict limits. To the casual observer, it appears to be a rather charming garden of Innocence, Eden in its pre-lapsarian state. However, things are not entirely what they seem.

At the intersection of the channels the visitor will notice an unusual object - a large glass globe which stands on a stone pedestal. Around the base of the pedestal, we have planted a patch of giant strawberries. You may be tempted to see this as a representation of the Tree of Knowledge. But that was not our intention. If you take a look at that extraordinary painting by Hieronymus Bosch, *The Garden of Earthly Delights*, among the many bizarre and outlandish images, will find both a giant strawberry (a symbol of earthly pleasure in Medieval iconography; the fruit looks very tempting, but tastes of nothing), and a naked couple copulating within a glass vessel.

What interests us about Bosch is not only his strange and beautiful painting, but also his supposed involvement with a heretical sect called the Adamites. This sect, according to de Perrodil's *Dictionnaire des hérésies, des erreurs et des schismes*, saw it as their sacred duty to violate the laws which the Creator had given to man. This neatly encapsulates the Decadent impulse. They also wished to rehabilitate Adam and Eve by seeking inspiration from their conduct in the garden of Eden. Nudity and sexual games formed part of their ritual. The Adamites were of course condemned and brutally persecuted by vindictive ecclesiastical authorities.

So, as you move around the Sacred garden, it is well to bear in mind the words of the epigraph which introduce this guide.

There is only one exit from the Garden of Eden. It is through the gate to the east. Above the gate has been fixed a gilded 'flaming' sword and the path leads across to **The Penitential Maze.**

We take great delight in the penitential maze at Mountcullen. It is an unusual feature. A very large rectangular area formed by a low box hedge extends along the east front of the house, across the lawns and reaches almost as far as the River Cull. It measures some 70 yds long by 30 wide. Within this rectangle, the path of the maze has been cut into the grass and filled with smooth gravel. On top of this has been spread a large quantity of crushed oyster and mussel shells. Even on overcast days, these shards of mother-of-pearl catch the light and make the pathway glitter. In fact, we have come to refer to the route through the maze as 'the path of shining light.' The dark green of the box hedge set against the grey, silver and black of the path creates a startling effect, as does the contrast between the sinuous path and the geometric precision of its frame. But the use of crushed shells has another effect. It makes the maze extremely painful to traverse. This is because penitents are expected to negotiate it on their knees. Ah, Pain and Beauty! To the Decadent there can be no more irresistible combination.

Penitential mazes were originally constructed as a single twisting path which eventually leads to the middle. In this, they represented the sinful world through which we must all pass on the way to redemption. Virtue, following the one true path, brings its own reward. However, it does not take long to realise that in the Mountcullen maze it is all too easy to lose your way, not knowing which way to turn, to find yourself constantly returning to the same spot. In effect, our maze is a celebration of blind, irrational fate, rather than of Christian virtue. Indeed, like the labyrinth at the court of Isabella d'Este, it is more closely related to the reversals of fortune, the ecstasy and despair experienced in the pursuit of earthly love.

There is another aspect of our maze which distinguishes it from its sacred antecedents. There are not one, but two exits. Normally in a penitential maze the penitents followed their *via dolorosa* from the outside to the centre. At Mountcullen, the unsuspecting penitents might easily follow a path which leads to a narrow exit about two-thirds the way up on the left hand side. At this point they will find themselves kneeling in front of a door which leads into the walled garden. The walled garden we have designated as the site for what we call the *Paradis artificiel*, in other words, the Narcotic garden (see chapter six).

But what of the other exit? What awaits the suffering penitent at the end of their path of pain by the river? Here the path enters a green 'room', created from a ring of closely-planted cypress trees. Within this room stands a statue which, for obvious reasons, one assumes to be the fat pagan, Priapus. But it's not! It's St Ters, of course. Our favourite saint! On his feast day, the women of Antwerp used to decorate the phallus of figures of St Ters with garlands of flowers (why do the women have all the fun?) and pray to him, that their gardens might receive a good forking, no doubt. We have approached the local parish priest with a view to reinstating this delightful custom.

As you leave the shrine to St Ters, you also leave the maze and find yourself on the banks of the river Cull. A narrow footbridge takes you across the river. On the other side the land rises sharply to a ring of wooded hills. Looking up, you see the water staircase which forms a wide path through the trees. Before reaching the bottom of the staircase, the water comes to a wall with an upward-curving lip along the top. This shoots the water forward in a semi-transparent curtain to the bassin below. Hidden behind this curtain of water, in the centre of the wall, is the entrance to the next feature of the sacred garden - **The Hermit's Cave.**

No sacred garden would be complete without a hermit's cave. Of course there is nothing new about this. In the 18th century, Charles Hamilton advertised for a person who was willing to become a hermit in his garden at Painshill, Surrey. The conditions were that he must...

'...*continue in the hermitage seven years where he should be provided with a Bible, optical glasses, a mat for his head, a hassock for his pillow, an hour-glass for his timepiece, water for his beverage, food from the house but never to exchange a syllable with the servant. He was to wear a camlet robe, never to cut his beard or nails, not ever to stray beyond the limits of the grounds. If he lived there under all these restrictions till the end of the term he was to receive seven hundred guineas. But on breach of any of them, or if he quitted the place at any time previous to that term, the whole was to be forfeited.*'

One person attempted it, but a three week trial cured him.

The abode that we have designed and decorated for the Mountcullen hermit is very different from the one Charles Hamilton had in mind. The interior is illuminated by natural light, as at Goldney House, via shafts in the roof, and the walls are covered with hundreds of thousands of small shells set in the most elaborate patterns, as in the Bain des Nymphes at the Château de Wideville. The shellwork is all a pun on Mrs Gordon's Christian name, Conchita, which (among other things) means 'little shell' in Spanish. This homage becomes even more explicit when one examines the statue which dominates the hermitage. This is a small-scale copy of the ecstasy of Saint Teresa by Bernini in the church of Santa Maria della Vittoria in Rome. On seeing the original statue for the first time, some wag felt bound to comment: "If that's religious ecstasy, I've seen it many times." Close inspection of the copy reveals the face of the statue to be unmistakably that of Mrs Gordon. Of course, one doesn't have to be a member of the Sigmund Freud fan club to understand the sort of connotations that a dark, moist opening like a grotto can have.

As for the rest of the cave, it is blatantly modelled on Cardinal Richelieu's grotto at Rueil.

In four of the angles there are satyrs, in the other four, nymphs, all life-size, prettily formed of sea-shells and snails; each character makes a strange gesture with the hand, sometimes putting a finger on the thigh, sometimes on the mouth, while the other hand directs the membrum virile in the air and water spurts from it; all that is treated with great realism. On four of the sides there are fountains with fine oval basins; near each stand three marble figures also discharging water from their genitals. ...

Our overt intention was to make life as difficult as possible for the Mountcullen hermit. Not for him a severely simple life uncluttered by the distractions of worldly concerns. Rather than the plain table with a wooden bowl and beaker, he has to make do with ...

... an octagonal marble table on which one could do all kinds of amusing things in that by pressing the instrument or tube coming from the centre, one made all kinds of figures with the water, for example, lilies, cups, flowers, glasses, moons, stars, parasols. When the whole grotto plays, water spouts from all parts (above, below, from the sides) ... as if a heavy shower was falling and the wind was blowing from all sides, mingling the jets, so that whoever does not immediately get to the benches does not escape a soaking.

On leaving the Hermit's Cave, you cross the river again by a second footbridge and come to an irregular-shaped enclosure created from a dry stone wall which is broken down in places. This is the **Garden of Gethsemane.** It is one of our favourite haunts. A place of agony, self-doubt and betrayal. A perfect location for anyone enveloped in 'a dark night of the soul.' Here one can kneel at a boulder for hours, languishing in the depths of religious agony, waiting for the flaming brands which betoken the arrival of the soldiers, their lightly-oiled muscles gleaming in the torch light.

Such a garden is *de rigueur*.

We have put a great deal of effort into this faithful recreation of the garden at the foot of the Mount of Olives. In order to improve the chances of the olive grove surviving in this part of Ireland, hot water pipes have been run through the walls and through the large boulders placed between trees. The idea came from the warmed garden walls of Beeleigh Abbey and is a technique which also ensures the survival of the Judas tree (*Cercis siliquastrum*) planted against the south-facing wall.

This particular section of the sacred garden has not reached its full potential as one important element is still lacking. We want this to be a 'night garden' but we are still awaiting the completion of our planting scheme. This includes night-flowering cacti (*Selenicereus grandiflorus*), eveningflower gladiolus (*Gladiolus tristis*) as well as Nicotiana, night-scented stocks (*Matthiola longi-petala*) and Mycelia fungus which glows in the dark. Planted in combination and in sufficient profusion the effect should be overpowering, or indeed, deliriously mystical.

From the exit to the garden of Gethsemane, you walk a short distance across the lawn towards the next section of the Sacred Garden. This lies to the north east of the house and should be the first thing that the visitor notices on arriving by the east drive. It is difficult to miss. It is a **Calvary**.

The Mountcullen Calvary did not start out as one. Originally, we wanted to follow in the footsteps of the 12th century Chinese emperor, Hui-Tsung. He was a fabulously decadent gardener, a man for whom the word 'excess' was devoid of meaning. When the imperial geomancers informed Hui-Tsung that the land to the north east of the capital was too flat, he ordered a mountain to be built.

Ken-yu, or the Impregnable Mountain, was more than ten *li* in circumference. It comprised ten thousand layered peaks with ranges, cliffs, deep gullies, escarpments and chasms. At its summit, the structure rose two hundred and twenty five feet above the surrounding countryside. From there it descended through foothills and excavated earth to ponds and streams bordered by orchards of plum and apricot trees densely planted.

To the east the emperor could stand on a high ridge looking

clear over the tops of a thousand plum trees. In spring he would be enveloped in the scent of blossom as the warm breeze wafted it up from below. High on the hillside was a smooth and gleaming precipice of purple rock which was reached by stone steps winding up along the cliff. As the emperor passed by, sweating lackeys would open a sluice gate in the hill which caused a man-made waterfall to tumble across the rock beside him.

The display of rocks on the mountain was extraordinary. One eye-witness account states :

'They were all in various shapes, like tusks, horns, mouths, noses, heads, tails, and claws, They seemed to be angry and protesting against each other. Among them were planted gnarled trees and knobbed, clinging vines and evergreens.'

A little further on, this same fascination with the grotesque gave rise to a display of fantastically contorted pine trees, 'their branches ... twisted round and knotted to form all kinds of shapes, like canopies, cranes, dragons.'

Although the cost in manpower and materials was immense, Hui-Tsung remained blissfully unconcerned. 'The hard labour of transporting earth in baskets was not felt, and the sound of hammer and axe not heard', he wrote. The building of the mountain bankrupted the empire, leaving it easy prey to marauding northern tribes. Hui-Tsung died a captive in a barbarian tent.

The Mountcullen calvary may not have cost an empire but it did require some major construction work. Large quantities of rock, rubble and earth were needed to produce a grassy knoll. Only when we realised that we could not come close to emulating the great Hui-Tsung did we decide to create a calvary and incorporate it into the Sacred garden. We began with the path which winds up from the bottom through swathes of bitter herbs - aloes, hyssop, rue, wormwood - to the three crosses on its summit. The central cross is embedded in a group of madonna lilies and early purple orchids. (The spots on its leaves are supposed to be drops of blood from the crucified Christ). Out of these grow several passion flowers, which entwine themselves around the crucifix. The whole effect is one of grotesque kitsch. Possibly one of our greatest triumphs to date.

Calvaries are of course a common sight in the catholic countries of southern Europe. Mont Valérien, outside Paris, comprised a cluster of churches, the Stations of the Cross and a crucifixion scene. During its heyday in the 17th century, it not only attracted a large number of pious and devout pilgrims but also a ragbag of mountebanks, tinkers, con men, indulgence sellers, holy water touts, bawds and drunkards. This farrago of sensibilities will no doubt appeal to the Decadent, but there was another reason for the building of the calvary at Mountcullen, another act of homage.

Placed at the foot of the central cross and almost hidden among the lilies is a carved stone pistol. This is a reference to that high priest of Decadence, J.K. Huysmans. After he had read Huysmans' *A Rebours*, Barbey d'Aurevilly commented: *Après un tel livre, il ne reste plus à l'auteur de choisir entre la bouche d'un pistolet ou les pieds de la croix*. [After such a book, the author is left with a simple choice - between blowing his brains out or kneeling at the foot of the Cross]. Some pious souls have argued that our calvary depicts the possibility of salvation for even the most debauched. We admit there is a certain ambiguity here.

The path down from the Calvary leads in two different directions. One leads away from the house and towards the cruel Garden. A most appropriate direction to take! (See chapter three). The other path returns to the front of the house and the Garden of Eden, from whence the whole dubious pilgrimage begins again.

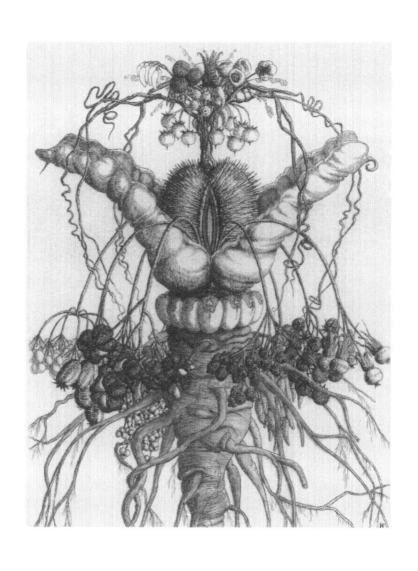

THE GARDEN OF VENUS

Editors' note: The design of the Garden of Venus resembles that of the Sacred garden in that it consists of a number of elements, seven in all, linked by a snaking path. (Medlar Lucan was insistent that the path should 'snake'). Its *point de départ* was somewhere to the south east of the house adjacent to the Garden of Histrion and its endpoint was the erotic hothouse built within the Garden of Oblivion, on the shores of Lough Doon. The reason why a garden devoted to the erotic should end up in a garden devoted to death is made clear at the end of this section. Durian Gray never tired of pointing out that 'nowhere are sex and death more intimately bound together than in the garden.' But one cannot help thinking that there is more than a hint here of that most decadent and taboo of subjects - necrophilia. Although little of the Garden of Venus was actually built, Gray and Lucan explained its theoretical basis and described its layout in significant detail. There remains little to do other than build it. The contents of the file are reproduced in full, but first a word of warning. The reader should under no circumstances attempt any of the recipes given in the Garden of Aphrodisia section.

———➤•◄———

An erotic garden - a tautology if ever there was one! Why we are even bothering to create an erotic garden, we don't know. Are not all gardens erotic - hotbeds of orgiastic excess presided over by the jolly little man with his phallus rampant? The executioner in Mirbeau's *The Torture Garden* put it very nicely:

"Flowers are violent, cruel, terrible and splendid ... like love!"
He gathered a nearby buttercup whose gold capitulum shook indolently above the grass and, slowly and lovingly, turned it between his large red fingers with extreme delicacy. In places dried blood flaked off his fingers: "Isn't it adorable," he repeated as he contemplated the flower. "So small and fragile - a microcosm of nature, with all the beauty of its strength. It contains the world. Ah, frail and relentless organism heading for its realisation! Flowers have no time for sentiment. They make love ... nothing but love ... and they do it all the time and in every way they can. It's all they think about. And they're right. Perverse? Because they obey

life's only need, which is love? But consider this! The flower is nothing but a sexual organ. Is anything healthier, stronger and more beautiful than a sexual organ? These marvellous petals, these silks, these velvets, these soft, supple and caressing fabrics - they are the curtains of the alcove, the draperies of the nuptial chamber, the perfumed bed where the sexes are united, where they pass their fleeting and immortal life enraptured with love. What an admirable example they set us!"

And when the poet of the Song of Songs wants to describe a woman's sexual arousal, what more apposite metaphor could have been chosen?

> A garden enclosed is my sister, my spouse;
> a spring shut up, a fountain sealed.
> Thy plants are an orchard of pomegranates,
> with pleasant fruits; camphire, with spikenard,
> Spikenard and saffron; calamus and
> cinnamon, with all trees of frankincense;
>
> I am come into my garden, my
> sister, my spouse: I have gathered
> my myrrh with my spice; I have
> eaten my honeycomb with my honey.

In planning this garden, we began by considering some large-scale changes in the landscape to the south east of the house. At West Wycombe, the property of Sir Francis Dashwood (he of Hell-Fire fame), by dint of raising a hummock here and a hillock there, judicious planting of shrubs and bushes, the park, when viewed from the house, resembled a naked woman lying on her back. The idea put us in mind of that wonderful sonnet by Baudelaire, *La Géante*.

> Du temps que la Nature en sa verve puissante
> Concevait chaque jour des enfants monstrueux,
> J'eusse aimé vivre auprès d'une jeune géante
> Comme aux pieds d'une reine un chat voluptueux.
> J'eusse aimé voir son corps fleurir avec son âme
> Et grandir librement dans ses terribles jeux;
> Deviner si son coeur couve une sombre flamme

Aux humides brouillards qui nagent dans ses yeux.

Parcourir à loisir ses magnifiques formes;
Ramper sur le versant de ses genoux énormes,
Et parfois en été, quand les soleils malsains,

Lasse, la font s'étendre à travers la campagne,
Dormir nonchalamment à l'ombre de ses seins,
Comme un hameau paisible au pied d'une montagne.

(In the days when Nature in her powerful spirit brought forth monstrous children every day I would like to have dwelt with a young giantess as a pleasure-loving cat dwells at the feet of a queen.

I would love to have seen her body and soul blossom together and grow freely in her terrible games. To have sought some dark flame lying hidden in her heart by gazing into the damp mists which cloud her eyes.

To have wandered at leisure over her magnificent curve, climbed the long slope of her knees, and sometimes, in summer, when the overwhelming sun caused her to lie down drowsily over the countryside to have slept sweetly in the shade of her breasts like a peaceful hamlet at the foot of a mountain.)

But back to Francis Dashwood. Now there was a Decadent gardener! He would have appreciated our efforts here at Mountcullen. The sort of man he was can be judged by a letter George Bubb Doddington wrote to him in 1745:

... We are all in love with your agreeable Defence of that Steady Course you are in, of employing 20 of the 24 hours either upon your own Belly, or from thence, like a publick Reservoir administering to those of other People, by laying your Cock in every private Family that has any Place fitt to receive it.

Of course, the Hell-Fire club was a good deal tamer than it has been portrayed. However, it is for his gardens at Medmenham Abbey that Sir Francis should really be remembered.

The motto set above the door of the abbey was taken from

Rabelais via St Augustine: 'Fay ce que voudras' [Do whatever you wish]. The favourite doctrine of the Abbey was summed up by another motto to be found in the middle of the orchard. There stood a very grotesque figure, *and in his hand a reed stood flaming, tipt with fire.* Below the figure were carved the words;

PENI TENTO

non

PENITENTI

This may be crudely translated as: Better a Stiff Prick than Penitence. At the entrance to a cave in the grounds there was a statue of Venus, bending over to pull a thorn out of her foot. The statue had her back to the viewer and just above the 'two nether hills of snow' were these lines of Virgil.

> *Hic locus est, partes ubi se via findit in ambas*
> *Hac iter Elysium nobis; at laeva malorum*
> *Exercet poenas, et ad impia Tartara mittit.*

(Here is the place where the way divided into two: this on the right is our route to Heaven; but the left-hand path exacts punishment from the wicked, and sends them to pitiless Hell.)

Within the cave, above a mossy couch, was the following exhortation:

> *Ite, agite, ô juvenes; pariter fundate medullis*
> *Omnibus inter vos; non murmurara vestra columbae,*
> *Brachia non hederae, non vincant oscula conchae.*

(Get on with it, you young things; put everything you've got into it together, both of you; may you be like doves in your cooings, ivy in your embraces, and oysters in your kissing.)

But let us return to our immediate concerns. Before embarking on any important activity in life - gardening, boy-scouting, sex - one should be well prepared before venturing forth. To this end we thought it best for any lovers who wish to explore this part of the Mountcullen estate to begin their erotic peregrination in the garden of Aphrodisia. The entrance to this garden, and indeed to all the spaces in the erotic garden, is marked by a stone slab standing on a broken classical column. Carved into the stone is a Japanese Geisha song. At the entrance to the Garden of Aphrodisia, the lovers will find the following:

> *Tonight would be quite a good night*
> *to taste the living flower,*
> *my lord, if you so wish.*

One of the most important elements of the Aphrodisiac garden will be the bed of nettles. This may seem perverse. So much the better! Among the Romans it was common knowledge that a brisk bout of flagellation with a bunch of nettles did wonders for their ardour. According to Juvenal, only dancing girls from Cadiz were capable of providing a comparable level of stimulation. The elder Pliny strongly recommended the male using nettles and the female, basil. Admittedly he was talking about persuading horses to couple, but there is no reason why it shouldn't work equally well for humans. Later, in 17th century Europe, the gallant was being advised to stuff his cod-piece with nettles. And should you require it, nettle seed in honey is a most effective cure for impotence.

In among the nettles we will plant the damask rose. It requires more preparation to extract the aphrodisiac qualities from this flower, but it's worth it. Firstly one has to run a very hot bath. Into the water one scatters a mixture of damask rose and vervain. One then has to wallow in it and carefully collect the resultant body sweat. This in turn should be added to wine or some sweetmeat and given to the one you desire. Ah, it takes us back to our days at the restaurant!

The garden of Aphrodisia could well double as a herb and spice garden, if so required. For instance, an Indian love potion recommends chewing caraway seeds and 'with the mouth thus sweetened, breathe on the beloved who will henceforth love you.' Not to be outdone, the Arabs mixed cardamom with saliva and spread it on the glans of the penis to excite the organ and increase its size.

It is vital to ensure that the garden produces a good crop of aniseed, known in India as shopa. The Ananga Ranga informs us that the aniseed should be 'reduced to an impalpable powder; strain and make into an electuary with honey. This being so applied to the lingam (male member) before congress that it may reach as far inside as possible, will induce venereal paroxysm in the woman and subject her to the power of man.'

For a woman, all she has to do is to crush a lotus flower to powder, add the rhizome of an iris, the root of a *Tabernaemontana coronaria,* the leaf of a *Colotropis gigantea,* and sugar. After she has applied this mixture as eye make-up, she will bring any young man into her power.

Next, in order to delay orgasm in the man, try levigating 'the root of the Lajjalu (*Mimosa pudica)* with milk of the cow or if none be found with the thick juice of the fine-edged milk weed *(Euphorbia pentagonia).* If this be applied before congress to the soles of the man's feet, his embraces will be greatly prolonged by the retention of the water of life'. Mind you, it works equally well using the bark of the blackwood tree, camphor and purified quicksilver, all applied to the man's navel. And don't forget, soaking a water-lily in milk, forming it into little balls and inserting these into the penis is one of the best ways of preventing premature ejaculation.

If possible, we must plant a Yohimbe tree (*Corynanthe yohimbine).* This is a most effective aphrodisiac. The dose is one ounce of yohimbe bark simmered in a pint of water for twenty minutes. It should then be strained and sipped. The initial effects are nausea followed by relaxed intoxication, and if you're lucky, hallucinations. It then increases the blood supply to the pelvic area and engorges the sexual parts.

Having dosed themselves up and rubbed themselves down sufficiently with amorous substances, the lovers should move on - for a little foreplay perhaps. Following the path they will eventually come across a second song carved in stone.

> *At Katushika the river water*
> *runs gently and the plum blossom*
> *bursts out laughing.*
> *The nightingale cannot withstand so many joys*
> *and sings, and we are reconciled.*
> *Our warm bodies touch,*
> *cane branch and pine branch,*
> *our boat floats in toward the bank.*

This stands at the entrance to the orchard. We thought it best to enclose the orchard with walls. The trees will grow much more successfully in such an environment, especially if the walls are heated (see page 20) It will also create a *hortus conclusus* shielded from prying eyes, not unlike those exquisite medieval gardens which appear in illuminated manuscripts. When we mentioned this to Mrs Gordon she insisted that small chinks are built into the walls for the benefit of voyeurs. What a woman! Her thoughtfulness is an example to us all.

The orchard will consist mainly, but not exclusively, of fruit trees. The connection between fruit and the erotic is long established. Pride of place should be given to the fig, a fruit which is sacred to Priapus. According to Florio, the latin word *fica*, a fig, could also be used in the sense of 'a woman's quaint'. The *abricot* or in Rabelais, the *abricot fendu* played very much the same role as the fig, and in Vandal mythology, their goddess of love was portrayed as a female in a reclining position holding out a pomegranate, a sign representing the female pudenda.

But it will not contain only fruit trees. Planted among them will be Spanish chestnut. This is on the recommendation of one Professor Gamber, who, in his fascinating book, *Ideal Marriage,* writes:

' *The semen of healthy youths of western European races has a fresh exhilarating smell, in the mature man it is more penetrating in type and degree. The very characteristic seminal odour is remarkably like that of the flowers of the Spanish chestnut.'*

At the heart of the orchard, we will plant a pear tree - the most decadent fruit of all. That priggish old cleric, the Curé d'Ars, would have *ce fruit diabolique* banned altogether, 'for it is the cause of of bodily lewdness and engenders debauchery'. In the 13th century, another killjoy, Bartolomeus Anglicus, repudiated the pear on the grounds that its shape was similar to that of the flames of Hell. Could one wish for a greater recommendation? Our pear tree will be planted in the hope that the lovely Conchita might one day make as fruitful a use of it as Lydia in Boccaccio's *Decameron*. Her story goes thus:

Lydia, wife of the aged Nicostratos, is consumed with desire for Pyrrhus, who is one of the old man's loyal servants. After setting Lydia a series of tests, Pyrrhus is convinced that her lust is genuine, he agrees to satisfy her desires in the not-too-distant future. Lydia however cannot wait that long. She wants Pyrrhus to make love to her that afternoon, and in front of her husband. Lydia has a plan.

Her first step is to feign illness. As she lies on her sick-bed, Nicostratos and Pyrrhus come to minister to her and she asks them to carry her into the garden. They set the bed down on the lawn at the foot of a beautiful pear tree. The two men then sit with her for a while. Before long, she turns to Pyrrhus and asks him to climb the tree to fetch down a pear for her. While up the tree, Pyrrhus looks down between the branches and in an astonished tone rebukes his master for the shameless and immodest way in which he is behaving with his wife. Nicostratos has no idea what his servant is talking about. He asks Pyrrhus to explain himself.

' I do believe,' said Pyrrhus, ' you take me for a cretin or a madman. Well, as you insist, I'll tell you. I saw you lying on top of your lady, and as soon as I started to climb down, you moved, to the spot where you are sitting now.'

In reply, Nicostratos said:

'You obviously are a madman. Because we haven't moved an inch since you went up that tree.'

'There's no point arguing about it,' said Pyrrhus. ' I am simply telling you what I saw - you were going at it hammer and tongs.'
Nicostratos grew more and more astonished. Finally he said:

' I think I'd better find out for myself whether or not this pear tree is enchanted, and what sort of strange things you can see from its branches.'

So saying, he climbed the tree. And no sooner had he reached a certain height than Pyrrhus and Lydia began to make love together. When Nicostratos saw what was happening, he shouted:

'You vile harlot, what are you up to? And you, Pyrrhus, you in whom I placed such trust!'

With this, he began to climb back down to the ground.

'We are just sitting here quietly,' said Pyrrhus and his mistress. But as they saw him descending the tree, they resumed their former positions. No sooner had Nicostratos reached the ground and found them in the places where he had left them than he began to heap abuse upon them.

'But Nicostratos,' said Pyrrhus, ' I admit that you were right, and that my eyes were deceiving me when I was up the tree. The reason I say this is that I know for a fact that you were suffering from the same delusion. If you are not convinced, then stop and think for a moment. Would a woman of such honesty and intelligence as your good lady, even if she wanted to besmirch your honour in this way, would she ever stoop to do so before your very eyes? As far as I'm concerned, I have nothing to say other than that I would rather be drawn and quartered than even contemplate such an act, let alone perform it in your presence. Obviously something is distorting our vision and whatever it is must come from the tree. For I was totally convinced beyond doubt that you were making love to your wife, until I heard you claim that I was apparently doing something which I most certainly was not, nor would it cross my mind to do.'

At this point, the lady interrupted. She rose to her feet and railed at her husband.

'May the devil take you! How could you hold me in such low esteem? To suppose that, even if I had wanted to disport myself in such a scandalous manner, I should do it before your very eyes! You may rest assured that if I should ever feel the urge to do it, I would not do it out here in the garden. On the contrary, I would find a nice, comfortable bed and arrange the whole thing in such a way that it'd would be highly unlikely that you would ever get to know about it.'

Nicostratos now accepted that they must both be telling the truth. They could never have brought themselves to perform such an act in his presence. So he ceased his shouting and raving, and began to talk about what a curious, not to say miraculous thing it was that a man's eyesight could be affected by climbing a pear tree.

It was not only in Italy that the garden was the locus for adultery. Manucci, the seventeeth century traveller to India, tells the following story of a garden called Dil-Kusha in front of the royal palace at Lahore.

To it went for recreation twelve officials and in lightness of heart, drunk as they were, they sent out in search of twelve women. One by one, eleven appeared and one man was left without a lady. As the sun was setting there appeared at the entrance to the garden, one who walked most graciously. She was very lovely and well-dressed so that she roused envy in the whole company. Drawing near to him to whom she was allotted, who had come forward to greet her, she perceived it was her husband! Vigorously hastening her pace, and with demonstrations of rage, she fell upon him, tore his clothes, beat and abused him and said that he must have lost his way out walking; the company he found himself in was not suited to a person of gravity. She dragged him home, making him out the sinner, although she was an adultress herself.

Having begun to experience a frisson of excitement in the orchard, the lovers must move on again. Further down the path they stop to read a third geisha song:

Will he be a fine chrysanthemum?
I will put him in a vase
and look at him.
He will be a plum blossom
having both scent and colour.

'Flower beds', 'bedding plants', everywhere in the garden you find nothing but rampant sexuality! Consider these as you make your way along the venereal path! Here is a clump of Lords and Ladies (*Arum maculatum*) also known as 'sweethearts' and 'silly lovers'. We must have lots of these. Its most common name is 'cuckoo's pintle'. [In French, *vit de chien, vit de prestre*]. Just the shape of the arum is enough to have it included in the erotic garden. But there is more! The phallic structure gives off a smell of decay which attracts flies. The insect crawls down inside the enveloping sheath of the plant and is trapped by hairs which line it and point downwards. Desperately looking for a way out, the fly then crawls around picking up pollen and pollinating the flowers until it dies, incarcerated in its floral prison. As if that were not enough, the berries of *Arum maculatum* can be fatal when eaten by small children, and the roots are used as a 'stiffening' agent. There is a whole novel here! Lords and Ladies is *the* Decadent plant.

Alongside these you may find the Bee orchid, which gets its name from the fact that the lip of the flower is coloured in such a way that it resembles a female bumble bee. A passing male bee spots the 'female' and swoops down with a view to sating his lust. In doing so, pollen from the orchid attaches itself to the bee's head. The male eventually gets fed up with the apparently frigid female and flies off with its head covered in pollen. In its sexually excited and unsatisfied state it is liable to try and mate with another flower.

The word 'Orchid' comes from the Greek for 'testicle', so any variety could be included in the beds. Many have charming country names, such as 'triple bullocks', 'sweet ballocks', 'sweet cods' and 'goat-stones'. And let's not forget those plants which resemble a bush of hair - a species of Adiantum known as *capillus veneris* (Maiden's hair, or Our Lady's hair). Also the *Asplenium trichomanes*. In his *Discourse on the Worship of Priapus*, Richard Payne Knight (or 'Dick Pain Night' as he came to be affectionately known) tells us *'There is reason for believing that the hair implied in these names was that of the pubes'*. Fumitory is another of these plants. In a 13th century vocabulary of plant names we found its Latin name, *fumus terrae*, its French name, *fumeterre*, and its English name, *cuntehoare*.

Having wandered around the beds, the lovers begin to increase their pace. A flush begins to redden their cheeks. Perhaps it's the heat. Their breathing begins to quicken slightly. Perhaps it's the exertion. Then, at the gate to the vegetable garden, they happen upon the fourth geisha song. Around the base of the column on which it stands grows Rocket Cress (*Eruca sativa*) as it used to be grown around the statues of Priapus.

> *The device of the two copper plums*
> *with silver in them*
> *slowly and very slowly*
> *satisfies.*
> *Just as all finishes*
> *dew falls on my clenched hand.*
> *I would rather the bean flowered yellow*
> *and he were here.*

Thomas Coryat, writing of India in the early 17th century, observed that the Mogul emperors were very careful about the sort of objects which were introduced within the confines of the harem.

Whatsoever is brought in of virile shape, as for instance radishes, so great is the jealousy, and so frequent the wickedness of this people that they are cut and jagged for fear of converting the same to some unnatural abuse.

Fifty years later, the Italian traveller Manucci made the same observation:

Nor do they permit into the palace radishes, cucumbers or similar vegetables that I cannot name.

This may sound bizarre, given that the only variety of radish you find today is the size of a gobstopper. We suspect that what Coryat and Manucci had in mind was the Black, or Spanish radish, known in France as *le pénis nègre*. This grows to 25 cms in length and 7 cms in diametre. It should not be confused with the horseradish which in Ancient Greece was used to punish couples caught in adultery. Yes, the culprits had a horseradish inserted into their backsides. Autolycus suffered this fate by order of Alexander the Great and in addition was made to ride around on a donkey. As a punishment, this proved counter-productive in that he appeared to derive considerable enjoyment from the experience.

Mannucci's mention of the cucumber is hardly surprising, any more than is the description of the banana in *1001 Nights* as 'the most compassionate of fruits, comforter of widows and divorcees'. We think the most inventive use of a cucumber, although not in an overtly sexual sense, was by Jimena, the lover of Rodrigo del Vivar, otherwise known as El Cid. After Rodrigo had inadvertantly killed Jimena's father, she avenged herself on Rodrigo by hitting him over the head with a cucumber filled with blood. Much more effective than cutting up his suits.

An asparagus bed is of course a must. In his *Herbal*, John Gerard highly recommends this vegetable.'... the young buds being steeped in wine and eaten, they stir up the lust of the body. 'As does Culpeper; ' a decoction of the roots being taken fasting several mornings together stirreth up bodily lust in man and woman. 'And Pierre Louÿs in his *Manuel de civilité pour les jeunes filles* states that well-bred young ladies should refrain from sliding the tip of an asparagus in and out of their mouths while gazing longingly at a young man to whom they may be attracted.

Fennel must be included not only because a concoction of fennel and vervain increases a lover's ardour, but also because *finocchio* in Italian refers to a perversely elegant gay. It's our sort of plant! What about a bed of fennel and wild pansies?

There is an old Arabic saying which goes: 'For duty a woman, for pleasure a boy, for ecstasy a melon.' And when it comes to erotic vegetables, the Arabs are great authorities. The Perfumed Garden informs us that:

The member of Abou el Heloukh has remained erect,
For thirty days without a break because he did eat onions.
And:
Abu el Heidja had deflowered in one night eighty virgins and he did not
eat or drink because he had surfeited himself first with chickpeas and had
drunk camel's milk with honey mixed.'
Need we say more!

The members of the squash family such as the courgette, often need to be fertilised manually, as do date trees. The traditional method consists in picking up pollen from the male plant with a feather and brushing it onto the female plant. Our friend Sebastian Bliss often performs this operation using his *membrum virile*.

Aubergines are possibly the most erotic of all vegetables - Robert Mapplethorpe obviously thought so - and Marie Rouanet in her *Cuisine amoureuse courtoise et occitane* agrees. An aubergine, smooth, purple and engorged, hanging amid its leaves, she compares to the exposed member of a donkey. And she is adamant about not peeling it - the aubergine, that is. The skin retains its beautiful colour. It is an ornament. But the important thing is to soap it well, a process she describes as *considérablement érotique*.

By now the lovers are getting impatient. Furtive glances are cast to see if they are alone. Clothing is being loosened or removed in an attempt to cool down. The stickiness of the climate is causing underclothes to cling and ride up. Stirrings have turned into longings. They hurry along the path to the site of the next song.

> *Spring flowers at the branch end*
> *over the water.*
> *Love is very deep,*
> *their reflection is very deep.*
> *I had to wet my sleeves*
> *to gather them,*
> *and I want to go on*
> *wetting my sleeves*

This stands by a water feature - a reference to the debauching of the emperor Ming Huang (712-56). Here was a man of vital intelligence. He was decisive and of sound judgment. He was also a great patron of the arts. He instructed court musicians, and under his influence poetry flourished. But when he fell in love with the beautiful concubine, Yang Kuei-fei, he became a man obsessed and gave in to her slightest whim. He built palaces for the lady and all her sisters, each with a garden. The best known was on the site of the ancient gardens of the Hua Ching hot springs. Here the emperor built 'a microscopic island mountain of lapis lazuli around which the girls of his seraglio sculled boats of sandalwood and lacquer'. Here too, the incomparable Yang Kuei-fei bathed in a marble pool attended by her handmaidens while the besotted emperor looked on through a peephole.

The lovers' imaginations are beginning frantically to explore each others bodies as they hurry onwards. The water garden has done nothing to cool their ardour. Looking desperately for a secluded spot they barely pause to read the sixth song.

> *Last night a peach petal was wetted by the rain,*
> *and when a girl after her toilet said:*
> *' Which is the more beautiful,*
> *I or the peach petal?'*
> *and he said:*
> *' Peach petal wetted by the rain is incomparable,'*
> *there were tears and a tearing of flowers.*

The garden is a small one. It will consist of a small garden 'room', the 'walls' of which will be made up of varieties of the shrub Hyperium, which grows to about five feet. This shrub is better known as St John's Wort, after the Baptist, and in late summer, especially the Hyperium 'Hidcote' variety, produces a spectacular show of glossy golden flowers. Not that these will ever be seen. For this is the Salome garden. The moment the head of a flower appears, the gardeners are under strict instructions to cut it off.

Salome is one of the great icons of Decadence, appearing and re-appearing in many different forms - the music of Richard Strauss, the writings of Wilde, Flaubert and Jean Lorrain, the images of Beardsley, Klimt and Jeanne Jacquemin who painted the woebegone heads of decapitated martyrs, placed on dishes like human cut flowers, lying in the blood-red water of an enormous chalice. Salome is the incarnation of *la volupté et la mort*, sex and death. She is the *Belle dame sans merci*, subjugating the noblest and fiercest of males through decapitation or castration.

The lovers barely register the Salome garden. Just as well, perhaps. They have only one thing on their minds. At the end of the path they see a magnificent domed glasshouse packed with green fecundity. At the entrance to the hothouse is the seventh song:

> *The flowers come to blossom, then*
> *we look at the flowers, then*
> *they wither, then ...*

The lovers burst in through the doors. Inside the heat is stifling. They throw themselves onto an earthy bed and surrender themselves to their lust. Their clothing is soiled as they writhe around in the soft earth, surrounded by Indian erotic statuary, amidst the dates and the avocado, the Mandrake, *Phallus impudicus*, the exploding puffball, the shooting fungus, the giant agave which copulates with the sky and then ... dies.

This is how we always envisage it, anyway! And this is why the hothouse is on the lakeshore next to the Garden of Oblivion. It is the climax of the erotic garden, the place of *la petite mort*, the little death. The garden, more than any other, is where sex and death are inseparably linked.

Appendix One

Editors' note: The following is a series of techniques recommended by Gray and Lucan to ensure fertility in the garden. They relate to the garden as a whole, but have a particular significance for the erotic garden. At the outset, the idea of subjecting the garden to clouds of artificial chemicals appealed greatly to Gray and Lucan's deep-seated antipathy to the natural. However, the invasion of the garden by the rational world of science and industry was abhorrent to them. An alternative presented itself in the shape of pagan ritual. As a way of promoting fecundity, they felt that this had been sadly ignored by horticulturalists and needed to be encouraged. They felt that the carrying out of pagan rites was the only seemly way for the Decadent gardener to proceed. If exotic plants were to be uprooted and introduced to the foreign soil of Mountcullen, then it made sense to import also the rituals which would promote their growth. Moreover, this supported their notion that the garden is fundamentally a place for 'acting', in all senses of the word, rather than a place of retreat and quiet contemplation.

CEREMONIES AND FESTIVALS DESIGNED TO ENSURE FERTILITY OF THE SOIL.

Before all else, we must seek out a couple who have recently had twins. They can guarantee the fertility of our garden thus: some little time after the birth of the twins, the woman lies down in the garden and places a plantain flower between her legs. The man then comes along and knocks away the flower with his penis.

For four days before doing any planting, the Decadent gardener should be kept apart from wife, husband or partner, in order that on the night before planting they might indulge their passions to the fullest extent. Alternatively, certain persons may be appointed to perform the sexual act at the very moment when the first seeds are deposited in the ground.

To ensure the fruitfulness of the ground, we adopt that old Chinese custom whereby wives or partners are placed at the disposal of any stranger who comes to stay. What warmer welcome could one provide? And it will be deemed an honour if the guest makes use of the opportunity. As an indication of just how effective this method is, it is sufficient to point out that when the Emperor heard of this practice, he forbade the people to observe it. For three years they obeyed. Then, finding that their lands were no longer fruitful and that many mishaps befell them, they implored the Emperor to allow them to reinstate the custom. According to Marco Polo 'for reason of this usage … their gods bestowed upon them all the good things that they possessed and without it they saw not how they could continue to exist.'

We are delighted to have come across indigenous rites which might be better suited to the location of Mountcullen. One of these is the Celtic custom of constructing colossal figures of wicker work or of wood and grass. The figures are filled with various animals and condemned criminals. They are then set alight and the wicker figures burned along with their contents. The greater the number of victims, apparently, the more fertile the land will be. The advantage of this particular custom is that it only has to be carried out once every five years. We have discussed with a local magistrate the possibility of reinstating this practice. He seemed to think we were joking.

HOW TO PROMOTE GROWTH
ONCE FLOWERS BEGIN TO APPEAR.

Try hanging a nine foot high flag of a man in a state of tumescence above your flower beds. We would like to say that this particular technique was recommended by Miss Gertrude Jekyll. But search as we have, we are unable to find a single reference to this in her numerous writings on the garden.

A delightful practice for promoting rapid growth is to create a Garden of Adonis. Adonis was the beautiful Greek youth with whom Aphrodite fell in love. He was born from a myrtle into which his mother, Myrrha, had been transformed after an incestuous affair with her father, Cinyras, king of Cyprus. When Adonis was killed by a wild boar, the anemone (or the rose) sprang from his spilt blood. Gardens of Adonis are baskets or pots filled with earth in which wheat, barley, lettuces, fennel, and various kinds of flowers are sown and tended for eight days exclusively by women. Having no roots but fostered by the sun, the plants shoot up but wither away rapidly. At the end of eight days, we carry the gardens, along with images of the dead Adonis, down to the lake shore and fling them into the waters of Lough Doon.

In effect, these are vegetable representations of Adonis and, by throwing them into the water, a plentiful supply of rain is guaranteed. We can claim that indeed the Garden of Adonis has proved spectacularly successful. We have never had any problem with rainfall at Mountcullen.

Another ritual intended to promote plant growth entails swathing a man from head to foot in straw and wrapping him round with straw ropes. He is then led from house to house to the accompaniment of music. In every house he dances with the women and the more and the higher they dance, the higher and more abundantly will grow the plants.

Alternatively, when the plants are beginning to show green above the ground, have them blessed by the priest in his vestments who is then rolled over the ground by the women of the village, without regard for the holes or mud he may encounter.

WHAT TO DO IF THE FRUIT CROP IS SCANT

Apparently, in Amboyna (wherever that is!), when the clove crop looks as if it might be scanty, the men go into the orchard by night and seek to fertilise the trees precisely as they would impregnate a woman. At the same time they call out: 'More cloves!' This is supposed to make the trees bear fruit more abundantly. We look forward to the time when our orchard will resound to such cries.

HOW TO RIPEN FRUIT QUICKLY

Another festival, to speed the ripening of hard fruit, requires a number of men and boys to assemble naked in an open space among the orchards and run from there to a distant hill. It may be necessary to hold this festival on a number of occasions should the pineapples at Mountcullen fail to ripen.

HOW TO ENSURE A SUCCESSFUL GRAFT

We found the following technique in the writings of the great Jewish philosopher, Maimonides. The grafting of one tree onto another of a different sort should be carried out by a young woman who at the very moment of inserting the graft in the bough should herself be subjected to treatment which can only be regarded as a direct copy of the operation she is performing on the tree. This is known as sympathetic magic.

BRINGING RAIN OR SUN

We cannot whole-heartedly recommend the next technique. Although it may be effective, it has proved difficult to set up and should definitely be conceived as a long-term measure. Firstly it requires setting up the cult of a python-god; then employing old priestesses armed with clubs to run frantically through the streets of local villages shrieking madly and carrying off young girls as brides-to-be for the serpent. Of course, pious people would at such times leave their daughters at their doors on purpose for the honour of being dedicated to the god. The consequent marriage enables the serpent god to discharge the function of bringing rain or sun at the appropriate moments.

POT PLANT CARE.

Finally, here is a simple tip for those who find it difficult to grow successful plants in pots. It was used by a young woman, Lisabetta, in another story from Boccaccio's *Decameron*.

Lisabetta has fallen in love with Lorenzo, who is employed by her brothers as a steward. When they find out about this liaison, they lead Lorenzo to a remote spot in the countryside and murder him, burying his body in a shallow grave. The ghost of Lorenzo appears to Lisabetta in a dream, in which she tells him what has happened and where he is buried. Lisabetta, together with her maidservant, set out for the lonely spot and ascertain the truth of Lorenzo's words. Unable to remove the entire body of her lover, she severs his head and takes it home wrapped in a cloth:

'Taking the head to her room, she locked herself in and cried bitterly, weeping so profusely that she saturated it with her tears, at the same time implanting a thousand kisses upon it. Then she wrapped the head in a piece of rich cloth and laid it in a large and elegant pot of the sort in which basil or marjoram is grown. She next covered it with soil in which she planted several sprigs of the finest Salernitan basil and never watered them except with essence of roses or orange blossom, or with her own teardrops. She took to sitting permanently beside this pot and gazing lovingly at it, concentrating the whole of her desire upon it because it was where her beloved Lorenzo lay concealed. And after gazing raptly for a long while upon it she would bend over it and begin to cry and her weeping never ceased until the whole of the basil was wet with her tears.

This particular form of horticultural care seems to work well.

Because of the long and unceasing care that was lavished upon it, and also because the soil was enriched by the decomposing head inside the pot, the basil grew thick and exceedingly fragrant.

Appendix Two

—————

Editors' note: The following story by decadent writer Jean Lorrain is thought to have been the inspiration for the Salome garden.

THE PRINCESS OF THE RED LILIES

—————

She was the daughter of kings, serious and cold. Barely 16 years old, with grey hawk-like eyes beneath haughty eyebrows. Her skin was so white that her hands could have been of wax and her temples of pearl. Her name was Audovere.

Her father was an old warrior king preoccupied with the conquest of distant lands, when he wasn't defending his own frontiers. She had grown up in an abbey, amid the tombs of her royal ancestors and from an early age had been looked after by nuns. Princess Audovere's mother had died in childbirth.

The convent where she had lived for 16 years stood amidst the shade and silence of an ancient forest. Only the king knew the route to this place and the princess had never seen the face of any man other than her father.

It was a severe place, even gypsies did not pass by it. Nothing entered the building except the light of the sun, and even that only dimly penetrated the thick vault of oak foliage.

After vespers, Princess Audovere sometimes left the confines of the abbey and walked slowly, accompanied by two lines of nuns in procession. She was serious and pensive, as if crushed by the weight of a proud secret, and so pale that it seemed that she was not long for this world.

She wore a long white wool dress with a hem embroidered with golden clover leaves. A headband of chiselled silver held in place a light veil of blue gauze or attenuated the nuance of her hair. Audovere was blonde like lily pollen or the pale vermilion of old altar vases.

Such was her life. Calmly, her heart filled with joyful hope, she waited in the convent for her father's return like another might have awaited the return of her betrothed. She would while away the time thinking of battles and the dangers of armies and the slaughtered princes over which her father had triumphed. These were her sweetest thoughts.

Around her, in April, the high mounds were covered in daisies, and in autumn the clay and fallen leaves turned them blood red; and still cold and pale in her white wool dress trimmed with golden clover, in April and October, in heat of June and in November, Princess Audovere spent her days, in silence, at the foot of the green or red oak trees.

In summer, she sometimes gathered up a handful of the white lilies that grew in the cloister garden, and she was so frail and white herself, she and the flowers might have been sisters. In autumn it was foxgloves that she tormented between her fingers - the violet digitalis gathered at the edge of woodland clearings, and the sick pink of her lips resembled the wine-red purple of the flowers. Strange to relate, she never pulled the leaves off the foxglove, but kissed it again and again almost mechanically, whereas her fingers seemed to take great pleasure in tearing the lilies to shreds. Her lips parted in a cruel smile. It was as if she was carrying out some dark ritual which was linked through space to some far-off event. It was later discovered that this was in fact a ceremony of blood and darkness.

At each gesture of the virgin princess a man would suffer and die. The old king was well aware of this. This was why he kept this deadly virgin hidden away in the unknown convent. The complicitous princess also knew this. Hence her smile when she kissed the foxgloves or slowly tore lilies to pieces between her beautiful fingers.

Each stripped lily was the body of a prince or a young warrior struck down in battle, each foxglove kissed was an open wound, a widening sore which led directly to the heart's blood, and Princess Audovere had lost count of the number of distant victories. For four years the secret of the spell had been known to her and during that time she had increased the number of kisses she had imparted to the poisonous red flowers. Without pity she had slaughtered the beautiful innocent lilies, dealing out death through a kiss. Acting as funereal aide-de-camp and mysterious executioner to her father, she would extinguish a life between her ever tightening grasp . Each evening the chaplain of the convent, an old blind Barnabite, heard her confession and absolved her of her sins; for the sins of queens only condemn peoples and the stink of corpses is incense at the *foot of the throne of God.*

Princess Audovere suffered from neither remorse nor sadness. Firstly she considered herself cleansed by absolution. Furthermore, young virgins are delighted by battlefields, where in the wake of defeat, princes, mercenaries and beggars, their bloody stumps held up toward the evening sky, scream out in their death agony. When confronted with blood, young girls do not feel the horrified anguish of mothers who shudder for their beloved sons. And moreover, Audovere was her father's daughter.

One evening (nobody knows how he stumbled upon the hidden convent), a wretched fugitive, crying like a child, came to hammer on the door, seeking asylum in this holy place. He was blackened with sweat and dust and he bled from the seven wounds he had received. The nuns welcomed him and, more through error than pity, led him to the cool of the crypt.

Next to him were laid a bowl of ice cold water which he could drink as he wished and a sprinkler dipped in holy water, with a crucifix to aid his passage from this life to the next. Already he was gasping, as his death agony began to tighten around his chest. At nine o'clock, in the refectory, the Reverend Mother told the nuns that prayers for the dead were to be said for the wounded man. The nuns, rather nervously, went back to their cells and silence descended on the convent.

Audovere was the only one who did not sleep. She was thinking of the fugitive. She had caught a glimpse of him as he had stumbled across the garden supported by two of the sisters. One thought obsessed her: this man in his last throes was undoubtedly an enemy of her father's, some deserter who had escaped the massacre, a piece of human wreckage washed up on the shores of this convent, panic-stricken. The battle must have taken place close by, nearer than the nuns realised, and the forest would be full of other deserters, more miserable wretches bleeding and groaning. From now until dawn a whole tide of ugly, suffering humanity with bloody and infected wounds would swamp the walls of the convent where they would be welcomed by the sisters with their indiscriminate charity.

It was already mid-July and the scent of lilies in their long beds filled the air. Princess Audovere went down into the garden.

Through the high stalks, which were bathed in moonlight and stood upright in the night like damps spears, Princess Audovere walked, and as she did so, she slowly began to strip the leaves from the flowers.

But what was happening? All around there arose the sound of sighs, the wailing and the rattle of the dying. The flowers, in her fingers, had the texture and the feel of flesh. One moment, she felt something warm fall on her hand which she took to be tears. The scent of the lilies was sickening. They had changed in some mysterious fashion, become dull and heavy, their flowers filled with a nauseating incense.

And although almost swooning, Audovere continued her murderous work. She stuck to her task, decapitating flowers without mercy, ceaselessly stripping calices and buds. But the more she slaughtered, the more the flowers grew back in numbers. Now it was like a field of tall rigid flowers, standing hostile in her path; a veritable army of pikes and halberds blossoming in the full moon. Cruelly tired, her head swimming, in the grip of a destructive rage, the princess continued tearing, murdering, grinding all in her path, until she was brought to a halt by a strange vision.

Out of a sheaf of taller flowers emerged a bluish transparence - the corpse of a man. His arms were extended, cruciform, his feet the one on top of the other. In the darkness the wounds in his left side and his bleeding hands were visible. He wore a crown of thorns and his temples were bespattered with mud and pus. The terrified princess recognised the wretched fugitive who had been given sanctuary that very evening, the wounded man dying in the crypt. He opened a painfully swollen eyelid and in a reproachful voice, asked;

"Why have you struck me down? What have I done to you?"

The following morning, the princess was found lying on the ground, lilies in her hand and pressed to her heart. Only the whites of her eyes showed. She was dead. She lay across a path at the entrance to the garden, and all around her the lilies had turned blood red. Never again would they flower white. Thus died Princess Audovere having breathed the scent of nocturnal lilies in a convent garden in July.

THE CRUEL GARDEN

Gardening and cruelty! Ah, but those two words go together so well! They are almost synonymous. You hear people talk of tending their gardens, of lavishing love and care on their gardens. What nonsense! Gardening is little more than systematic violence in pursuit of beauty. (At least, that's what it should be!) Leopardi understood this perfectly.

Go into a garden - full of plants, herbs and flowers. As charming as you please, in the loveliest season of the year. Everywhere you look you'll find pain. The whole vegetable kingdom is in a permanent state of suffering. Over there is a rose - tortured by the sun that gave it life; it shrivels, languishes, fades. And that lily over there is being cruelly sucked by a bee - in its tenderest, most vital parts...

This plant is too hot, that one too cold; another has too much light, or too much shade; the soil is too damp, or too dry. This plant is uncomfortable, its growth is obstructed or crowded; another has no support, or struggles to find it. Nowhere in the entire garden will you see a plant in perfect health ...
Meanwhile you are wrecking the grass with your boots; crushing, battering, squeezing out the blood, smashing, killing. And that beautiful, sensitive, kind-hearted girl over there is gaily shattering stems as she walks. Even the gardener - that model of prudence and good sense - is busy lopping off sensitive limbs, reducing them to stumps with his shears and nails ...
We think of the garden as a happy place. But in truth its life is a sad and wretched thing - every garden is an enormous hospital (far more pitiful than a cemetery). If the plants were capable of thinking as well as feeling, they would soon realise that they would be better off not existing at all.

Doesn't history prove time and again that gardening and viciousness go hand in hand? Consider the emperor Nero, who developed that singular form of garden illumination - human torches. And, if the Bible is to be believed, the first murder, indeed the first fratricide, was carried out by a gardener. Perhaps all gardeners carry the mark of Cain. Show us a lover of gardens and we will show you a sadist. And nowhere did these qualities combine to more dramatic effect than in the Mogul emperors.

Babur, the first of the great Moguls, was fourteen when he laid siege to and captured Samarkand, the golden capital of his ancestor, Timur Leng, or Tamburlaine. After his victory, Babur spent much of his time visiting the nine gardens which surrounded the walled city. These had been created by Timur Leng himself and caused Babur to remark that few towns in the habitable world are as pleasant as Samarkand. But this 'builder of pleasant gardens', Timur Leng, was also the man who, in 1399, had led a merciless attack on Delhi. After his army departed, it was said that nothing moved in the city, not even a bird, for two months.

The perfect conjunction of horticulture and sadism was achieved by Jahangir, who governed the Mogul empire at its zenith from 1605 - 1627. As a young man he had accompanied his father, Akbar, on many journeys to the outposts of empire, and it was on one such trip that he discovered and fell in love with Kashmir. Jahangir's writings overflow with praise for the province.

Kashmir is a garden of eternal spring ... a delightful flower bed and a heart-expanding heritage for dervishes. Its pleasant meads and enchanting cascades are beyond all description. There are running streams and fountains beyond count. Wherever the eye reaches there are verdure and running water; the rose, the violet and the narcissus grow of themselves: in the fields there are all kinds of flowers and sweet-scented herbs - more than can be numbered. In the soul-enchanting spring, the hills and the plains are filled with blossom; the gates, the walls the courts and the roofs are lighted up by the torches of banquet-adorning tulips. What shall we say of these things or of the wide meadows and the fragrant trefoils?

Clearly a sensitive soul, and as Lord Blake once said of Ali Bhutto, 'he would never strike you as the sort of chap who'd commit atrocities.'

But Jahangir was a true Decadent. After his first cup of yellow wine at the age of seventeen, he began to drink so heavily that wine no longer affected him. He changed to *arrack*, and from that to double-distilled spirits, of which by his late twenties he was drinking twenty cups a day. In an effort at self-discipline, he switched to a cocktail of one part arrack to two parts wine, and reduced his daily intake to six cups. He also consumed enough opium every day to befuddle an elephant.

When it comes to gardening, Jahangir was exactly the sort of reliable authority to whom the Decadent would want to turn for advice. Take this example of man-management. In the twelfth year of his reign he recorded the following incident:

'At this time the gardener represented that a servant of Muqarrab Khan had cut down some champa trees above the bench alongside the river. On hearing this I became angry and went myself to enquire into the matter and to exact satisfaction. When it was established that this improper act had been committed by him I ordered both his thumbs to be cut off as a warning to others'.

This was not an isolated incident. Jahangir was very keen on punishment, and regarded it (quite properly in our view) as a spectator sport. Sir Thomas Roe, the English ambassador to the Mogul court, felt that Jahangir's practice of watching criminals being crushed to death by elephants below his balcony was done 'with too much delight in blood'. But Jahangir was also a bit of wag. He once sent a servant who had broken a china cup to China to fetch another one. And in at least two instances, the emperor managed to combine his delight in punishment with his enthusiasm for planting. Again it was Sir Thomas Roe who wrote:

'... a gentlewoman was taken in the King's house in some improper act with an eunuch ... the poor woman was set up to her armpits in the ground ... to remain there three days and two nights in that situation without sustenance, her head and arms being exposed to the violence of the sun. If she survived, she was then to be pardoned.

The second case occurred when Jahangir

'happened to catch an eunuch kissing one of his women whom he had relinquished. He sentenced the lady to be put into the earth, with only her head left above ground, exposed to the burning rays of the sun, and the eunuch to be cut in pieces before her face.'

Of course, criminals, eunuchs and women of the harem were dispensible. With his own family he was a model of generosity and gentleness - up to a point. There is no doubt that he was deeply in love with his queen, Nur Jahan, to whom he showed the greatest consideration when she arrived at his court as an impoverished widow. He was probably responsible for her state of widowhood in the first place, but then what more effective way of proving his love for her than by having her husband murdered? The act speaks for itself.

And then there were Jahangir's dealings with Prince Khusrau, his eldest son. Five months after Jahangir had become emperor, Khusrau rose in open revolt against him. He besieged Lahore, but was unable to capture it and was then defeated in battle. He was captured with two of his closest friends. They were brought before Jahangir - in a garden outside Lahore. As usual in such family gatherings, there was a great deal of weeping and embracing and remorse on both sides, and the prince got off quite lightly. He was forced to ride an elephant down a street lined with his supporters, each one impaled live upon a stake. Meanwhile the prince's two friends were sewn into the wet skins of a newly slaughtered ox and ass, complete with head and ears, seated backwards on donkeys and paraded around the city all day. Under the hot sun, the skins dried and shrank and one of the men died from suffocation and constriction.

Prince Khusrau spent a year in chains after his first rebellion, but failed to learn his lesson. No sooner had he been released than, between August and September 1607, he plotted the assassination of his father. Some four hundred nobles were said to be involved, although Jahangir executed only the ringleaders. By now his patience was wearing thin. He ordered his son to be blinded, preferably by his own brother. But the task was incompetently done and Khusrau later regained partial sight. The Prince still lived around the palace and was brought into his father's presence from time to time in the hope of effecting a reconciliation. But this failed to occur as the emperor was depressed by his son's appearance . According to Jahangir,' he showed no signs of openness and happiness and was always mournful and dejected in mind. 'Curious, really! Anyway, the emperor found his attitude irritating and sent him away.

Khusrau died when still a young man. After his son's death, Jahangir had the body disinterred and brought from the Deccan to Allahabad for re-burial. At every point where the cortege stopped on the journey, Jahangir gave orders for a shrine and a garden to be laid out. These gardens became places of pilgrimage where women in particular would gather to ask favours of the dead rebel, now turned secular saint. The Prince was finally laid to rest in a garden-tomb, the Khusrau Bagh, along with his mother and sons.

So perhaps Jahangir wasn't such a monster after all. He loved flowers, his wife, and (once he was safely underground) his son. Above all he loved gardening.

During the first half of the 17th century, the Vale of Kashmir was said to contain 777 gardens on the lakesides and mountain slopes, all built by Jahangir, his son Shah Jehan, and their nobles.

Central to these gardens was water, and they were designed to be approached in boats. Thus François Bernier in the 17th century described Shalimar Bagh:

The entrance from the lake is though a spacious canal, bordered with green turf and running between two rows of poplars. Its length is about five hundred paces, and it leads to a large summer house placed in the middle of the garden.

Shalimar Bagh means 'The Abode of Love'. Here Jahangir would sit on his black marble throne and receive visitors. The throne was placed across the central water course, thus ventilating the emperor with the coolness of the flowing stream.

Jahangir's gardens were intended as pieces of earthly paradise. 17th century European visitors found no reason to disagree with the emperor's assessment. As François Bernier was returning from Send-Brary:

I turn'd a little aside from the road to go and lye at Achiavel, which is the house of pleasure of the ancient kings of Kachemire, and at present of the Great Mogol ... The garden itself is very fine, there being curious walks in it, and a store of fruit-bearing trees, of Apples, Pears, Prunes, Apricocks and Cherries and many jets of waters of various figures and Ponds replenished with Fish together with a high cascata of water which by its fall maketh a great Nape of thirty or forty paces long, which hath an admirable effect, especially in the night, when under this Nape is put a great number of little lamps fitted in holes purposely made in the wall; which maketh a curious shew.

This is the very effect we sought to recreate in the Mountcullen garden at the bottom of the water staircase (See chapter four, page 76).

The favourite garden of Jahangir and Nur Jahan was Vernag. Vernag's great claim to fame was its fishponds. This is Bernier again:

From Achiaval went I yet a little more out of my way to pass through another Royal Garden which is also very beautiful, and hath the same pleasantness with that of Achiaval, but this is peculiar in it, that in one of its Ponds there are Fishes that come when they are called, and when you cast bread to them; the biggest whereof have golden rings in their Noses with inscriptions about them which they say that renowned Nour-Mehalle, the Wife of Jehan-Guire, the grandfather of Aureng-Zebe, caused to be fastened in them'.

If one is going to keep pets, that's the way to do it! In fact, when it came to pets, Jahangir rivalled Snow White in slushiness. After the death of one of his pet deer, he had a large garden pavilion erected to its memory.

The son who succeeded him, Shah Jehan, was a chip off the old block. He had his brother, two nephews and two male cousins murdered on his way to the throne. He also improved on some of his father's horticultural achievements. At Shalimar Bagh, he extended the garden and built the black marble pavilion on the zenana, or topmost terrace. He even created one or two gardens of his own. At the fort at Agra, he built Anguri Bagh, the Grape Garden. The name derives from the decorative inlay of vines on the buildings nearby. In 1684, Jean-Baptiste Tavernier, the jeweller, described what he saw:

Before the divan is a gallery that serves for a Portico; which Cha-Jean had a design to have adorn'd all over with a kind of latice-work of emeraulds and rubies that should have represented to the life Grapes when they are green and when they begin to grow red. But this design which made such a noise in the world and requir'd more riches than all the world could afford to perfect, remains unfinish'd; there being only three stocks of a vine in gold with their leaves as the rest ought to have been; and enamel'd in their natural colours with emeraulds, rubies and granates wrought into the fashion of grapes.

Shah Jehan was also responsible for the modest little garden tomb he built to commemorate his wife. This is otherwise known as the Taj Mahal. But he was not really in his father's league as a truly Decadent gardener. His problem was simple: he was too soft. For example, there was one garden, Nishat Bagh (Garden of Gladness) which he coveted greatly. He tried to persuade the owner, Asaf Khan IV, to make it over to him, but Asaf refused as it was his most precious possession. Shah Jahan was unable to enforce his demand because of a belief among the Moguls that a garden can only be bought for a fair price or given as a token of friendship. In his fury, Shah Jehan ordered that the stream above Nishat Bagh be diverted, cutting off its lifeblood. Asaf Khan was left wandering sadly among his silent fountains and dying garden, before one of his servants dared to defy the emperor and restore the flow. Unbelievably, Shah Jehan not only allowed Nishat Bagh to return to its former glory, but even spared the servant's life. No wonder the dynasty went into decline.

CUTTINGS FROM THE TORTURE GARDEN.

Despite the cruelties perpetrated by the Mogul emperors, nothing can compare with the horrors created in the imagination of the French novelist Octave Mirbeau. His *Jardin des Supplices* (The Torture Garden), which was described by Oscar Wilde as 'a green adder of a book', portrays a world in which gardening and sadistic brutality are taken to nightmarish extremes. The narrator is a corrupt and cynical Frenchman who journeys by sea to the far East on a spurious scientific mission. On the voyage he meets a beautiful and enigmatic Englishwoman called Clara. Deeply attracted to her lack of conventional morality, he lives with Clara in her house in China. But it is only when she takes him on a visit to the Torture garden that he begins to understand the depths of her depravity.

The garden sloped down gently ornamented everywhere with rare species and precious plants. An avenue of enormous camphor-trees led from the pavilion I was in to a red door, shaped like a temple which opened out to the countryside. Between the leafy branches of gigantic trees which partly concealed the view to the left, I caught glimpses of the river gleaming like polished silver in the sun. I tried to take an interest in the garden's multiple decorations, in its strange flowers and monstrous vegetation. A man crossed the avenue with two indolent panthers on a lead. In the middle of the lawn stood an immense bronze representing some obscene and cruel divinity. There were birds there - cranes with blue plumage, red-throated toucans from tropical America, sacred pheasants, ducks with golden casques and clad in brilliant purple like warriors from long ago, tall multi-coloured wading birds seeking the shade of the thickets. But neither the birds nor the wild beasts, nor Gods, nor flowers could hold my attention, nor could the bizarre palace on my right which between the cedars and bamboos superimposed its light-filled terraces adorned with flowers, its shaded balconies and vivid roofs. My thoughts were elsewhere, far, far, away ...

Laughter in the foliage, little cries, the friskiness of a dog ... Clara appeared, dressed half in Chinese fashion, half in European. A pale mauve silk blouse faintly spangled with golden flowers enveloping her in a thousand folds, outlining her slender body and rounded curves. She wore a large pale straw hat below which her face appeared like a pink flower in the pale shadow. And she was wearing yellow leather shoes on her little feet.

When she entered the pavilion it was like an explosion of scents.

"You think I look weird, don't you? Oh such a sad man of Europe, who hasn't laughed once since he's been back. Aren't I beautiful?"

I did not rise from the settee where I was reclining.

"Quickly! Quickly! Darling, we must do the grand tour. I'll put my gloves on along the way. Let's go."

And we walked in the sun - that frightful sun which blackened the grass - withered the peonies in the garden and weighed on my skull like a heavy iron helmet.

<hr>

The Chinese are incomparable gardeners, infinitely superior to our clumsy horticulturists whose only thought is to destroy the beauty of plants by disrespectful practices and criminal hybridisation. They are the real criminals and I can't understand why the most severe penal laws have not been enacted against them in the name of universal life. I would be quite happy to see them guillotined mercilessly in place of those tame murderers whose social 'selectionism' may be somewhat praiseworthy and noble since for the most part their targets are only ugly old women and the most disgusting part of the bourgeoisie who are a permanent outrage to life. In addition to pushing infamy to the point of defaming the moving and pretty grace of simple flowers, our gardeners have dared that debased practical joke in which the names of old generals and dishonoured politicians are given to the fragility of the rose, the stellar radiance of clematis, the heavenly glory of the delphinium, the heraldic mystery of the iris and the modesty of the violet. In our flower beds you frequently come across an iris, for instance, baptised General Archinard! There are narcissi - narcissi! - grotesquely designated: The Triumph of President Félix Faure; hollyhocks that unprotestingly accept the appellation of 'Mourning for Monsieur Thiers'; violets - timid sensitive and exquisite violets - which have not felt insulted with nicknames like General Skobeleff and Admiral Avellan! Flowers, all beauty, light and joy - all tenderness too - evoking sullen moustaches and heavy soldiers' tans or politicians' parliamentary effrontery! Flowers reflecting political opinions and helping to spread election propaganda! To what aberrations and intellectual debility do we owe such blasphemy and outrage against the divinity of things? If a being could possibly be so devoid of soul as to feel hatred for flowers then European gardeners (and in particular French gardeners) have justified this inconceivably sacrilegious paradox.

Being perfect artists and resourceful poets, the Chinese have piously conserved the love and devoted cult of flowers: one of the rarest and most ancient traditions to have survived their decadence. And, as flowers have to be distinguished from one another, they have used graceful analogies, dream images, pure or pleasurable names which perpetuate and harmonise in our minds the sensations of gentle charm and violent intoxication which they inspire in us. This is how the Chinese honour their favourite flower, the peony, according to its form and colour with such delightful names that each one is a complete poem or novel in itself: 'Young Girl Offering Her Breasts' or 'The Water Sleeping Under The Moon' or 'The Sun In The Forest' or 'The First Desire of the Reclining Virgin', or 'My Dress is no longer completely white because the Son of Heaven left behind a little of his rosy blood when he tore it', or how about 'I have swooned with my Lover in the Garden'?

And Clara, who recounted these charming things to me, cried indignantly as she stamped the ground with her small feet in her little yellow slippers.

"And they consider these divine poets who call their flowers 'I swooned with my Lover in the Garden' to be apes and savages!"

———⟫●⟪———

The Chinese are right to be proud of their Torture Garden, perhaps the most absolutely beautiful in all China where there are many marvellous gardens. The rarest and the most delicate and robust species of flora are collected from the mountain snow line and the parched furnace of the plains as well as those mysterious and wild plants which hide in the most impenetrable forests and which popular superstition considers as being the souls of evil genies. From mangrove to saxatile azalea; from horned and biflorous violet to distillatory nepenthe; from voluble hibiscus to stoloniferous sunflower; from androsace invisible in its rocky fissure to the most wildly tangled liana - each species represented by numerous specimens which, gorged upon organic food treated to the rituals of gardening experts, assume abnormal forms and colourings, the wonderful intensity of which, with our sullen climates and insipid gardens, we are unable to imagine.

———⟫●⟪———

Clara pointed out strange plants growing in the ground across which water gushed forth from all sides. I approached. On high stalks, scaly and stained black like snakeskins were enormous spars, kind of funnel-shaped cornets with the dark violet of putrefaction inside, and the greenish-yellow of decomposition outside, like the open thoraxes of dead animals. Long, blood-red spadices, imitating monstrous phalluses, came forth from these cornets. Attracted by the corpse-like odour that these horrible plants exhaled, flies hovered in concentrated swarms, swallowed up at the bottom of the spar which was adorned from top to bottom with silky projectiles that enlaced the flies and held them prisoner more effectively than any spider's web. Along the stem, the digitalised leaves were clenched and twisted like the hands of men under torture.

" You see, darling," declared Clara. "These flowers are not the creation of a sick mind or a delirious genius - they're of nature ... Didn't I tell you *that nature loves death?"*

━━━►●◄━━━

We had now entered into bamboo palisades along which ran honeysuckle, odorous jasmine, begonia, mauve tree ferns and climbing hibiscus that had not yet blossomed. Moonseed wrapped itself around a stone column with its countless liana. At the top of the column the face of a hideous divinity grimaced, its ears stretched like bats' wings, its hair ending in fiery horns. Incarvillea, day-lilies, moraea and delphinium nudicaul concealed the base with their pink bells, scarlet thyrses, golden calyxes and purple stars ...

Here and there in the indentations of the palisade, appearing like halls of verdure and flower-beds, were wooden benches equipped with chains and bronze necklaces, iron tables shaped like crosses, blocks and racks, gibbets, automatic quartering machines, beds laden with cutting blades, bristling with steel points, fixed chokers, props and wheels, boilers and basins above extinguished hearths, all the implements of sacrifice and torture covered in blood - in some places dried and darkish, in others sticky and red. Puddles of blood filled the hollows in the ground and long tears of congealed blood hung from the dismantled mechanisms. Around these machines the ground had absorbed the blood. But blood still stained the whiteness of the jasmines and flecked the coral-pink of the honeysuckles and the mauve of the passion flowers. And small fragments of human flesh, caught by whips and leather lashes, had flown here and there on to the tops of petals and leaves. Noticing that I was feeling faint and that I flinched at these puddles whose stain had enlarged and reached the middle of the avenue, Clara, in a gentle voice, encouraged me:

"That's nothing yet, darling ... Let's go on!"

━━━►●◄━━━

We reached an avenue leading to the central pond and the peacocks, which hitherto had followed us, suddenly abandoned us and scattered with a great noise through the flower-beds and the garden lawns.

The broad avenue was bordered by dead trees on both sides - immense tamarinds whose massive bare branches interlaced in hard arabesques across the sky. A recess was hollowed out in every trunk. The majority remained empty but some enclosed the violently contorted bodies of men and women subjected to hideous and obscene tortures. Some sort of clerk dressed in a black robe stood gravely in front of the occupied recesses with a writing-case on his chest and a police register in his hands.

"It's the avenue of the accused," Clara told me. "And these people you see standing here come to take the confessions which only prolonged suffering could tear out of the wretches ... It is an ingenious idea. I really do believe they got it from Greek mythology. It's a horrible transposition of the charming fable of the wood nymph trapped in the trees!"

Clara approached a tree in which a woman who was still young was growling. She was hanging by her wrists from an iron hook and her wrists were held between two blocks of wood clasped with great force. A rough rope of coconut thread covered with pulverised pimento and mustard and soaked in a salt solution was wound around her arms.

"That rope is kept on," Clara was kind enough to explain, "until the limb is swollen to four times its usual size ..."

Shadows descended across the garden, trailing blue veils that lay lightly over the bare lawns and more thickly over the flower-beds whose outlines had clarified. The white flowers of the cherry and peach trees - whose whiteness was now moon-like - had elements of slippage and wandering, the strangely stooping aspect of phantoms. And the gibbets and gallows raised their sinister casks and black frames in the eastern sky that was the colour of blue steel.

Horror! Above a flower-bed, against the purple of the dying evening, endlessly turning on the stakes, slowly turning, turning in the void and swaying like immense flowers with stalks visible in the night, I saw, endlessly turning, the silhouettes of five tortured men.

"Clara! Clara! Clara!"

Ah yes! The Torture Garden! Passions, appetites, personal interests, hatreds and lies, along with laws, social institutions, justice, love, glory, heroism and religion. These are its monstrous and hideous flowers - instruments of eternal human suffering. What I saw that day, what I heard, exists and cries out and yells outside that garden, which for me is *no more than a symbol of the whole earth. I have vainly sought a lull in crime and a rest in death, but I have found them nowhere.*

THE WATER GARDEN

It is the omnipresent rush of water which give the Este gardens their peculiar character. From the Anio, drawn up the hillside at incalculable cost and labour, a thousand rills gush downward, terrace by terrace, channelling the stone rails of the balusters, leaping from step to step, dripping into mossy conches, flashing in spray from the horns of sea-gods and the jaws of mythical monsters, or forcing themselves in irrepressible overflow down the ivy-matted banks.

Edith Wharton, *Italian Villas and Their Gardens*

It was that little phrase 'incalculable cost and labour' which really attracted us. Suddenly we knew how the Mountcullen water garden should work. Substitute the Cull for the Anio and there you have it - except that Mountcullen will be infinitely more impressive.

We want to use water as a kind of liquid 'nervous system' for the entire garden. A huge head of water will be created in the hills above the house. From here it will come cascading down to the garden in a vast, battering torrent. The surge of energy will power the of fountains, automata and mechanical devices, and the flow of water through the garden will connect and animate its different parts before trickling away to mingle with the dark waters of Lough Doon.

This will not be workable without extra hands. We don't want clodhoppers either, but finely-tuned spirits who know how to manipulate a stopcock. At Versailles, Louis XIV had a staff of eleven to look after the fountains: the *Intendant de la Conduite et Mouvements des Eaux et Fontaines*, the chief fountainer, three assistants and six boys. The chief fountainer, Denis Joly, issued his boys with keys, ladders, whalebone rods and other tools for clearing blocked pipes and keeping the fountains going. If the king came along and they didn't have their tools about them, they were swiftly and severely punished. The same applied if they weren't at their posts when the order came to activate the displays. Since

POOLS OF HEROD

I

FOUNTAIN OF IMBECILITY

I

GROTTO   WATER STAIRCASE   GROTTO

I

THÉÂTRE D'EAU

I

BASSIN DE FOLIES

I

CURVE OF RIVER CULL AT REAR OF HOUSE

I

DINING-TABLE

I

FOUR RIVERS OF EDEN

I

WATER AVENUES

I

LABYRINTH

I

CHADARS

I

ENSTONE ROCK

I

RUEIL DRAGON

I

LOUGH DOON

I

ISLANDS OF THE IMMORTALS

I

THE GODALMING SURPRISE

The sequence of waterworks at Mountcullen

there wasn't enough pressure to run all the fountains at once, they had to be turned on in series as the king and his guests came into view, then off again as soon as they disappeared. The boys stood at strategic points and blew whistles to signal when the visitors were approaching.

The first operation is to divert the River Cull further upstream in order to fill a pair of reservoirs at the highest point above the house. This will give good head, as the water engineers say, as well as avoiding the vulgarity of electric pumps. The reservoirs will also double as bathing pools, to be known as the Pools of Herod.

THE POOLS OF HEROD

Many people believe that King Herod was nothing but a bloodthirsty tyrant in the pay of the Romans, who murdered babies and lusted after his step-daughter. But this is to do him a disservice. He was also a great builder of swimming-pools. We once climbed up to his fortress at Masada and took in the view - salt, rocks, desert, the poison mineral blue of the Dead Sea thousands of feet below. Herod saw all that from his poolside. Obstacles and impossibilities attracted him as the reek of the stinkhorn attracts the fly. Scholars doubt if he really did order the Massacre of Innocents, but there's no doubting the man's decadent credentials - his mania for luxury and building in strange places, his paranoia, egotism, visionary aestheticism, and the final madness. The view from the hills above Mountcullen may not match that from Masada, but looking out over the house and Lough Doon to the blue mountains in the distance should create the sensation of swimming in mid-air.

At the top of the water system we shall install a set of barrels containing dyes, so that the colour of the waters flowing through the garden can be varied at will. (An idea from one Monsieur de Brunoi, who, when he went into mourning over the death of his mother, put his garden into mourning as well. He had barrels of ink sent from Paris so that his jets d'eau might spout black water.) Other barrels will hold different-coloured oils for marbled water or indeed flammable liquid so that the canals, fountains and cascades can burst spectacularly into flame with a single match. As well as providing garden lighting of a particularly ghostly and memorable kind, it should be possible to poach trout thus for a large number of guests.

FOUNTAIN OF IMBECILITY

This will be located between the Pools of Herod and is a key emblem in the iconography of the garden. A madman with water squirting from phallic jets all over his head. Could be Herod himself, or a favourite politician? The jets will be lengths of leather hose-pipe with copper nozzles, as described by the philosopher Charles de Brosses, visiting Villa Mondragone in 1739:

These pipes were lying innocently about until someone turned on a tap and they suddenly stood up in the strangest way and began pissing fresh water in a continuous stream. Migieu seized one of them and squirted Lacurne in the face. Lacurne squirted him back and soon we were all at it - we had tremendous fun for half an hour until every one of us was soaked to the skin.

At Villa Aldobrandini on the same day they found another good trick which we might put in hereabouts:

At the top of the steps we had our revenge on Legouz who had wetted us earlier at the Belvedere. He was trying to turn on another tap to soak us again, but it was designed to trick the trickster, and it flung out a ferocious jet of water, thick as your arm, straight into Legouz's stomach. Legouz went squelching off in great haste, with his trousers and shoes full of water ...

WATER STAIRCASE

A wide path down the hill for this has already been cleared. It is just a matter of deciding on a design for the staircase. Chatsworth, Caserta, and Peterhof (where the water flows between gold-painted statues into the Gulf of Finland) provide suitable models. At Bagnaia in Italy there's the water-chain: a shallow rill racing through tulip-shaped troughs of stone. Our favourite, though, is the cascade squirting from Fame's trumpet at Villa Garzoni, which feeds a steep double staircase of deep, overflowing pools stuffed with tadpoles, with viewing steps for walkers either side.

GROTTOES

'Such that have convenient places in their Villes', says John Worlidge in his *Systema Horti-Culturae* (1677), *'make themselves Grotto's or Caves in the Earth, either in the side of some declive of a Hill, or under some Mount or Terrace artificially raised, may you make a place of repose, cool and fresh in the greatest heats … It is a place that is capable of giving you so much pleasure and delight, that you may bestow not undeservedly what cost you please on it … '*

We fully intend to. Two or three 'grotts' will be excavated at different levels alongside the staircase as it descends the hill.

The Grotto of the Flood at Pratolino would go well here. When you sit down on a bench to look at the sculpture, the whole place floods at once 'and all the seats squirt water into your backside' (Montaigne). Some people pay large sums for that sort of treatment. The escape route is also booby-trapped - a staircase with 'a thousand jets of water from every two steps'.

We might model another on the Grotto of the Winds at the Villa Torrigiani, near Lucca. Here our visitors can be showered from the roof, hosed by statues round the walls, and squirted between the legs by invisible jets on the threshold. If they've managed to escape all this, there's the fail-safe of an extra set of nozzles along the approach path. These squirt two ways, catching spectators as well.

One function of the grotto is for dining in comfort on hot days. So a small kitchen and pantry flank the entrance. Floors are cobbled with black and white pebbles. Walls are lined in volcanic rock and shells form lurid masks. There is an air of ambiguity everywhere - 'do I wake or sleep?' Daylight enters, dim and damp, from a lantern in the roof where a crystal sphere hangs, as it once did in the Boboli grotto, filled with darting fish.

THÉÂTRE D'EAU

This is a semicircular retaining wall over which the water comes cascading from a lip of stone stuck out about a foot from the vertical wall, thus forming a semi-transparent curtain. The wall is studded with a set of Mogul *chini-kanas* (niches behind the waterfall with lights in them to glimmer through the water at night. This should look most ethereal from the house on clear summer evenings.

On either side of the théâtre d'eau is a series of four nude Decadent figures in the act of pleasuring or being pleasured. On the left, Decadents of the Ancient World (Salome, Nero, Heliogabalus, Cleopatra) On the right, Decadents of the Modern World (Empress Wu, Durian Gray, Medlar Lucan, Conchita Gordon). The statues are on revolving plinths so that on hot days they can be replaced by live human beings. Behind the curtain of water is the entrance to the Hermit's cave (see the Sacred Garden page 22).

BASSIN DE FOLIES

This is a pool into which tumble the waters from the Théâtre d'Eau - and anything else that may have come down the water staircase. As the effusions of Decadence they are greeted by a set of grinning stone apes perched on the balustrade. Again, these might be supplemented by real apes on party days.

We must think carefully about fish (e.g. Jahangir's giant carp with gold rings through their noses, or Nathanael Ward's monster tadpoles, bred in the dark). Investigate rare species. We have heard that one of the great lakes, Erie perhaps, has become so polluted that a degenerate, mutant species of fish has developed in the waters there. Such creatures would be most suitable.

RIVER CULL AT REAR OF HOUSE

From the bassin de folies, the water will drain back into the river

Cull about a hundred yards from the rear facade of the house. We need to replace the present bridges, however, which are graceless and dull. We are looking into alternative designs: small scale versions of the Bridge of Sighs, or the suicide bridge in the Parc des Buttes-Chaumont.

DINING TABLE

Behind the house **stands** a long stone dining table with a channel of water running down the centre, for cooling wine, dipping fingers and other overheated parts of the anatomy. You will have seen such a thing at the Ville Lante. In the background a mobile fountain wheels too and fro resonantly dispensing gin. Arcs of

water, shot from powerful concealed jets in the ground, form a vault over the diners' heads. In the benches, 'enema seats' squirt water, as at the palace of Archbishop Sittikus at Hellbrunn. Pliny the Younger at his Tuscan villa had dishes floating on model ships and birds in a nearby pool.

FOUR RIVERS OF EDEN

The water will then be channelled underground to the Sacred Garden at the front of Mountcullen house. There the four rivers of Eden will be reproduced. For details see the Guide to the Sacred Garden.

WATER AVENUES

What we have in mind are the avenues created by the last of the d'Este Dukes of Ferrara, at a time when their power was in terminal decline, and all that seemed to be left to a rotting élite was the pursuit of ever more rarified pleasures... Ella Noyes tells the story with feeling in her *Story of Ferrara:*

The gulf between sovereign and subjects widened as the Duke, embittered by disappointments, grew sombre and selfish in his old age. Caring only to wring all the revenue he could out of the dominions slipping from the grasp of his House, he allowed abuses to multiply unchecked. The poor were ground down by ever-increasing exactions. The terrible harshness of the game laws, which Alfonso instituted to satisfy his measureless appetite for the chase, was ruining the land. Wild creatures multiplied and consumed the harvests, wolves infested the fields, fertile stretches became wastes, while peasants hung in bunches on the Piazza, with the pheasants they had stolen suspended to their feet. No wonder the people regarded with delight the prospect of a change of government. All sympathy between them and their old lords was dead.

In his later years the Duke withdrew himself more and more from the vulgar gaze, and, surrounded by his courtiers, abandoned himself to a forced gaiety, close hidden within the ducal gardens and wildernesses, where no unprivileged eye might penetrate. There the pleasures of that elect circle grew ever more unrestrained. The joyous, vigorous, madcap Marfisa, now wife of the Marchese Cybo Alderano, led the revels, presiding over them like some Maenad with her flushed cheeks and unveiled golden hair, which Tasso had once sung. Alfonso had linked together the scattered pleasaunces round the city by a wide 'viale' some miles in length, which made a girdle of beauty and delight within the formidable circuit of the walls, with their mighty bastions and earthworks. Luxury and pleasure girt round by a warlike strength unequalled in Italy, such was the Ferrara of Alfonso II. The ducal alley was hedged by a thick pleached growth of vines and olives, and along the middle ran a clear stream, so that the prince and his guests could pass as they would, in boats or in carriages, from one place of delight to another, uninterrupted by the curious crowd, the roads leading out of the city being carried over it on bridges. From the Castle, which stood itself among gardens, ... the Viale led southwards by groves of plane trees and pomegranate-covered walls to the Castellina with its marble chambers and sculptured baths. Then through orchards, shut in by thickets of roses, it passed on beside a little hill of box trees and a garden full of exquisite flowers to a thick ilex wood, where birds of rare kinds were gathered together to make sport for the fowler. Thence to a grove of precious fruit trees - oranges, citrons and lemons - seldom seen in that part of Italy, and enclosed on one side by the city walls , and on another by marble loggias, frescoed and sculptured by the best masters. A flight of marble steps descended here to a large fish pond, where the Duchess, with her ladies and cavaliers, delighted to lean over the parapet and feed the fish, which had learned to glide close to the surface of the water at the sound of a little bell.

[Ella Noyes, *The Story of Ferrara* (London, 1904), pp. 245-6.]

THE LABYRINTH

This will be one of the principal architectural features visible as one stands on the front steps of the house and looks towards the lough. The idea came from *Hypnerotomachia Poliphili*, a mystical-erotic dream romance written by a Dominican friar, Francesco Colonna, and published in Venice in 1499. The book is long and densely written in an almost indecipherable mixture of Italian and Latin although there are many amusing and explicit woodcuts in

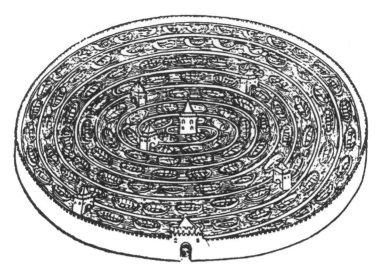

it - which may help to explain why it was so 'influential' for the following 200 years.

It's the story of a young man, Poliphilus, who sets off in a dream to find Polia, the woman he adores. Before their blissful union on the Island of Venus, Poliphilus wanders through some bizarre and opulent gardens. One consists of a huge water-labyrinth.

According to the text, you go round this thing in a rowing boat, with flowers and fruits dropping in from trees and bushes planted along the walls. But, pleasant as it sounds, the labyrinth is mortal to enter. There are seven concentric rings, each guarded by a tower. In the first sits a kindly matron who gives you your 'fate'. You drift on through calm water to the second, where girls read your fate for you and accompany you to the next tower. Here are 'more voluptuous damsels', who tempt many travellers to abandon their first guides. Now the water becomes rougher and you have to row. At the fourth tower the girls are 'athletic and pugnacious', and the water gets rougher still. At the fifth you pick up a partner and have an easy ride on mirror-like waters, enjoying the pleasures of conversation with a companion soul. Number six has an elegant and modest matron, intent on the cult of an unnamed god. In the final ring, the air becomes dark and oppressive, the rowing gets harder (because you're at the centre of a vortex and the circle is so tight), and your mind is afflicted with memories of the beautiful places and people you have left behind ('cum suprema afflictione d'animo per reminiscentia degli belli lochi et societate relicta'), a feeling which is made worse by the knowledge that you can't turn back because there's a long line of boats following behind you. At the seventh tower is a matron who judges your progress through the labyrinth. Somewhere on this journey - it could be hiding in any of the towers - you will meet a deadly dragon - a 'mortifero draco voracissimo et invisibile' - who will devour you.

CHADARS

As the water flows out of the labyrinth, it links a cascade of alternating rectangular pools and Mogul *chadars* (45-degree slopes of stone with raised patterns of scales or shells to fret the water for sparkle & music). Each of the pools contains a 'drowned sculpture', including a sunken Studebaker in cream and gold, a Masonic Pyramid, and a Rolls Royce Silver Cloud. From here we follow the course of the stream to a reproduction of Mr Bushell's celebrated:

ENSTONE ROCK

Thomas Bushell (1594-1674) was one of the great obsessive gardeners of England. He worked as a secretary to Francis Bacon, leading a debauched life, breaking every commandment except the one against murder. In 1620 he decided to reform. He left London and the court, opting for 'a Cottagers habit and low condition', first on the Isle of Wight, then on the Calf of Man, then at Enstone in Oxfordshire, where he found an unusual rock buried under a field. This was the nucleus of his garden.

I discovered and perfected nature's ingenious design upon my Rock at Enstone ... I beautyfied the same with the Ornaments of contemplative Groves and Walks, as well as artificial Thunder and Lightning, Rain, Hail-showers, Drums beating, Organs playing, Birds singing, Waters murmuring, the Dead arising, Lights moving, Rainbows reflecting with the beams of the Sun, and watry showers springing up from the same

View of 'The Rock' from Robert Plot, *Natural History of Oxfordshire.*

Fountain: these were then my sole Companions ... I ate only oil, honey, mustard, herbs and biscuit, like those long-lif'd fathers before the flood.

The Rock no longer exists , but we have a picture to help us reconstruct it.
KEY
1 Shew the water of the rivulet
2 The island in the middle of it
3 The pales round it standing on a standing wall
4. An artificial rock erected in the middle of the island, covered with living aqueous plants
5. The keeper of the waterworks that turns the cocks
6. A canopy of water cast over the rock by
7. An instrument of brass for that purpose
8. A column of water rising about 14 foot, designed to toss a ball
9. The streams of water from about 30 pipes set around the rock, that water the whole island, and sportively wet any persons within it: which most people striving to avoid, get behind the man that turns the cocks, whom he wets with
10. A spout of water that he lets fly over his head: or else if they endeavour to run out of the island over the bridge with
11, 12. Two other spouts whereof that represented at 11, strikes the legs, and that at 12 the reins of the back
13. The bridge over the water lying on two trestles
14. The steps leading into the grove, and towards the house, where you pass by
15. A table of black marble
16. A cistern of stone, with 5 spouts of water issuing out of a ball of brass, in which a spaniel hunts a duck, both diving after one another, and having their motion from the water
17. The way up from the banqueting room over the rock, and other closets, etc.

RUEIL DRAGON

This will be, or appear to be, the final element in the water garden. It will take the form of a whirling water cannon in the shape of a dragon and stand on the lakeshore, to repel any unwelcome guests who think they can arrive unannounced at the jetty. The original was a great favourite for visitors to Cardinal Richelieu's garden at Rueil in the 17th century. John Evelyn described it as 'a basilisk of copper which, managed by a fountainer, casts water near sixty feet high, and will of itself move round so swiftly, that one can hardly escape wetting.'

ISLANDS OF THE IMMORTALS

Having animated the dragon, the stream, by now reduced to a mere trickle, will flow out into the lough. Offshore a little way, we intend to build a number of artificial islands.

There are a number of possible islands to choose from, apart from the Island of the Dead. Hadrian's Marine Theatre at Tivoli - a private place of study and rest; The Boboli island, forested with lemon and orange trees in terracotta urns; Jahangir's throne on a marble slab above a waterfall; Isola Bella, floating like a stepped green Zapotec pyramid in the waters of Lake Maggiore.

Most bizarre of all are the Chinese Islands of the Immortals - moving islands in the Eastern Sea which turned to mist when a human traveller came near. (The Han Emperor Wudi built replicas, hoping to attract the immortals to come down and tell him their secrets as they flew past on storks.) We like this notion of shifting islands. Can we build some on rafts like the ancient Mexican floating gardens *(chinampas)*, anchor them for a while in certain spots, then move them around? Should be possible. Making them dissolve into mist may be more difficult.

As was said earlier, the Reuil dragon will be apparently the last element of the water garden. However, on the lawn, by the lake side, is to be seen a small glass pyramid sheltering the head of a spiral staircase. This leads to ...

THE GODALMING SURPRISE

This is perhaps the ultimate use of water in a garden, heroically extending the frontiers of Decadence and setting a formidable technical challenge to all who follow. Whitaker Wright, a financier, bought Lea House, near Godalming, Surrey, in the early 1890s. He knocked down the old manor house and built a new one, described by Barbara Jones (in her majestic *Follies & Grottoes*) as 'heavy without magnificence, squat in all its proportions'. He also transformed the park, adding three artificial lakes - a square lake, a bathing lake and a 'big lake'. But the real treat was under the water. This is how it was described in *The Royal Magazine* (1903):

Descending the stairs one comes to a subway, 400 feet long, lighted by electric lamps. The passage, which is wide enough for four people to walk abreast, leads into a great chamber of glass 80 feet in height - a beautiful conservatory with a wondrous mosaic floor, settees and chairs, palms, and little tables.

It is a wonderful place - a fairy palace. In summer it is delightfully cool - in winter, delightfully warm, for the temperature is always fairly even. Outside the clear crystal glass is a curtain of green water - deep, beautiful green at the bottom, fading away to the palest faintest green at the top, where little white wavelets ripple. Goldfish come and press their faces against the glass, peering at you with strangely magnified eyes. On summer nights one looks through the green water at the stars and the moon, which appear extraordinarily bright and large, for they are magnified quite ten times by the curved glass and the water.

This submerged fairy-room with appendages cost fully £20,000. It was built, of course, with the utmost care - for if one of the square panes of three-inch glass should break, the place would be filled with water within five minutes.

But these submerged houses do not exhaust the wonders of the Lake of Surprises. Mr Wright built a beautiful boathouse of stone by the lake side, wherein were kept a number of boats - electric launches, sailing craft, rowing boats - for he was fond of boating, and has achieved some notable triumphs with his racing yachts.

Sailing round the lake, one would come unexpectedly upon an opening in the bank almost hidden by shrubs and trees. This gave entrance to a subterranean passage, lined with white tiles, covered in places with creepers, deep water rippling at the bottom. Proceeding cautiously up this strange channel running underground, one was reassured by the sight of daylight at the end: and, pushing on, came at length to a wondrous grotto, a fairy-like cavern, with trees, high above, forming a roof with their branches. Leaving the boat, one stepped on to a path carved out of the solid rock, which led, by steps, into an extraordinary labyrinth of galleries and hidden chambers, some of which were beautifully fitted with Oriental decorations.

Poor Mr Wright was not allowed to enjoy his underwater

palaces for long. In 1904, at the Old Bailey, he was sentenced to seven years in prison for fraud, and swallowed arsenic before he could be taken from the court. His death was a tremendous loss to the gardening world. Though unmourned, unrecognised, and almost unbeliev-able, his achievements remain supreme to this day.

One underwater structure at Lea House was used as a smoking-room, another as a ball-room. Jean-Jacques Lequeu, the French Revolutionary architect, left designs for an underwater Indian brothel. Like most of his designs, this was far too visionary - too 'mad' - to be built. Perhaps now at Mountcullen, its time has come.

THE GARDEN OF HISTRION

Editors' Note: This is one of the least complete yet most shocking of Lucan and Gray's plans for Mountcullen - not so much for the design of the garden as for what they intended to do in it. Surviving notes make it clear that they were planning the world première of the Earl of Rochester's pornographic farce *Sodom, or The Quintessence of Debauchery.* This was to be the climax of a surprise party to celebrate Mrs Gordon's return from Kashmir.

Sodom was considered too obscene for publication for nearly 300 years. It involves actors 'frigging with dildoes', kissing and doing obeisance to each other's genitals, and copulating on stage. The scenery is as priapic as the action - one scene is set in 'a grove of cypress and other trees cut in shapes of pricks' - and the language is a dazzling shade of barrack-room blue throughout. Lucan and Gray had cast themselves in the parts of Bolloximian and Buggeranthus, and Mrs Conchita Gordon was to play Queen Cuntigratia. Various London friends of Mrs Gordon were invited to fill the other roles, and several had already arrived at Mountcullen for rehearsals.

Although the last few days of Lucan and Gray's residency have proved impossible to reconstruct with any certainty, it seems likely that the final débâcle was triggered by what Medlar Lucan described as an 'undress rehearsal' of the play. This coincided with the arrival at Mountcullen of Father O'Malley and a group of parishioners. Their intention was to hand over a petition demanding the dismantling of the Sacred Garden. They were horrified to find 'a horde of debauchees cavorting in the nude' on the front lawn. This led to an angry demonstration in which several villagers claim to have been psychologically traumatized. Whatever the truth of this, the trauma must have affected both sides. Within a few hours the house party had broken up, and the next morning Lucan and Gray were gone.

Of the Garden of Histrion only a jumbled file remains. It contains the text of *Sodom*, a cast list, a newspaper article about D'Annunzio, extracts from various literary and scientific works and a number of design notes. All of these are reproduced below (with the exception of the cast list, which Mrs Gordon has asked us not to publish). We have added nothing except the occasional historical note where this seemed necessary.

The garden was planned in four sections, each a recreation or reinterpretation of a famous historical precedent. As no work was carried out on this part of the garden, it is impossible to say how much of it was seriously intended to be built, and how much was merely an experiment with ideas.

A GREEN THEATRE

This is the centre of the theatrical garden, a womb in shape and

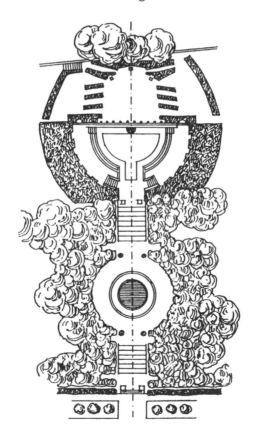

symbol, a wooden O with the leaves left on.

We model it on the theatre at Villa Reale, Marlia. This is a 17th century creation which escaped the vandalizing Romantic hand of Napoleon's sister, Elisa Baciocchi. (She bought the villa, planted a park around it, and spent her summers there from 1806 to 1814). It is an intimate circle of clipped yew, hushed and secret inside its tall, dark-leaved walls. Anything can happen here, and no doubt will.

Half the circle is auditorium, with balconies and boxes cut out of the hedge. The other half is a stage, a raised turf platform with exits and entrances for actors through the surrounding foliage. Niches in the back wall contain terracotta statues of Commedia dell'Arte figures: Arlecchino, Pulcinella and Colombina.

The acoustics are excellent. The 'devil incarnate' Paganini used to come and play his violin here, to the delight of Elisa. He recalled that she 'sometimes fainted at my playing, and would often withdraw so as not to deprive others of the pleasure.'

THE PLEASURE GARDEN

This is a highly social form of garden theatre which has now, alas, died out - the London pleasure-garden. Its heirs are the theme parks and children's Valhallas of Disneyland, Legoland, the Natural History Museum, etc. But in London from the Restoration to 1880, there was fun of a different kind to be had - at the Ranelagh in Chelsea, Cuper's, the Colisseum, the Cremorne at Fulham, the Eagle in City Road, and, most famous of all, the New Spring Gardens at Vauxhall. There were scenic effects, booths, pavilions, boat-rides, grottoes, walks, pavilions, pyramids, temples, mazes, obelisks, waterfalls, supper-boxes, music and stalls.

Says Boswell, describing Vauxhall in his *Life of Johnson:* 'It is peculiarly adapted to the taste of the English nation, there being a mixture of curious shew, - gay exhibition, - musick, vocal and instrumental, not too refined for the general ear; for all which only a shilling is paid; and, though last, not least, good eating and drinking for those who choose to purchase that regale.'

One owner of Vauxhall, Jonathan Tyers, had a macabre park

laid out at his country house in Surrey to make up for all the vanity and frippery of his public pleasure-garden. He visited on Sundays for the purposes of solemn meditation. There was a Temple of Death, with a clock striking the hours once a minute and black leather-bound editions of Young's *Night Thoughts* and Robert Blair's *The Grave* chained to a desk. There was a Valley of the Shadow of Death, guarded by gateposts made of stone coffins with human skulls set on top: one belonged to a highwayman, another to a Covent Garden prostitute. Everywhere visitors' thoughts were directed by inscriptions, statues and pictures to the contemplation of mortality and the shortness of human life. It must have been quite a relief for Tyers to get back to work on Mondays.

Thackeray's *Vanity Fair* gives a sense of the atmosphere and the acts on offer, circa 1810.

The party was landed at the Royal Gardens in due time. As the majestic Jos stepped out of the creaking vehicle, the crowd gave a cheer for the fat gentleman, who blushed and looked very big and mighty, as he walked away with Rebecca under his arm. George, of course, took charge of Amelia. She looked as happy as a rose-tree in sunshine.

"I say, Dobbin," says George, "just look to the shawls and things, there's a good fellow." And so while he paired off with Miss Sedley, and Jos squeezed through the gate into the Gardens with Rebecca at his side, honest Dobbin contented himself by giving an arm to the shawls, and by paying at the door for the whole party.

William Dobbin was very little addicted to selfish calculation at all; and so long as his friend was enjoying himself, how should he be discontented? And the truth is, that of all the delights of the Gardens; of the hundred thousand extra lamps, which were always lighted; the fiddlers, in cocked hats, who played ravishing melodies under the gilded cockle-shell in the midst of the gardens; the singers, both of comical and sentimental ballads, who charmed the ears there; the country dances, formed by bouncing cockneys and cockneyesses, and executed amidst jumping, thumping, and laughter; the signal which announced that Madame Saqui was about to mount skywards on a slack-rope ascending to the stars; the hermit that always sat in the illuminated hermitage; the dark walks, so favourable to the interviews of young lovers; the pots of stout handed about by the people in the shabby old liveries; and the twinkling boxes, in which the happy feasters made-believe to eat slices of almost invisible ham - of all these things, and of the gentle Simpson, that kind, smiling idiot, who, I daresay, presided even then over the place - Captain William Dobbin did not take the slightest notice.

He carried about Amelia's white cashmere shawl, and having attended under the gilt cockle-shell while Mrs. Salmon performed the Battle of Borodino (a savage Cantata against the Corsican upstart, who had lately met with his Russian reverses), Mr. Dobbin tried to hum it as he walked away; and found he was humming the tune which Amelia Sedley sang on the stairs, as she came down to dinner.

It is to be understood, as a matter of course, that our young people, being in parties of two and two, made the most solemn promises to keep together during the evening, and separated in ten minutes afterwards. Parties at Vauxhall always did separate, but ;'twas only to meet again at supper-time, when they could talk of their mutual adventures in the interval.

Captain Dobbin had some thoughts of joining the party at supper: as, in truth, he found the Vauxhall amusement not particularly lively - but he paraded twice before the box where the now united couples were met, and nobody took any notice of him. Covers were laid for four. The mated pairs were prattling away quite happily, and Dobbin knew he was as clean forgotten as if he had never existed in this world.

"I should only be de trop," said the captain, looking at them rather wishfully. "I'd best go and talk to the hermit," and so he strolled off out of the hum of men, and noise, and clatter of the banquet, into the dark walk, at the end of which lived that well-known pasteboard Solitary. It wasn't very good fun for Dobbin; and, indeed, to be alone at Vauxhall, I have found, from my own experience, to be one of the most dismal sports ever entered into by a bachelor.

The two couples were perfectly happy then in their box: where the most delightful and intimate conversation took place. Jos was in his glory, ordering about the waiters with great majesty. He made the salad: and uncorked the champagne; and carved the chickens; and ate and drank the greater part of the refreshments on the tables. Finally, he insisted upon having a bowl of rack punch; everybody had rack punch at Vauxhall.

"Waiter, rack punch."

That bowl of rack punch was the cause of all this history. And why not a bowl of rack punch as well as any other cause? Was not a bowl of prussic acid the cause of fair Rosamond's retiring from the world? Was not a bowl of wine the cause of the demise of Alexander the Great, or at least, does not Dr. Lempriere say so? - so did this bowl of rack punch influence the fates of all the principal characters in this "Novel without a Hero," which we are now relating. It influenced their life, although most of them did not taste a drop if it.

The young ladies did not drink it; Osborne did not like it; and the consequence was that Jos, that fat gourmand, drank up the whole contents of the bowl; and the consequence of his drinking up the whole contents of the bowl, was a liveliness which at first was astonishing, and then became almost painful; for he talked and laughed so loud as to bring scores of listeners round the box, much to the confusion of the innocent party within it; and, volunteering to sing a song (which he did in that maudlin high-key peculiar to gentlemen in an inebriated state), he almost drew away the audience who were gathered round the musicians in the gilt scollop-shell, and received from his hearers a great deal of applause.

"Brayvo, Fat un!" said one; "Angcore, Daniel Lambert!" said another; "what a figure for the tightrope" exclaimed another wag, to the inexpressible alarm of the ladies, and the great anger of Mr. Osborne.

"For heaven's sake, Jos, let us get up and go," cried that gentleman, and the young women rose.

"Stop, my dearest diddle-diddle-darling," shouted Jos, now a as bold as a lion, and clasping Miss Rebecca round the waist. Rebecca started, but she could not get away her hand. The laughter outside redoubled. Jos continued to drink, to make love, and to sing; and winking and waving his glass gracefully to his audience challenged all or any to come in and take a share of his punch.

If you can't bear the thought of all those people, you could always have a theatre of automata, like the water-driven marionette theatre at Hellbrunn, near Salzburg (1748-52, by Lorenz Rosenegger); or the performance of 72 scenes from Chinese history by costumed mechanical figures gliding along in boats, which was built for the 7th century Emperor Yangdi; or a selection of Hero of Alexandria's automata ...

LIBATIONS AT AN ALTAR PRODUCED BY FIRE.

To construct an altar such that, when a fire is raised on it, figures at the side shall offer libations. Let there be a pedestal, A B C D (fig11) on which the figures stand, and also an altar, E F G, perfectly air-tight. The pedestal must also be air-tight, and communicate with the altar at G. Through the pedestal insert the tube H K L, reaching nearly to the bottom at I, and communicating at H with a bowl held by one of the figures. Pour liquid

into the pedestal through a hole, M, which must afterwards be closed. Now if a fire be lighted on the altar E F G the air within it, being rarefied, will descend into the pedestal and exert pressure on the liquid it contains, which, having no other way of retreat, will pass through the tube H K L into the bowl. Thus the figures will pour a libation, and will not cease so long as the fire remains on the altar. When the fire is extinguished, the libation ceases; and as often as the fire is kindled the same will be repeated. The pipe through which the heat is to pass should be broader towards the middle, for it is requisite that the heat, or rather the vapour from it; passing into a broader space, should expand and act with greater force.

BIRDS MADE TO SING, AND BE SILENT ALTERNATELY BY FLOWING WATER.

The construction is after this manner. Let A (fig 15) be a stream perpetually running. Underneath place an air-tight vessel, B C D E, provided with an inclosed diabetes, bent siphon F G, and having inserted

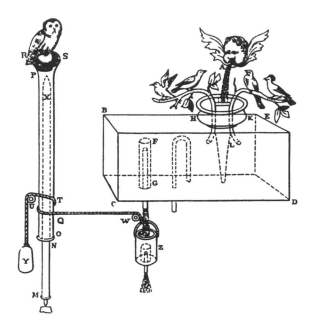

in it a funnel, H K, between the extremity of the tube of which and the bottom of the vessel a passage is left for the water. Let the funnel be provided with several smaller pipes, as described before, at L. It will be found that, while B C D E is being filled with water, the air that is driven out will produce the notes of birds; and as the water is being drawn off through the siphon F G after the vessel is filled, the birds will be mute.

We are now to describe the contrivance by which the owl is enabled to turn herself towards, or away from, the birds, as we have said. Let a rod N X turned in a lathe rest on any support M: round this rod let a tube O P be fitted, so as to move freely about it, and having attached to it the kettle-drum top R S, on which the owl is to be securely fixed. Round the tube O P let a chain pass, the two extremities of which, T U, Q W, wind off in opposite directions, and are attached, by means of two pullies, the one T U, to a weight suspended at Y, and Q W to any empty vessel Z, which lies beneath the siphon or inclosed diabetes F G. It will be found that while the vessel B C D E is being emptied the liquid being carried into the vessel Z causes the tube O P to revolve, and the owl with it, so as to face the birds: but when B C D E is exhausted, the vessel Z becomes empty likewise by means of an inclosed or bent siphon contained within it; and then the weight Y, again preponderating, causes the own to turn away just at the time when the vessel B C D E is being filled and notes once more issue from the birds.

An Automaton, the head of which continues attached to be body, after a knife has entered the neck at one side, passed completely through it, and out at the other; the animal will drink immediately after the operation.

An animal shall be made to drink while it is being severed in two. In the mouth of the animal (fig 78), let there be a tube, A B, and in the next another, C D, passing along through one of the outer feet. Between these tubes let a male cylinder, E F, pass, to which are attached toothed bars, G and H. Above G place a portion of a toothed wheel K, and, in like manner, beneath H a portion of a toothed wheel, L. Over all let there be wheel, M,

the inner rim of which is thicker than the outer; and let sections be cut out of this wheel by the three circles M, N and X, so that the interval between each division may be equal to the radius of the wheel. Let the rim or felly be likewise divided by the circles, so that the circumference of the wheel will no longer be a circle. Having made an incision, O P, in the upper part of the neck, and severed the head within the incision, make in it a circular cavity broader below than above, as it were a

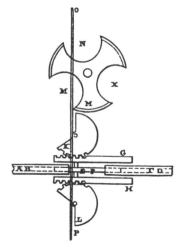

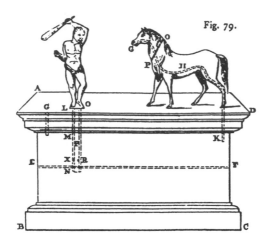

Fig. 79.

female tube shaped like an axe, which will contain two sides of the hexagon inscribed in the circle. Let this cavity be R S, in which the entire rim M N X will revolve in such a manner that, before one division disappears, the beginning of the next will succeed, and similarly with the third: so that, if a pin be inserted through the wheel the wheel will revolve, and the head of the animal adhere to the neck. Now, if a knife is passed down through the incision O P, it will enter one of the clefts of the wheel M, and confine it in the circular cavity; and, descending lower, it will touch the projecting tooth of the part K of the wheel, which, being forced downwards, will fit its teeth into those of the bar G, and the bar being pushed back will bring the cylinder out of the tube A B. the knife, passing though the intervening space, will still descend and fall upon the projecting tooth of the part L of the wheel; and this, being forced downwards, and fitting its teeth into the toothed bar H, will drive the cylinder out of C D and fit it into A B. This cylinder is an interior tube fitted into the two tubes, that, namely, in the mouth of the animal, and that reaching from the incision in the neck to the hinder foot. When the knife has passed quite through the neck, and the tube E F has touched both A B and C D, let water be offered to the animal, and a pair of sliding tubes, placed under the herdsman, be turned round. When the herdsman revolves, the water above will flow downwards along the tube C D E F A B, and the current of air caused by the stream of water will attract the water offered to the mouth of the animal. Of course the sliding tubes are *so arranged that, as the herdsman turns round, the holes in them coincide. The same result can be brought about without the aid of a stream of water in the following manner. Take once more a pedestal perfectly air-tight, A B C D (fig), having a partition across the middle, E F. Let the tube from the mouth of the animal, G H K, lead into the pedestal, and another tube, L M N, pass through the surface A D and the partition E F. In the tube, L M N perforate a hole, X, just above the partition E F, and let another tube, O P, fit into it closely, having a hole, R, corresponding with the hole X. To the tube O P attach a figure of Pan, or some other figure with a fierce look and, when the figure is turned towards the animal, it shall not drink, as though frightened; when the figure turns away, it shall drink. Now, if we pour water into the compartment A D E F through a hole G, which must afterwards be carefully closed with wax or some other substance, it will be found that, if the holes R and X are made to coincide, the water which was poured in will pass into the compartment E B C F. As A D E F becomes empty, it will attract the air through the mouth of the figure, which will then drink when a cup is presented to it.*

We will be adapting these ingenious mechanisms to represent some favourite scenes from our schooldays. These will include: 'Choir practice', 'Six of the best', 'After lights out' and 'In the Fives Court'.

D'ANNUNZIO'S GARDEN

Gabriele D'Annunzio, 'conqueror of women, of cities, of men', moved to the Villa Cargnacco on Lake Garda in 1921. He renamed it 'il Vittoriale' (Victory Monument) in memory of his 'glorious defeats'.

D'Annunzio's lifestyle as a young man is a model to aspiring Decadents: 'served by fifteen domestics and surrounded by ten horses, thirty greyhounds, two fox-terriers, one spaniel and more than 200 pigeons: working and loving restlessly, venturing out rarely and then on horseback; seeing guests at rare intervals, and spending at least ten times what he was earning.' He fed his greyhounds on 'prime cutlets and old Cognac', which the animals greatly enjoyed. He lived in overheated luxury, among hundreds of cushions covered in rare silks and damasks, the air heavy with incense and perfumes.

We found an amusing piece about D'Annunzio in the *New York Times* recently. The writer, Roderick Conway Morris, kindly sent us this special version for the Mountcullen archive.

Born in 1863 in Pescara on the Adriatic coast, D'Annunzio went to study in Rome in 1881 and first won fame as a lyric poet. A dandy, shameless self-publicist and incorrigible philanderer, he embraced during his lifetime both fin-de-siècle aesthetic hedonism and the Futurists' fascination with machines and technology. His career was characterised by his infatuation with women, motor cars, aeroplanes, high-powered boats and other writers (including Nietzsche, whose philosophy encouraged him to try to prove himself a modern Superman). D'Annunzio's prose works soon established him as a leading representative of Decadence, and after he wrote 'The Martyrdom of St Sebastian', a scenario (with music by Debussy) infused with a vaguely perverse eroticism, all his works were placed on the Papal Index of forbidden books.

The literateur's fiery nationalistic exhortations were influential in bringing Italy into the conflict on the Allied side in 1915, and although his subsequent war record was more marked by dramatic gestures than solid results, D'Annunzio displayed consistent physical courage and was good for morale. During the hostilities Italy was promised Dalmatia as a spoil of war (before the creation of Yugoslavia had been envisaged). Exasperated by his country's failure to press this claim afterwards, the writer rallied a band of volunteers, whom he dubbed his 'Legionaries' and commanded a private expedition to seize Fiume (Rjeka), a city with a majority Italian population but with an overwhelmingly Slav hinterland. They held Fiume between September 1919 and January 1921, when they were forced to withdraw.

Disillusioned by this débâcle, D'Annunzio ostentatiously turned his back on the world, renting, and soon buying, a villa and gardens on Lake Garda, which had been confiscated during the war from a German art critic, Henry Thode. He spent the rest of his days there, his much-vaunted solitude alleviated by an entourage of female admirers, visiting lovers, former comrades-in-arms, friends and other guests.

To assist him in his ambitious scheme for the transformation of the villa and grounds, D'Annunzio recruited the young local architect Giancarlo Maroni, himself a decorated war veteran. Maroni continued to work on this fantastic conglomeration of houses, pavilions, tombs, memorials, museums, follies, theatres and landscaped gardens until his own death in 1952.

After the Vittoriale's main gateway is a double arch in the form of a bridge pier on the River Piave - the line held by the Italians against the Central Powers between 1917 and 1918. (To the right is a 1,500-seat open-air amphitheatre.) Beyond is a large courtyard, within which is the front door of D'Annunzio's house, which he called the 'Prioria' (Priory), a suitably preposterous allusion to his new, supposedly monklike, existence - the facade of which is virtually covered with coats of arms.

In a portico to the left are two splendid vintage motor cars: the maroon 1913 Fiat Type 4 in which D'Annunzio drove from Italy to Dalmatia to conquer Fiume, and his blue 1931 Torpedo Isotta Fraschini. The door beside them leads to the Auditorium, suspended from whose dome is the biplane he flew in his 'Raid on Vienna' during the First War. This flamboyant but militarily ineffectual gesture culminated with the dropping not of bombs but tricolour propaganda leaflets. Apart from manuscripts and memorabilia, the neighbouring Museum also contains some of D'Annunzio's martial outfits, which remind us that their owner was remarkably diminutive in stature. (In fact, the Polish portrait painter Tamara de Lempicka having rebuffed the Great Seducer's advances on her visit to the Vittoriale, referred to D'Annunzio as 'that ghastly dwarf in uniform'.)

The author's house itself, which is more or less just as he left it on the night of his death, with his clothes still hanging in the closets, medicines in his cabinet and glass and bottle of mineral water on a tray in his study, is an extraordinary warren of rooms crammed with books, pictures, bronzes, plaster casts, wood carvings, chinoiserie, brocades, tapestries, oriental carpets, ceramics, musical instruments, war trophies, and assorted knick-knacks. Given that these total tens of thousands of items - there are 900 alone in the Blue Bathroom - it is not surprising that one can enter here only on guided visits in small groups.

D'Annunzio lost his right eye crash-landing an aeroplane in the Adriatic during the war, and subsequently suffered photophobia, hence the Romantic gloom into which most of the Priory is plunged, with diffused light coming from outside through stained glass windows, and a variety of exotic lamps, including illuminated bowls of glass fruit. Odd-ball mementos further enliven the weird scene: in the Globe Room (a library), for example, an Austrian heavy machine-gun, rifle and plumed helmet, and in the Relics Room, where statuettes of Buddhas and Christian saints vie for attention with a marble relief of the Lion of St Mark and a leopard skin, the central gilded baroque altar displays the twisted steering wheel of the boat in which Sir Henry Segrave was killed in England on Lake Windermere in 1930 trying to break the water speed-record.

A walk in the Vittoriale's extensive and diverting Park confirms D'Annunzio's extraordinary powers of persuasion when soliciting souvenirs. For here, among the cypresses and olives, is the entire bow section and bridge of the warship 'Puglia', projecting out of the mountainside and pointing across the lake to the Adriatic, where the vessel was involved in an incident in 1920 in which the Captain and Engineer heroically lost their lives rescuing some sailors trapped ashore. When the ship was decommissioned, D'Annunzio asked if he could have it, and the Italian Navy duly obliged, dismantling the forward section so that the architect Maroni could have it built into the hillside.

Yet another nautical gift, in which the writer at one time used to take visitors on high-velocity tours of the lake, is now in a nearby pavilion. This is the celebrated MAS 96, the MTB with which he made an audacious raid, braving minefields, on an Austrian naval installation - but finding no ships to torpedo, he had to retire, leaving behind three bottles of Italian wine, adrift on cork floats, with a provocative message.

At the summit of the Park, which contains many other curiosities, wooded paths, streams, fountains and tranquil corners, stands the Mausoleum. This substantial circular ziggurat - which blends elements of classical, eastern and Futurist forms - is crowned with the raised sarcophagi of ten of D'Annunzio's Fiume Legionaries, with his own tomb raised above them at the centre. Like everything else at the Vittoriale, the monument is somewhat over-the-top. Yet the views from here over Lake Garda are truly majestic, and Maroni's architecture finally transcends the eccentricity, not to say egocentricity, of D'Annunzio's dottily engaging bid for Immortality.

Of course there's no point having a garden theatre without something exciting to perform there. There are plenty of suitable texts, from the safe *(Twelfth Night)* to the frankly obscene. A charming music-hall piece is *The Cockney's Garden* by Edgar Bateman, with music by Geo Le Brunn. This is not only amusing, but has tremendous inverted snob-appeal, and may induce the effect nicely described by William Empson in one of his essays on Shakespeare whereby listening to early blues songs made him yearn for luxurious silk underwear.

We are in no doubt as to what our first production will be - Rochester's filthy little gem, *Sodom*. This will make a sparkling pornographic premiere for our Decadent Garden Theatre.

———————

THE FARCE OF
SODOM
or
The Quintessence of Debauchery

JOHN WILMOT, EARL OF ROCHESTER.

London
1689
printed by Mr. Joseph Streater
to be sold by
Mr. Benjamin Crayle
bookseller

Prosecuted and fined £20
all stocks seized & incinerated
1690

DRAMATIS PERSONÆ

BOLLOXIMIAN	King of Sodom
CUNTIGRATIA	His Queen
PRICKETT	Young Prince
SWIVIA	Princess
BUGGERANTHUS	General of the Army
POCKENELLO	Pimp, Catamite, and the King's Favourite
BORASTUS	Buggermaster-general
PENE & TOOLY	Pimps of Honour
LADY OFFICINA	She-pimp of Honour
FUCKADILLA CUNTICULA CLITORIS	Maids of Honour
FLUX	Physician-in-ordinary to the King
VIRTUOSO	Dildo and Merkin Maker to the Court

Dogs, Rogues, Caterpillars, etc.

ACTUS PRIMUS

SCENA PRIMA

The Scene: an antechamber hung with Aretine's postures

Enter BOLLOXIMIAN, BORASTUS, POCKENELLO, PENE and TOOLY

BOLLOXIMIAN: Thus in the zenith of my lust I reign,
I drink to swive, and swive to drink again,
Let other monarchs who their sceptres bear,
To keep their subjects less in love than fear,
Be slaves to crowns - my nation shall be free,
My pintle only shall my sceptre be.

My laws shall act more pleasure than command,
And with my prick I'll govern all the land.

POCKENELLO: Your Grace at once hath from the powers above
A princely wisdom and a princely love,
Whilst you permit your subjects to enjoy
That freedom which a tyrant would destroy,
By this your royal tarse will purchase more
Than all the riches of the Kings of Zoar.

BORASTUS: May your most gracious cods and tarse be still
As boundless in your pleasure as your will.
May plentiful delights of cunt and arse
Be never wanting to your royal tarse.
May lust incite your prick with flame and sprite,
Ever to fuck with safety and delight.

BOLLOXIMIAN My prick, Borastus, thy judgement and thy care
Requires, in a nice juncture of affair.

BORASTUS: My duty's still my service to prepare.

BOLLOXIMIAN: Ye are my Council all.

POCKENELLO: The bliss we own.

BOLLOXIMIAN: But this advice belongs to you alone
Borastus. No longer I my cunts admire,
The drudgery has worn out my desire.

BORASTUS: Your Grace may soon to human arse retire.

BOLLOXIMIAN: My pleasures for new cunts I will uphold,
And have reserves of kindness for the old.
I grant in absence dildo may be used
With milk of goats, when once our seed's
infused.
My prick no more to bald cunt shall resort -

Merkins rub off, and often spoil the sport.

POCKENELLO: Let merkin, sir, be banished from the court.

PENE: 'Tis like a dead hedge when the land is poor.

TOOLY: It is not fit a cunt should wear a tower.

BOLLOXIMIAN: As for my queen, her cunt no more invites,
Clad with the filth of her most nasty whites.
Borastus, you spend your time I know not how.

BORASTUS: The choice of buggery, sir, is wanting now.
I would advise you, sir, to make a pass
Once more at Pockenello's loyal arse.
Besides, sir, Pene has so soft a skin
'Twould tempt a saint to thrust his pintle in.

TOOLY: When last, good sir, your pleasure did vouchsafe
To let poor Tooly's hand your pintle chafe,
You gently moved it to my arse - when lo!
Arse did the deed which light hand could not do.

BOLLOXIMIAN: True, I remember how my sperm did flow.
Truly, I'm in arrears to thy rewards.
But let's be active while the time affords,
And Pockenello for a mate I'll choose.
His arse shall for a minute be my spouse.

POCKENELLO: That spouse shall, mighty sire, though it be blind,
Prove to my lord both dutiful and kind.
'Tis all my wish that Pockenello's arse
May still find favour from your royal tarse.

BOLLOXIMIAN: And next to Tooly, I will have a touch
With Pene.

PENE: Oh sire, you honour me too much!

It was enough when me you did entrust
As harbinger unto your royal lust.
But as from heaven, your will can make us blest
Though we're unworthy. When we have done
    our best
Nor your affections dare we claim our right.

BOLLOXIMIAN: Those who my pleasure serve I must requite.
Henceforth, Borastus, set the nation free.
Let conscience have its force of liberty.
I do proclaim, that buggery may be used
O'er all the land, so cunt be not abused.
That's the provision. This shall be your trust.

BORASTUS: All things shall to your orders be adjust.

BOLLOXIMIAN: To Buggeranthus let this grant be given,
And let him bugger all things under heaven.

BORASTUS: Straight your indulgence shall be issued forth
From East to West, and through the South to
    North.

BOLLOXIMIAN: Let Pene assist you in this grand affair,
Then to our royal citadel repair.

BORASTUS: We shall obey.
             [Exeunt BORASTUS and Pene]
POCKENELLO: Great Sir, when last you were entombed
Within the straits of Fuckadilla's womb,
You told her that her sperm did slowly come.

BOLLOXIMIAN: And what of that?

POCKENELLO: I would a plot reveal.

BOLLOXIMIAN: Against my honour? Pockenello, tell!

POCKENELLO: No wonder she don't fuck as she was wont -
                 Pene has been too familiar with her cunt.
                 My liege, he swived her in her time of term.
                 I saw him wipe the gleanings of her sperm.
                 His reaking tarse in tail of shirt he packed,
                 Sneaking to shelter't from the treacherous act.
                 But the strange dye the traitor did relate,
                 Which stiff with menstr'ous blood stood up in
                      state.

BOLLOXIMIAN: Alas, poor Pene! I cannot blame the deed
                 Where Nature urgeth by impulse of seed.

POCKENELLO: Yet 'twas a trespass without leave to swive
                 Upon his sovereign's prerogative.

BOLLOXIMIAN: His little tarse doth but for mine prepare,
                 So lightning before thunder clears the air.
                 With crimes of this sort I shall soon dispense -
                 His arse shall suffer for his prick's offence.
                 In ropy seed my spirit shall be sent
                 With joyful tidings to his fundament.
                 Come, Pockenello, ere my pintle burns,
                 In and untruss. I'll bugger you by turns.

                                                    [Exeunt]

ACTA SECUNDA

*The scene changes to a fair portico joining to a pleasant garden
adorned with naked statues of both sexes in various postures.
In the middle of the garden is a woman representing a fountain,
standing on her head and pissing bolt upright.
Soft music is played, after which is sung, by a small voice,
in a mournful key:*

                 Unhappy cunt, oh comfortless,
                 From swilling plenty, fallen into distress;
                 Deprived of all its ornamental hair,

Fed with the empty diet of the air.
Divorced and banished from its dearest duck,
That proselyte to pagan fuck.
Assist ye powers
That bring down monthly flowers,
Come, come away, and in a trice,
Congeal these thoughts of ice.
Comfort my cunt, or give me your advice.

*Enter CUNTIGRATIA, OFFICINA, FUCKADILLA, CUNTICULA
and CLITORIS*

OFFICINA: Sure, Madam, he must fuck with some remorse
                 Since your divorcement from his royal tarse.
                 The day of marriage you may justly rue
                 Since he will neither swive nor suffer you.

CUNTIGRATIA: That tyranny does much augment my grief,
                 I can command all but my cunt's relief.
                 My courses have been stopped with grief and
                      care.
                 In all his pleasures I can have no share.

OFFICINA: These girls, I'll warrant you, have enough to
                 spare.

CUNTIGRATIA: I am not jealous, but my envy must
                 Declare to all: your pleasures are unjust.
                 Not that I would deprive your cunts of food.
                 For you like me are women, flesh and blood.
                 Yet youth nor beauty can your crimes excuse.

FUCKADILLA: What woman can a standing prick refuse?
                 When love makes courtship, there it may
                      command.
                 What soul such generous influence can
                      withstand?
                 I least offend you in your royal seed -

He fucked for pleasure and for very need.
He pressed it hard, I would have turned the
    spring,
But that my duty was to obey my King.

OFFICINA: This I must needs in her defence declare -
To reconcile the King it was her care.

CUNTIGRATIA: Had I a pintle privilege to choose,
His prick for any other I'd refuse.

CLITORIS: Madam, I wonder such a noble mind
Should be to singularity inclined?
He's but a man, and if you'll credit me,
There's many others swive as well as he.

CUNTIGRATIA: All that and more, Clitoris, I allow,
And do my faith to thy experience owe.

OFFICINA: Troth, were I you, a pintle I would have,
Though he deprived me of the crown he gave.
Your cunt may claim a subject's liberty,
Though he a tyrant to your honour be.

CUNTIGRATIA: Your counsel bravely does my care expel -
Whom could you recommend to swive me
    well?

OFFICINA: Your cunt Buggeranthus to a hair would nick.

CUNTIGRATIA: The General! I long to see his prick.
They say he swives all women to a trance!

FUCKADILLA: Madam, you'll say so when you see his lance.

CLITORIS: He is a man, no doubt!

CUNTICULA: He has such charms

	You'll swear you have a stallion in your arms.
	He swives with so much vigour, in a word,
	His prick is as good mettle as his sword.
OFFICINA:	Truly I've heard it is both long and large.
CUNTIGRATIA:	Then with my open cunt I'll give him charge.
	I'll hug and kiss and bear up till I die.
	Oh, let him swive me to eternity.
	Come, come, dear General! Oh heavens, I fear
	Twelve hours will pass before I find him here.
	Twelve hours? Twelve years! Oh, I shall ne'er contain -
OFFICINA:	Sit down and frig a while - 'twill ease your pain.
CUNTIGRATIA:	I spring a leak. All hands to pump amain!

Here the QUEEN, sitting in a chair of state, is frigged with a dildo by Lady OFFICINA. And the rest pull out their dildos and frig too, in point of honour.

CUNTIGRATIA:	So there, yet more, you do not make it spurt.
	You do as if you were afraid to hurt.
OFFICINA:	Madam, the fault in Virtuoso lies -
	He should have made it of a larger size.
	This dildo by a handful is too short.
CUNTIGRATIA:	Let him with speed be sent for to the Court.
FUCKADILLA:	Madam, your dildos are not to compare
	With what I've seen.
OFFICINA:	Indeed, they're paltry ware.
CUNTICULA:	Short dildos leave the pleasure half begun.

CUNTIGRATIA: Oh, how the General in my mind does run!
Let's to the grotto for a while repair.
And sing a bawdy song. Perhaps the air
May echo news the General is come,
To whose stiff tarse I'll sacrifice my womb.
Sing, Fuckadilla, charm us with a touch.
See it not treat of chastity too much.

FUCKADILLA: That's a strange word! But if you bawdy crave,
I've choice.

CUNTIGRATIA: Aye, that's what we would have.

SONG

FUCKADILLA: Rouse stately tarse,
And let thy bollocks grind
For seed.
Heave up fair arse,
And let they cunt be kind
To the deed.

Thrust, pintle, with a force
Strong as any horse.
Spend, till her cunt o'er flow,
Joined with the neighboring flood of sperm
below.

There in a swound
We'll lie as drowned
And dead upon the shore,
Rather than we wake
We should our sad leave take
'Cause we can spend no more.

CHORUS: When pintle cannot gain new breath
Resurrection is worse than death.

ACTUS SECUNDUS

Six naked women and six naked men appear, and dance, the men
doing obeisance to the women's cunts, kissing and touching them
often, the women doing ceremonies to the men's pricks, kissing
them, dandling their cods, etc., and so fall to fucking, after which
the women sing, and the men look simple and sneak off.

Enter PRICKETT and SWIVIA

SWIVIA: Twelve months must pass ere you will yet arrive
            To be a perfect man. That is, to swive
            as Pockenello does.
            Your age to fifteen does but now incline.

PRICKETT: You know I would have stripped my prick at
                nine.

SWIVIA: I ne'er saw't since. Let's see how much 'tis
                grown?
            By heavens, a neat one! Now we are alone,
            I'll shut the door, and you shall see my thing.

PRICKETT: Strange how it looks - methinks it smells like
                ling:
            It has a beard, yes, and a mouth all raw -
            The strangest creature that I ever saw.
            Are these the beasts that keep men so in awe?

SWIVIA: 'Twas such a thing, philosophers have thought,
            That all mankind into the world has brought.
            'Twas such a thing our sire the King bestride,
            Out of whose mouth we came.

PRICKETT: The devil we did!

SWIVIA: This is the workhouse of the world's chief trade

On this soft anvil all mankind was made.
Come, 'tis a harmless thing, drawn near, and try.
You will desire no other death to die.

PRICKETT: Is't death, then?

SWIVIA: Aye, but such a pleasing pain
That it straight tickles you to life again.

PRICKETT: I feel my spirits in an agony -

SWIVIA: These are the symptoms of lechery.
Does not you prick stand, and your pulse beat
    fast?
And you desire some unknown bliss to taste?

PICKETT: My heart incites me to some new desires,
My blood boils o'er -

SWIVIA: - I can allay the fire.
Come, little rogue, and on my body lie -
A little lower yet - now, dearest - try!

PICKETT: I am a stranger to these unknown parts,
And never versed in love's obliging arts.
Pray guide me, I was ne'er this way before.

SWIVIA: There, can't you enter now, you've found the
    door.

PICKETT: I'm in, I trow. It is as soft as wool.

SWIVIA: Thrust then, and move it up and down, you
    fool.

PICKETT: I do, oh heavens, I am at my wit's end.

SWIVIA: Is't not such pleasure as I did commend?

PRICKETT: Yes, I find cunt a most obliging friend.
                    Speak to me sister, ere my soul depart.

SWIVIA: I cannot speak - you've stabbed me to the heart.

PRICKETT: I faint. I can't one minute more survive.
                    I'm dead.

SWIVIA: Oh! Brother! But I am alive
                    And why should you lie dead t'increase my
                        pain?
                    Kiss me, dear bird, and you shall live again.
                    Your love's grown cold, now you can do no
                        more.
                    I love you better that I did before:
                    Prithee be kind.

PRICKETT: Sure I did lately dream,
                    That through my prick there flowed a mighty
                        stream,
                    Which to my eye seemed like the whites of eggs.

SWIVIA: I dreamt too, that it ran betwixt my legs.

PRICKETT: What makes this pearl upon my pintle's snout?

SWIVIA: Sure, you fucked lately. Now your dream is out.

PRICKETT: That I should lose my sense, heaven forbid!
                    And yet, I scarce remember what I did.

SWIVIA: It was this cunt that made your pintle weep,
                    And lulled you into such a gentle sleep.
                    Gave you those pleasures which your waking
                        thought
                    On all your senses has amazement wrought.

PRICKETT: 'Tis strange, me thinks, that such a homely feat

With such delight should all my senses treat,
That such a gaping, hungry, hairy beast
Should from its maw give squeamish prick a
    feast.
But its strange influence I do admire -
My heart is glutted, yet I still desire -
Which turns my freezing body into fire.

SWIVIA: All unknown pleasures do at first surprise.
Try but one more, you'll find new joys arise.
It will your heart with more contentment fill.
Besides the pleasure, 'twill improve your skills.
Come, try again, 'twill gratify your pain,
When you enjoy what half the world refrain.

PRICKETT: I feel an air, which does my blood unfold,
Betwixt a summer's heat and winter's cold.

SWIVIA: And no erection yet - prithee, let's feel.
Poor little thing, it is as cold as steel.
I'll manage it. Dispose it to my trust,
I'll make it strong to act as well as lust.
Stroke cunt and thighs.

PRICKETT: I do.

SWIVIA: 'Twon't do, I doubt.

PRICKETT: Oh, never fear.
Thrust out your spirit, with might and main

Noise within

PRICKETT: I hear someone coming.

SWIVIA: Put it up again.

Enter CUNTICULA, and drunkish she sings:

CUNTICULA:	'Twas the touch of the finger and thumb, And pretty soft palm That ushered the balm And made it the sooner to come.
SWIVIA:	You did my thoughts surprise.
CUNTICULA:	Did my presence disturb your privacies?
SWIVIA:	No. We dare let you know what we have done. Come, we'll continue what we have begun. Sure I have lost the virtue of my hand.
CUNTICULA:	Madam, I'll hold a piece, I'll make it stand.
PRICKETT:	Sister, let go! Cunticula shall try. Great virtue from her hand I prophesy.
SWIVIA:	I'll not my goods into her hands entrust, But on these terms: that she who first Does by the power of her prevailing hand Make cods shrink up, and pintle stiffly stand, Shall have the flowing juice.
CUNTICULA:	With all my heart - What says his princely grace?
PRICKETT:	Agreed: sister, I fear you've lost your place. Now for your credit. Hold, not quite so fast! The pleasure of itself is apt to waste- She does't with art.
SWIVIA:	Look how his cheek glows.
PRICKETT:	There, there —— *[He spends]*
CUNTICULA:	Oh death, if overflows!
PRICKETT:	'Tis done, and you may thank your treacherous hand.

CUNTICULA: I would have held it, if you had given
command.
That I should lose a blessing of this price,
For this loss I in tears could spend my eyes.
Pardon, sweet prince, pardon this mistake.
If all that I have recompense can make
Here, prostrate at your foot you may command
My cunt or arse, where'er your prick will stand.

PRICKETT: You've let out all the spirits of my blood,
You've ruined me, and done yourself no good.

SWIVIA: 'Twas your new office did ambition move
To hasten to the centre of your love.
When in her journey she received a fate
Which hope and pleasure did anticipate.
Muster your spirits up, and try again.

PRICKETT: Where power is wanting, will is but in vain.
I've spent my last, and would fain retire,
To sleep an hour.

SWIVIA: Will that restore desire?

PRICKETT: If it deceitful prove -
Adieu to fucking. Sleep will all care remove.

SWIVIA: Come cousin, we'll convey him to my bed.
You see his spirits with our hopes are fled.
Though he be living, he's as bad as dead.

[Exuent, leading him mournfully]

ACTUS TERTIUS

Enter CUNTIGRATIA and BUGGERANTHUS

CUNTIGRATIA: Let the last siege with this content be crowned,
                That what your prick has lost, my cunt has
                    found.
                Your seed, sir (with my pleasure) I will own
                Was in my cunt so plentifully thrown
                That had all mankind - whose pintles I adore -
                With well-filled bollocks swived me o'er and
                    o'er -
                None could in nature have obliged me more.

BUGGERANTHUS: If kings are gods on earth, their queens may
                    claim
                Of goddesses an usurped name.

CUNTIGRATIA: And Fate in him must great perfection show
                Whose tarse can please a deity below.

BUGGERANTHUS: If I have pleased in so sublime a sense-
                I owe it to your cunt's omnipotence.

CUNTIGRATIA: This modesty in you does ill appear,
                Whose virtues are to dare, and not to fear.
                Whose arms the strength of mighty Mars can
                    prove.
                Whose prick's the standard of the Queen of
                Love,
                Whose bollocks (like a twin of worlds) contain
                Those millions of delight in every vein.
                This, and much more, Lord General, is due
                To those perfections which I find in you.
                You must oblige me in this very hour -
                You know 'gainst all denial cunt has power.

BUGGERANTHUS: Your favours, madam, are so far above

The utmost merits of my vassal-love,
That should I court in lechery to obey,
And in obedience swive my soul away,
All my endeavours would at last become
A poor oblation to your royal womb.

CUNTIGRATIA: Still from my love you modestly withdraw,
And are not by my favours kept in awe.
When friendship does approach, you seem to fly.
Do you so before your enemy?

BUGGERANTHUS: No, by my head, and by this honoured scar.
But toils of cunt are more than toils of war.

CUNTIGRATIA: Fucking a toil! Good lord! You do mistake.
Of ease and pleasure it does all partake,
'Tis all that we can dear or happy call.

BUGGERANTHUS: But love, like war, must have its interval:
Nature renews the strength by kind repose,
Which an untimely drudgery would lose.
Madam, with sighs I celebrate the hour
That stole away my love and robbed me of my
power.
                                    [Offers to go]

CUNTIGRATIA: You shall not go thus, dear Lord General. Stay!

BUGGERANTHUS: In what my power admits, your will I must obey.

CUNTIGRATIA: In the first place, give me a parting kiss,
And next, my lord, the consequence of this -
Once for a parting blow, once and no more.

BUGGERANTHUS: Could that have been I had obeyed before.
Your menstr'ous blood does all your veins
  supply
With unexhausted lechery, whilst I
Like a decrepit lecher, must retire,

With prick too weak to act what I desire

[Exit]

CUNTIGRATIA: Does my new passion to contempt remove
The trophies of his honour and my love?
Ah, Buggeranthus, had my passion been
Decked with the state and grandeur of a queen
So loose a love I had not then betrayed!
My love had more my majesty obeyed.
My passion, like a prodigal, did treat
With all the choice variety of meat -
And now the glutted lecher scorns to eat.

[Exit]

Enter BOLLOXIMIAN, BORASTUS, POCKENELLO, TOOLY.

BOLLOXIMIAN: Since I have buggered human arse I find
Pintle to cunt is not so much inclined
What though the lechery be dry, 'tis smart -
And turkey's arse I love with all my heart:
The lust which in those animals I see
Does far exceed all human lechery.
Their cunts by use improve their influence
Whilst ours grow void of pleasure and of sense.
By oft formenting, cunt so big doth swell,
That pintle works like clappers in a bell:
All vacuum. No grasping flesh doth guide
Or hug the brawny muscles of its side,
Tickling the nerves, the prepuce or glans,
Which all mankind with great delight entrance.

BORASTUS: Nature to them but one poor way doth give,
But man delights in various ways to swive.

POCKENELLO: How simple was the lechery of old,
How full of shame, how feeble, and how cold.
Confined to a formality of law -
When wives their husbands pintles never saw,
But when their lust or duty made 'em draw.
They fucked with such indifferent delight,
As if prick stood against its will, in spite,

First rubbed, then spent, then groaned, and bid
    goodnight.
We the kind dictates of our sense pursue,
We study pleasures still, and find out new.

BORASTUS: May as the gods his name immortal be
                 That first received the gift of buggery.

BOLLOXIMIAN: Faces may change, but cunt is but cunt still,
                 And he that fucks is slave to woman's will.
                 And why, Borastus, should we daily bring
                 One dish to feast the palate of a king?
                 And strive with various sauces to invite
                 The grandeur of his critic appetite -
                 And still the meat's the same? The change doth
                    lie
                 But in the sauces' great variety.
                 'Tis so with cunt's repeated dull delights -
                 Sometimes you've flowers for sauce, and
                    sometimes whites,
                 And crab-lice, which like buttered shrimps
                    appear,
                 And may be served for garnish all the year.

                 Enter BUGGERANTHUS

BORASTUS: My liege, The General.

BOLLOXIMIAN: Brave man of war!
                 How fares the camp?

BUGGERANTHUS: Great sir, your soldiers are
                 In double-duty to your favour bound.
                 They own it all, they swear and tear the ground,
                 Protest they'll die in drinking of your health,
                 And creep into the other world by stealth,
                 Intending there among the gods to vie
                 Their Sodom King with immortality.

BOLLOXIMIAN   How are they pleased with what I did proclaim?

BUGGERANTHUS: They practise it in honour of your name,
                     If lust presents, they want no woman's aid.
                     Each buggers with content his own comrade.

BOLLOXIMIAN: They know 'tis chargeable with cunts to play.

BUGGERANTHUS: It saves them, sir, at least a fortnight's pay.
                     But arse they fuck, and bugger one another,
                     And live like man and wife, sister and brother.
                     Dildos and dogs with women do prevail -
                     I saw one frigging with a dog's bob-tail.
                     'My lord,' said she, 'I do it with remorse,
                     For I had once a passion for a horse,
                     Who in a moment grieved and pleased my heart.
                     I saw him standing pensive, in a cart,
                     With padded eyes, and back with sores
                         oppressed,
                     And heavy halter hanging on his crest.
                     I grieved for the poor beast, and scratched his
                         mane,
                     Pitied his daily labour and his pain,
                     When on a sudden from his scabbard flew
                     The stateliest tarse that ever mortal drew,
                     Which clinging to his belly stiff did stand.
                     I took and grasped it with my loving hand,
                     And in a passion moved it to my cunt.
                     But he to womankind being not wont
                     Drew back his engine, though my cunt could
                         spare
                     Perhaps as much room as his lady mare.
                     At length I found his constancy was such
                     That he would none but his dear mistress
                         touch.
                     Urged by his scorn I did his sight depart,
                     And to despair surrended up my heart.
                     Now wandering o'er this vile cunt-starving land

I am content with what comes next to hand.'

BOLLOXIMIAN: Such women ought to live, pray find her out.
She shall a pintle have, both stiff and stout,
Bollocks shall hourly by her cunt be sucked,
She shall be daily by all nations fucked.
Industrious cunts should never pintle want -
She shall be mistress to my elephant.

BUGGERANTHUS: Your honour's matchless!

BOLLOXIMIAN: I'll do't. Let her swive!
I will encourage virtue while I live.

POCKENELLO: Were Officina here she would aver
The title of Grand Cunt belonged to her.
With ease you may thrust in your double-fist.

BUGGERANTHUS: She has as good a cunt as ever pissed.

BOLLOXIMIAN: That mighty orifice of Nature's gate
Gave once delight, but ne'er did propagate.
Products spoil cunts. Flux does allow
That what like woman was, it makes like cow.

POCKENELLO: But fruitless cunts by frigging may be spoiled
When they use dildos big as new-born child.

Enter TOOLY

TOOLY: My liege, a stranger at your royal gate
Does from Gomorrah for a message wait,
Who forty striplings now does with him bring.

BOLLOXIMIAN: Oh, 'tis a present from our brother-king.
Conduct him in. 'Twas very kindly done
Of brother Tarsehole. This has saved my son.
I love strange flesh. A man's prick cannot stand

Within the limits of his own command,
And I have fucked and buggered all the land.
Pleasure should strive as much in time of peace
As power in time of battle to increase.

TOOLY *enters with the striplings*

BOLLOXIMIAN: So beautiful a troop I have not seen!
How fares our brother Tarsehole and his Queen?

MESSENGER: All hail and health from these were sent by me,
And this from them vouchsafe, O King, to see.
[Delivers a letter]

BOLLOXIMIAN *Of the fairest of the damsels, for the remembrance,*
[*reads*] *- in manifold expressions -*
Joy in your gates, honour in your high places
And in your retirements, pleasure in adundance.
Gomorrah.   Tarsehole.
'Tis well, stranger. Thanks, and go tell thy lord
That what the limits of my land afford
He may command like me what cunts do live
Within my precincts that are fit to swive.
By Tooly we intend to send a score
Of modern virgins - if we can find more,
We shall with careful expedition send.
Meanwhile, our love and honour recommend.
Tooly, divert the stranger while he stays,
With wine, and with our Sodominian plays.
Receive him kindly, my commands fulfil,
And let him fuck and bugger what he will.
Here are my valued gems, these are to me
More than the riches of the treasury.
[Pointing to the boys]
What! Does my crown and jewels do me good?
Jewels and gold are clay to flesh and blood.
Grace every chamber with a handsome boy,
And here's my pretty darling and my joy!

[Pointing to one of the boys]
Go, and prepare what to my pleasure's due:
The choice of their apartment's left to you.
[Exeunt all but the King and a boy]

BOLLOXIMIAN: Come, my soft flesh, and Sodom's dear delight,
To honoured lust thou art betrayed tonight.
Lust with thy beauty cannot brook delay.
Between thy pretty haunches I will play.
[Exeunt omnes]

ACTUS QUARTUS

*Enter OFFICINA, FUCKADILLA, CUNTICULA, CLITORIS and
VIRTUOSO*

OFFICINA: Let's see the late improvement of your art -
These dildos are not worth a fart.

FUCKADILLA: They are not stiff.

CUNTICULA: The muzzle is too small.

CLITORISl: Nor long enough.

OFFICINA: Lord! That's all in all.
Wherefore, Virtuoso, do you bring
So weak, and such a bauble of a thing?

VIRTUOSO: Madam, the philosophical demonstration:
These are invented with a full intention
To gratify the most ingestive veins
That course in blood or seed in yoke restrain.

OFFICINA: Oh fie! They scarce exceed a virgin's span,
Yet should exceed what Nature gives to man.

FUCKADILLA:	I'll hold a fucking! Let the truth be known,
	He made it by the measure of his own.
VIRTUOSO:	Madam, 'tis done, and I'll be judged by all.
	The copy does exceed th' original.
OFFICINA:	Who shall try first?
CLITORIS:	I'll -
OFFICINA:	- Think no disgrace
	If I before your ladyship take place.
	More pricks have I enjoyed, I'll make appear,
	And I have more experience by five year.
FUCKADILLA:	If by seniority you claim you due,
	I had a cunt when no man thought of you.
	It makes me laugh to see those gossips strive
	For an estate when the true heir's alive.
	All your properties are secure, I think -
	I bore a child when you was meat and drink.
	Produce, sweet sire, a lively yard. I'll vow
	I would pawn honour to make trial now.
	So long, so trim -
OFFICINA:	So plump, so lily-white -
CUNTICULA:	So rough, so stiff -
FUCKADILLA:	So jointly, so upright.
	Damn silly dildos, had I but the bliss
	Of once enjoying such a prick as this,
	I would his will eternally obey,
	And every minute cunt should tribute pay.
OFFICINA:	You are too amorous, fie, look off away.
FUCKADILLA:	Let me look on until my thoughts do give
	By strength of fancy what I should receive.

OFFICINA:	Time and experience does my judgment tell,
	Though you work dildos and make merkins well,
	You have the finest yard that e'er I saw.

FUCKADILLA:	A god to rule and keep our sex in awe.
	Oh let me kiss't - I'll have it in my hand.

VIRTUOSO:	Madam, you are all power, all command.
	In every charm you rally and surprise.
	From your kind looks such influence does arise,
	You raise my prick and frig it with your eyes.

FUCKADILLA:	Oh now my dearer part of womankind
	Can give what your abortive love can find,
	My loving cunt will give more joys to you
	Than all the beauty of mine eyes can do.
	[Takes him by the prick]
	This engine made of human flesh and grain,
	My drudging pleasure, our delight and pain,
	The prince's profit, the poor man's joy and care,
	The cuckold's surety, the rich man's despair.
	Direct thyself to my indulgent cunt,
	Thou kind reliever of all women's want.

VIRTUOSO:	My power long since was in the puddle drowned,
	See and behold - the seed lies on the ground.

FUCKADILLA:	Hell on't, 'tis so! Oh, madam, I am cursed!
	[She seems indisposed]
OFFICINA:	What now, not well?

FUCKADILLA:	Now prick has done his worst,
	That bliss for which my cunt so long did stay,
	He gave to fancy, and 'tis thrown away.

OFFICINA:	Thus 'tis, with lovers young and full of fire.

Fruition is as forward as desire.
They're apt to make their compliments before
They come to see the keyhole of the soor.
Oh cursed imposter, quashed to perfect joy
That does love's fruit before 'tis ripe destroy.
The worst of tarses well may make such moan
When the prick-maker cannot rule his own.

[Exeunt omnes]

ACTUS QUINTUS

*A grove of cypress and other tress cut in shapes of pricks. Several
arbours, figures, and pleasant ornaments. In a banqueting-house
are discovered men playing on tabours and dulcimers with their
pricks, and women with jews harps in their cunts.*

A youth, under a palm-tree sitting, in a melancholy manner sings:

Oh! Gentle Venus, ease a prick
That owns thy cunt a Queen,
That lately suffered by a lass,
And spit out blood as green as grass
And cankers has fifteen.

Under her hand it panting lies
And fain it would, but cannot rise.
And when it's got betwixt her thighs,
It grieves to feel such poxy pain,
And it draws back again.

Enter BOLLOXIMIAN, BORASTUS and POCKENELLO

BOLLOXIMIAN: Which of the gods more than myself can do?

BORASTUS: Alas sir, they are pimps compared with you.

BOLLOXIMIAN: I'll heaven invade, and bugger all the gods,
And drain the springs of their immortal cods.

I'll make them rub till prick and bollocks cry -
'You've frigged us out of immortality.'

Enter FLUX

BOLLOXIMIAN: Man of philosophy, who pricks repairs,
How chance so long thy counsels and thy cares
Have been a stranger to our courts?

FLUX: O King,
I have these ten days been a-simpling,
Endeavouring with all my art to cure
The crying pains your nation does endure.
The heavy symptoms have infected all -
I now may call it epidemical.
The pricks are eaten off, the women's parts
Are withered more than their despairing hearts.
The children harbour heavy discontents,
Complaining sorely of their fundaments.
The old do curse and envy all that swive,
Any yet - in spite of impotence - will strive
To fuck and bugger, though they stink alive.
The young who ne'er on Nature did impose
To rob her charter or pervert her laws,
Are taught at last to break all former vows,
And do what Love and Nature disallows.

BOLLOXIMIAN: What act does Love and Nature contradict?

FLUX: That for which Heaven does these pains inflict.
Nor do the beauties of thy throne escape -
The Queen is damned, Prince Prickett has a
    clap.
Raving and mad the Princess is become,
With pains and ulcerations in her womb.

BOLLOXIMIAN: Curse upon Fate to punish us for nought.
Can no redress, no punishment be sought?

FLUX: To Love and Nature all their rights restore,
               Fuck no men, and let buggery be no more.
               It does the propagable end destroy,
               Which Nature gave with pleasure to enjoy.
               Please her, and she'll be kind; if you displease,
               She turns into corruption and disease.

BOLLOXIMIAN: How can I leave my own beloved sin,
               That has so long my dear companion been?

FLUX: Sir, it will prove the shortening of your life.

BOLLOXIMIAN: Then must I go to the old whore, my wife?
               Why did the Gods, that gave me leave to be
               A King, not grant me immortality?
               To be a substitute for heaven at will -
               I scorn the gift - I'll reign and bugger still.

The clouds break up and fiery demons appear in the air.
They dance and sing:

               Frig, Swive, and dally,
               Kiss, rise up, and rally,
               Curse, blaspheme, and swear,
               Here are in the air
               Those will witness bear.

               Fire your bollocks singes,
               Sodom on the hinges.
               Bugger, bugger, bugger.
               All in hugger-mugger,
               Fire does descend.
               'Tis too late to mend.

                              [They vanish in smoke]
               The Ghost of CUNTIGRATIA appears

CUNTIGRATIA: Tyrant, thy day of doom just now is come,
               When thou, and all thy skill,

	Shall be one funeral pile.
	My wretched spirit fears
	Thy want of penitence and tears.
	I now hell's miseries partake
	For thy damned sake.
	We'll shortly meet again
	With howlings, plague, and pain.
	I'll stay for you on t'other side of the lake.
	[Descends]
POCKENELLO:	Pox on these sights - I'd rather have a whore.
BORASTUS:	Or I a cunt's rival.
FLUX:	For heaven's sake, no more.
	Nature puts me in prophetic fear.
	Behold, the heavens in a flame appear.
BOLLOXIMIAN:	Let heaven descend, and set the world on fire-
	We to some darker cavern will retire.
	There on thy buggered arse I will expire
	[Leering all the while on POCKENELLO]

Enter FIRE *and* BRIMSTONE, *and a* CLOUD OF SMOKE *appears*

The curtain is drawn

FINIS

THE 'PARADIS ARTIFICIEL'

Editors' note: The *Paradis artificiel* was the name given to the Narcotic garden and was taken directly from the title of the book by the notorious poet and consumer of narcotic substances, Charles Baudelaire. Gray and Lucan produced copious notes on the planting, propagation and harvesting of narcotic plants. They also did extensive research into the preparation of these plants for use as hallucinogenics. Unfortunately, in the aftermath of the complaints made by the local residents concerning the 'goings-on' at Mountcullen House, the local constabulary impounded these papers, and despite our best efforts, we have failed to obtain their release for publication. [An interesting, and possibly unconnected, footnote to this episode is that residents living around Mountcullen have recently noticed a significantly more relaxed attitude on the part of the Gardai to their law enforcement duties. As one resident put it; "Ah, 'tis like an angel painted a smile on their faces."]

Of all the papers concerned with the Narcotic garden, only a few fragments remain. They begin with the following short note on the design of the garden. The rest of this chapter is made up of a series of passages from various writers about the effects of using narcotic plants. These include an account by Medlar Lucan of his own experiment with henbane, the most powerful of the ingredients that witches used in their 'flying ointments'.

DESIGNING A 'PARADIS ARTIFICIEL'

Our thinking on the Narcotic garden is beginning to take shape. We know where the garden will be sited - in the old walled garden to the east of the house - and it will be accessible from the Penitential maze. Only those who have undergone the painful initiation of the maze will be allowed to enjoy the fruits of the artificial paradise.

For us, it is important that the narcotic plants are not only grown within the garden, but that they are consumed *in situ*. To this end we are designing and building a number of pavilions which will provide an appropriate location for experiencing the full benefit of the narcotic plants to be grown at Mountcullen. The idea of appropriateness is important here. Thus we envisage in one corner of the garden will stand a small green and gold Chinese pagoda, surrounded by incandescent red opium poppies. Next to it we propose a small Aztec temple with a stash of peyote or mescalin. (We will need a hothouse within the garden). Alongside that, a Gabonese hut with some *ibo'a (Tabernanthe iboga)* shrubs growing around it. *Ibo'a* is not only a narcotic but also an aphrodisiac. So it could be used in the Garden of Venus as well, especially as one of the ritualistic objects connected with the use of *ibo'a* is an eight-string harp gleaming with sacrificial blood, which is a symbol of the First Woman.

In fact, there are a few such narcotic plants which may be appropriate for other gardens. Dutry (*Datura stramomium*), for example, could also appear in the Cruel Garden, as it was used by the Hindus of Masulipatam (on the Coromandel coast of the Bay of Bengal) as a method of punishment. According to the 17th century writer John Fryer, important people who had committed a crime were sent to a place called the Post, *'where the Master of the Post is acquainted with the heinousness of the Crime; which being understood he heightens by a Drink, which at first they refuse, made of Bang (Cannabis indica) ... and being mingled with Dutry (the deadliest sort of Solanum or Nightshade) ... after a week's taking they crave more than they ever nauseated ... [This] makes them foolishly mad. Then are they brought into the Inner Lodgings of the House in which folding doors open upon delicious Gardens where Apes and Cats, Dogs and Monkeys are their Attendants, with whom they maintain their dialogues, exercising over them their humour of an Assassin, Usurper, Miser, or what their Genius led them to whilst themselves. After this manner are they imprison'd during the King's pleasure, or he orders their cure, to restore them to their senses again.*

Fryer also mentions that amusing old custom of the Mogul emperors of sending state prisoners to Gwalior to be subjected to a slow death from doses of an infusion of poppy.

Some pavilions will cause us problems no doubt. The Tartar hut, for example. We have no idea what it might look like. However, it is indispensible for the consumption of Fly-agaric. What appeals to us about Fly-agaric is that it is such a sociable substance. Everybody gets to partake. Oliver Goldsmith gives the following description of how to make sure there is always enough to go round.

Rich Tartars lay in large quantities (of the mushroom) for the winter, and when a nobleman makes a mushroom feast all the neighbours around are invited. The mushrooms are prepared by boiling, by which the water acquires an intoxicating quality, and is the sort of drink which the Tartars prize beyond all other. When the nobility and ladies are assembled, and the ceremonies usual between people of distinction over, the mushroom broth goes freely around; they laugh, talk double entendre, grow fuddled, and become excellent company. The poorer sort, who love mushroom-broth to distraction as well the rich, but cannot afford it at the first hand, post themselves on these occasions round the huts of the rich and watch the opportunity of the ladies and gentlemen as they come down to pass their liquor; and, holding a wooden bowl, catch the delicious fluid, very little altered by filtration, being strongly tinctured with the intoxicating quality. Of this they drink with the utmost satisfaction, and thus they get as drunk and as jovial as their betters.

A problem arises when mixing narcotics. Opium in the Chinese pagoda is straight-forward enough, but what about narcotic 'cocktails'? In what setting does one partake of a mixture of mandrake, henbane and thornapple? This particular concoction, by the way, comes from our old friend, the 16th century Neapolitan, Giovanni Battista della Porta. It is particularly effective *'to make a man believe he was changed into Bird or Beast; and cause madness at his pleasure. For by drinking a certain Potion, the would seem sometimes to be changed into a Fish; and flinging out his arms, would swim on the Ground: sometimes he would seem to skip up, and then to*

dive down again. Another would believe himself turned into a Goose, and would eat Grass, and beat the Ground with his teeth, like a Goose: now and then sing and endeavour to clap his Wings. And this he did with the aforenamed plants ... I remember when I was a young man, I tried these things on my Chamber-fellows: ... [One] man by drinking a potion, flung himself upon the earth, and like one ready to be drowned, struck forth his legs and arms endeavouring as it were to swim for life: but when the strength of the Medicament began to decay, like a shipwrack'd person, who had escaped out of Sea, he wrung his Hair and Clothes to strain the Water out of them; and drew his breath, as though he took such pains to escape the danger. These, and many other most pleasant things, the curious Enquirer may find out: it is enough for me only to have hinted at the manner of doing them.

As ever in the Decadent garden, the solution to any problem is to be found in the darker recesses of the imagination. For taking henbane, we intend to build a chicken coop - but not just any old chicken coop. This one was designed by the French Revolutionary architect, pornographer and surrealist *avant la lettre*, Jean-Jacques Lequeu.

MEDLAR LUCAN ON HENBANE
(*HYOSCYAMUS NIGER*)

*A few years ago, Durian, Heinrich and I took a house in Slovenia with
no intention other than idling away the summer. It was a peasant house
with a small garden and along one side of the house there grew in
abundance a plant which I recognised as henbane, Hyoscyamus niger. I
watched the plant with an interest bordering on obsession throughout the
summer, as I waited for its seeds to ripen. When this occurred I collected
a quantity and set about preparing them.*

*I discovered that there are two ways of experiencing henbane. One is
to make a sort of paste from the seeds and to rub it into an area of the chest
close to the heart. The other is to roast the seeds and inhale the fumes.
Feeling unconvinced about the first method, I decided to start with the
second. I took a handful of the flat, greyish seeds and placing them on a
metal plate, I heated them slowly from below using a spirit stove. I
watched with anticipation and unease as the seeds began to swell. Shortly
after, their shells burst and the fumes began to rise. I inhaled deeply...*

*It was not long (although I cannot say how long) before it became clear
that the fumes were beginning to penetrate my consciousness. The first
effects were physical - I began to feel very unsteady on my feet. My head
was aching and I experienced a sickening dizziness. Also my mouth and
throat became parched, to the point where I could barely swallow, let alone
speak. I began to feel frightened. One might have thought that this was
related to having taken the henbane, that it was a fear of poisoning or
death. But it could not have been, as I no longer had any idea how I had
got into this state. No, it was just a vague, unspecific terror.*

*I remember looking in a mirror and this increased my anxiety. My face
had swollen and become livid. The flesh on my head had grown much
heavier and I could feel the bulk of it weighing about my cheeks, distorting
the shape of my face. My eyes stared out at me, enlarged and black. I had
trouble fixing my gaze on the mirror as it kept moving back and forth.*

*Soon not just the mirror but the entire room was on the move. I had
to clutch hold of something to stop myself from sliding rapidly first to the
left then to the right. My senses were diminishing. Sounds began to fade
and the objects in the room began to darken. My peripheral vision became
lost in a grey fog, I was drenched in perspiration by now and as the*

darkness deepened, sight was replaced by a series of terrifying hallucinations.

A thin stone column with an elaborately carved capital suddenly presented itself to my sight. It stood in front of me and was looking at me. I tried to move my head to avoid its gaze but found I was unable to. My body no longer responded to my wishes. I was paralysed. The gaze of the column became unbearable. I was overcome with a terrible sense of shame and terror towards this. My whole body seemed to be shaking uncontrollably.

As I stood there, unable to move, the column slowly dissolved and reformed in the shape of a grotesque infant. Its face was hideously contorted in a silent scream. It appeared to be in great pain, but I felt no sorrow or pity for it. I knew that it bore me ill-will and I desperately wanted to escape its malevolence. There was something deeply violent and almost satanic about it.

At this point, a whole host of images crowded around me - weird animals, talking plants, a cloud of tiny black insects, demented voices whispering urgently to me, as if semi-human creatures were trying to crawl inside my ears. It was as if I was inhabiting the world of a medieval text, a bestiary of madness. All the time I was trying to move, to escape, but my legs refused to respond. A wave of sickness rose up in me, to the point where I was sure I would collapse, although at the same time I knew that this would not bring me unconsciousness. The grotesque visions would continue to haunt me.

The next stage which I remember was both the most horrifying and also the most exultant. Between the waves of nausea, I experienced moments of profound well-being. These were accompanied by a feeling of bodily disintegration. Although I was paralysed, it appeared that parts of my body were beginning to detach themselves and take on a separate existence. My head was stretching upwards and at any moment would be parted from my body. Simultaneously, a sensation of flight began to take hold of me. With this came a relaxation. As I experienced the terror of my dissolving body, I abandoned myself to my hallucinations and I was soon at one with them, drifting through a gloomy sky and over a strange, crepuscular landscape. This was little short of euphoric. The terror had lifted and I accepted the horror of the images which presented themselves as a matter of course.

When I returned to consciousness, I was totally disoriented. Durian and Heinrich must have carried me to my bed, where I lay for some days languishing in deep gloom. My body was racked with discomfort and the nausea remained with me. Even several days later I was still unsteady and found it difficult to walk or take hold of objects.

This account is inevitably sketchy and incoherent. One consequence of henbane narcosis is memory failure, so all that I was left with are one or two particular hallucinations and a general sense of the physical effects. This may be for the best. I shudder to think what nighmarish images I have forgotten.

OPIUM

One fascinating aspect of the *paradis artificiel* is that often consumption of narcotic plants creates another garden - a visionary garden produced by a mind hallucinating on a plant grown and consumed in a real garden. This was the common experience of the Mogul emperor Babur. Babur, garden lover and drug addict, used to take a substance called Majun. He writes of the effects: 'While under its influence wonderful fields of flowers were enjoyed ... We sat on a mound near the camp to enjoy the sight.'

In this vein, undoubtedly our favourite narcotic-induced garden is that described by Coleridge in *Kubla Khan*.

In Xanadu did Kubla Khan
A stately pleasure-dome decree:
Where Alph, the sacred river, ran
Through caverns measureless to man
    Down to a sunless sea.
So twice five miles of fertile ground
With walls and towers were girdled round:
And there were gardens bright with sinuous rills,
Where blossomed many an incense-bearing tree;
And here were forests ancient as the hills,
Enfolding sunny spots of greenery.

But oh! that deep romantic chasm which slanted
Down the green hill athwart a cedarn cover!
A savage place! as holy and inchanted
As e'er beneath a waning moon was haunted
By woman wailing for her demon-lover!
And from this chasm, with ceaseless turmoil seething,
As if this earth in fast thick pants were breathing,
A mighty fountain momently was forced:
Amid whose swift half-intermitted Burst
Huge fragments vaulted like rebounding hail,
Or chaffy grain beneath the thresher's flail:
And 'mid these dancing rocks at once and ever
It flung up momently the sacred river.
Five miles meandering with a mazy motion
Through wood and dale the sacred river ran,
Then reached the caverns measureless to man,
And sank in tumult to a lifeless ocean:
And 'midst this tumult Kubla heard from far
Ancestral voices prophesying war!

    The shadow of the dome of pleasure
    Floated midway on the waves;
    Where was heard the mingled measure
    From the fountain and the caves.
It was a miracle of rare device,
A sunny pleasure-dome with caves of ice!

MONSIEUR DE PHOCAS
Jean Lorrain

The Javanese servants had provided each of us with a small pipe crammed with greenish paste. A negro dressed entirely in white, who suddenly appeared between the tapestries, lighted each of them in turn with brightly-glowing charcoals from a small silver brazier. Seated in a semi-circle on cushions set upon the Asian carpet, with our hands resting on squares of embroidered silk or Persian velvet, we smoked in silence, concentrating our whole attention on the progressive effects of the opium.

The company gathered in the studio, which had earlier been so noisy, had now fallen into silent mediation. At Ethal's signal the agile hands of the Javanese had unbuttoned our waistcoats and loosened the collars of our shirts in order to facilitate the effects of the drug. I was seated next to Welcome. Maud White - whose figure, freed from restraint, moved sinuously beneath her black velvet peplum - was stretched out beside her brother. The English formed a separate group, already subdued by the increasing oppression of the narcotic. Still seated in her armchair, rigidly encased in her armour of precious stones, the old Duchess of Althorneyshire was the only one present who was not smoking. Pipe in hand, Ethal was still caught up in the comings and goings, giving orders.

All the candles in the chandeliers had been extinguished. Only two had been replaced and relit, burning brightly in the middle of the room. Their flames lit up two opposite corners of a carpet laid out there, about which the negro had distributed flower-petals. He had strewn them around like a shower of rain, then retired.

Candles and flower-petals! One might have thought that we were at a wake. The smoke from our pipes ascended in bluish spirals. A dreadful silence weighed upon the studio. Ethal came at last to stretch himself out between Welcome and myself, and the ceremonial dancing began.

In the mute and heavy atmosphere of that vast vapour-filled hall the two Javanese idols began to sway on the spot, the rhythmic movements of their feet extending through the length of their bodies into the contortions of their arms. Their extended hands seemed boneless and dead.

Standing in the midst of the flower-petals, in the spectral glow of the two candles, they feverishly crumpled the wool of the carpet beneath their hammering toes. Their legs glistened from their narrow ankles to their slim thighs in a flux of transparent gauzes. They were now wearing strange diadems on their heads, like comical tiaras, which made their faces seem triangular and intimidating.

While they silently shook themselves, with slow and cadenced undulations of their entire bodies, the scallopshell breast-plates slipped gently from their torsos, and the jade rings slid along their bare arms. The two idols gradually divested themselves of their garments. Their finery accumulated at their feet with a light rustling sound, as of seashells falling on sand. The tunics of white silk followed the slow fall of the jewellery. Now, as they stood on tiptoe, very slender in their exaggerated nakedness, it was as if two long black serpents shot forth from the cones of the two diadems had begun a delicious and lugubrious dance within the bluish vapours.

The sound of snoring was already audible, but amid the

plucked petals the naked idols continued to dance.

All of a sudden they took hold of one another at the waist, twirling while tightly interlaced, as though they had but a single body with two heads ... and then they suddenly evaporated. Yes, *evaporated, like smoke* - and at the same time the hall was filled with a new light.

A whole section of the tapestry was moved aside. Dressed as a stage, Claudius's model table appeared: cold and waved like a parquet floor, lit from behind by the pearly and frosty glow of a wan nocturnal sky.

It was a sky padded with soft clouds, against which stood out the sharp black silhouettes of roofs and chimney-stacks: an entire horizon of chimney-pots, acute angles and attics, formed in salt and iron filings. In the distance, the dome of Val-de-Grâce could be seen. It was a silent and fantastic Paris, as seen by a bird in flight - the same panorama that could be seen from Claudius' windows, framed like a stage-set by the skylight of his hall.

Above this improvised stage, as if sprung from a dream, a whiteness appeared: a flocculence of tulle or of snow, something silver and impalpable. This frail whirling thing, which leapt and fluttered delicately beneath the moon, in the *ennui* of that corner of a deserted studio, was the slender naked form of a dancer.

She spun around in the mute air like a winter snowflake, and nothing disturbed the fearful silence save for the soft pitter-pat of her footfalls. Were it not for the silky rustling of her tulles she would have seemed supernatural in her transparence and thinness. Her legs like slender stems, the rigid projection of her bosom, her pallor blue-tinted by the moonlight and her astonishingly fragile waist combined to give her the appearance of a phantom flower: a phantom and perverse flower, funereally pretty. The scenery of Parisian roofs and chimneys completed the illusion. It was some little ghost strayed from Montparnasse or Belleville which danced there, in the cold of the night. Her flat yet delicate face had the ghastly charm of a death's-head; long black hair descended to either side of her head, and in her hollow eyes there burned an intense alcoholic flame, whose blue ardour made me shudder.

Where had I seen that girl before? She had the slenderness of Willie and the smile of Ize Kranile, that triangle of ironic pink flesh revealing the hardness of enamel ... Oh, the shadows playing about those shoulder-blades — it was as if the skeleton were showing through beneath her breasts!

All around me, the rattle of heavy breathing emerged from somnolent chests, but they were no longer snoring. My head was heavy, and the moistness of icy sweat was all over me... and the snowflake danced on and on.

She flared up suddenly in a flash of violet, as if bathed in projected limelight ... and instantly flew back up into the sky as the chimneys and the roofs invaded the studio. They were now in the friezes and in the bay-window dazzlingly lit by the same flash of light. It was as if the invisible houses beneath the roofs and chimneys had suddenly surged up from the ground - and I was lying, among my Asian cushions, on the pavement of a street in the middle of a deserted Paris.

No, not Paris, but at a road-junction in some lugubrious suburb: a place bordered with newly-built houses as yet uninhabited, their doors boarded up and their grounds concealed, stretching into the distance ... it was cold and frosty night. The sky was very clear, the pavement very hard. I had a harrowing impression of absolute solitude.

From one of the streets, all of whose buildings were white, two horrid louts were emerging. They wore velvet coats, linen jackets, red handkerchiefs tied around their necks and had vile fishy profiles beneath their high-peaked caps. They hurtled forward like a whirlwind, dragging with them a struggling woman in a ballgown. A sumptuous fur-lined cloak slid from her bare shoulders. She was blonde and delectable, but her face could not be seen and I dreaded that I might recognise it. The violent scene was utterly noiseless.

I could see nothing of the silent and brutalised woman but her lustrous back and the soft blonde hair at the back of her head. The two thugs were gripping her tightly by the arms. She had fallen to her knees, paralysed by terror. I wanted to call out, to run to her aid, but I could not: two invisible hands, two talons, took me by the throat also. Suddenly, one of the bully-boys knocked the woman down, pressed her face into the ground, and kneeling on top of her, swung at her neck with a cutlass. Blood spurted out, splashing the green velvet pelisse, the white silk dress and the delicate golden hair with vivid red. I woke up, choking hoarsely on my stifled cries.

The other smokers were all around, sleeping heavily, with their faces contorted. The tapestry had fallen back into place over the studio skylight. The night was dark. The two candles were still burning, but the greenish light they emitted was distorting the faces. What a sight they were, those stretched-out bodies! Ethal's studio was strewn with them. We were not like that to begin with; whence came all these cadavers? For those people were no longer sleeping; there were all dead, just so many corpses. A veritable human tide of cold green flesh had risen to the flood and broken like a wave ... but an immobile wave, cast at the feet of the Duchess of Althorneyshire - who still remained, rigid, with her great eyes wide open, seated in her armchair like some macabre idol!

She too was greenish beneath her make-up; it was as if the purulence of all the bodies heaped at her feet cast a humid glow upon her flaccid skin; her corruption was phosphorescent. Her diamonds had become so livid that she now seemed to be embellished with emeralds, like some bloated green goddess - and in her hieratic face, the colour of hemlock, only the gleaming eyes remained white.

I watched that abomination. The ancient idol - so stiff that she seemed to be on the point of breaking up - was leaning over the body of a young girl prostrate at her feet; a supple and white cadaver outstretched upon the floor, of whom nothing could be seen but the back of the head. The back of the head was blonde and broad, like that of Maud White. Althorneyshire, with a sinister mocking laugh, put her voracious mouth to the nape of the neck as though to bite it - or, rather, to suck at it like some vile cupping-glass, for in her haste the teeth had fallen from her rotten gums.

'Maud' I cried, brought bolt upright by anguish - but it was not Maud that the horrible hunger of the idol was lusting after, for in that same instant I saw , shining in a violet halo, the smile and oblique expression of the tragedienne. Her mysterious mask was all aflame in that aureole above the horrid Althorneyshire ... and everything faded away into the shadows, while a familiar voice murmured in my ear:

The chastity of Evil is in my limpid eyes.
It was her voice - the voice of Maud White!

The Synthetic Garden

In our Golden Book of Decadents, certain names have a way of recurring. One of these is 'Mad' Ludwig, King of Bavaria from 1864 to 1886. History remembers him for his patronage of Wagner and a series of romantic castles; we remember him for his remarkable success in avoiding reality. He was an obsessive, moody, neurasthenic type, with a single-minded devotion to having his own way. He lived, entirely by night, in resplendent surroundings - he was the ultimate connoisseur of overheated, velvet-and-gold, peacock-feathered, orientalised luxury kitsch. His achievements in this field represent a kind of Decadent Absolute by which all other attempts have to be measured.

As a Decadent Gardener he outstrips all comers. Sir Francis Dashwood, Ippolito d'Este, Jahangir ... they scarcely begin. Even Louis XIV quails before the Swan King.

Three projects earn him his pre-eminence. The Blue Grotto at Schloss Linderhof, the Winter Garden in Munich, and the cable-car at Chiemsee - every one a monument to his dark genius.

The Winter Garden is our starting point. A big iron hothouse (say 3,000 square metres) filled with tropical gardens, pools, sofas, alligators, etc., kept at a stifling temperature all year round. In England they boast of Sir Joseph Paxton's Crystal Palace, built for the Great Exhibition of 1851, but similar constructions went up all over northern Europe at the time. The French and Germans did very stylish things - imagine a spiked helmet the size of a football stadium, or a replica of the dome of St Peter's with a glass doughnut bulging round the rim. But all of these, however bold or imposing, had one fundamental limitation: they were built on the ground. Ludwig built his on the roof of a palace.

Contemporary pictures show a lush interior: a painted backdrop of the Himalayas, a lake, a jungle, a rowing boat. Ludwig began building the Winter Garden in 1867 as a place of refuge from official business. Access was through his private apartments, and few visitors were allowed. The Spanish Infanta was one of the lucky ones:

With a smile the King drew the curtain aside. I was dumbfounded, for I saw an enormous garden, lit in the Venetian manner, with palms, a lake, bridges, pavilions and castellated buildings. 'Come,' said the King, and I followed him fascinated, as Dante followed Virgil to Paradise. A parrot swinging on a golden hoop cried 'Good evening!' to me, while a stately peacock strutted past. Crossing by a primitive wooden bridge over an illuminated lake we saw before us, between two chestnut trees, an Indian town ... Then we came to a tent made of blue silk covered with roses, within which was a stool supported by two carved elephants and in front of it a lion's skin.

The King conducted us further along a narrow path to the lake, in which was reflected an artificial moon that magically illuminated the flowers and water-plants ... Next we came to an Indian hut, from whose roof native fans and weapons were hanging. Automatically I stopped, but the King urged me forward. Suddenly I felt as if I had been transported by magic to the Alhambra: a little Moorish room, in the centre of which was a fountain surrounded by flowers, carried me to my homeland. Against the walls were two splendid divans, and in an adjoining circular pavilion behind a Moorish arch, supper had been laid. The King invited me to take the centre seat at the table and gently rang a little hand-bell ... Suddenly a rainbow appeared. 'Heavens!' I involuntarily cried. 'This must be a dream!'

Life below stairs was less dreamlike. The Winter Garden was too heavy for the walls of the palace, and eventually had to be demolished. But even while it stood it caused inconvenience. Theodor Hierneis, an apprentice cook in the royal kitchens, shared a bedroom with another boy directly under the lake:

There must have been some weak spots in the masonry, for water often dripped down on to us from the heavy supporting girders and we could only protect ourselves slightly by going to bed under umbrellas. If we had reported the matter, it would certainly have been put right, but as kitchen-boys we were not bold enough, so it had to be the umbrella.

Impeccable Decadent practice! The roof-garden threatening to engulf the palace, the kitchen-boys trembling with fear and cold - one can hardly ask for more.

In our winter garden for Mountcullen, the movement is from hard to soft. We start with a garden of Venetian glass, then pass through stone, metal, plastic, wax, paint and silk - to culminate in a sticky Turkish confectionery garden in the fragrant shadow of the Mountain of Venus.

THE GLASS GARDEN

A staircase leads up into a hallucinatory Renaissance scene: a garden built entirely of glass. It is described by Francesco Colonna in the *Hypnerotomachia Poliphili*:

And vppon the lefte side of the incomparable pallace, they brought mee into a fayre Orchyard of excogitable expence, tyme, and subtletie of woorke-manshippe, the contynent and cyrcuite whereof was as muche as the plot of the pallace, wherein was the resydence and abiding of the Queene.

Round about fast by the walles of the Orchyard there were set conuenyent garden pots in which in stead of growing plantes, euerie one was of pure glasse, exceeding a mans imagination or beleefe, intorpiaried boxe the rootes and stalkes of golde, whereout the other proceeded.

Betwixt one and other of the which was placed a Cyprusse tree, not aboue two paces high, and the boxe one pace full of manyfolde maruellous symples, with a most excellent imitation of nature, and pleasaunt diuersitie in the fashions of flowers in distinct colours verie delyghtfull.

The playne labiall compassing about the quadrant Orchyard comming out from the walles as a seat for these aforesayde garden pottes and trees to stande vppon, was subcoronized with golde by excellent lyneamentes wrought and adorned. The vpper face whereof, and whereuppon those pottes and trees did stande, was couered with a playster of glasse gilte, and a curious historographie to be seen in the same, and compassed about and holden in with wyering and netting of golde.

The wall that compassed about the Orchyard with a conuenient distance, was bellyed out with columnes of the same matter, and inuested with flowring bindings naturally proportioned, and heere and there were quadrangulate columnes of golde chamfered, arching from one to an other, with a requisite beame Zophor and coronice, with a meete and conuenient proiecture ouer the chapter of glasse vppon the round.

The substance of which subiect proiecture of the bryttle matter, was of counterfayte diasper diuersly coloured and shining. Which bryttle substance had some void space betwixt that and the other.

The mouth of the arches were stopped with rombyes of cleare glasse in forme of a tryangle, and the pypes beautified all ouer with an Encaustick painting, verie gratious to the sight of the beholder.

The ground was here and there couered with great round balles of glasse lyke gunne stones, and other fine proportions much pleasing, with a mutuall consent vnmoouable lyke pearles shining without adulteration by folyature. From the flowers did breath a sweet fragrancie by some cleare washing with oyle for that purpose.

This may seem daunting to reproduce - few garden centres these days carry 'a requisite beame Zophor and coronice' - but it's worth trying to order one if only to enjoy the reactions of the shop-assistants.

An alternative is to think small: in 18th century Venice, miniature glass gardens were made as *trionfi da tavola* or centre-pieces for the Doge's banquets. They had glass pools, fountains, urns, statues and balustrades, all very finely worked. One such 'triumph' may be set at a picnic table under the tinkling leaves of a full-size glass tree.

THE STONE GARDEN

The ultimate in low-maintenance horticulture, this garden is built entirely of white marble and will have a strange and ghostly effect.

Imagine a terrace overlooking a lake, 50 yards in length, with marble divans, tables, fountains and pools, all decorated with sculptures and floral inlays in the Mogul style. The inlays are made with precious and semi-precious stones. In order to reach the highest standards, the level of realism must be extreme. Petals, leaves, visiting insects, etc, must quiver with life. Master craftsmen, willing to fly to Ireland for a suitably handsome commission, can no doubt be found in the Agra yellow pages.

The 'Against Nature' Garden

J-K Huysmans, in his vademecum of Decadence, *A Rebours*, details the horticultural tastes of his aesthete-hero Des Esseintes, a man who 'has discovered in artificiality a cure for the worries of life and the American manners of his time'. The restless extremism, the contempt for bourgeois taste, the plush and lurid pathology of the botanical descriptions, make this a key text for the anti-gardener of today.

He had always adored flowers, but his passion had been indiscriminate, without distinction between genera and species. Now it had narrowed, purified, to a single caste.

It was already some time since he had learned to despise the vulgar plants that bloomed in dripping pots beneath green awnings or russet sunshades on market stalls in Paris.

At the same time as his literary and artistic tastes had become refined, accepting only works filtered through the finest sieves, distilled by the most subtle and tormented minds - and when he had finally lost patience with commonly-held ideas - this was when his love of flowers had freed itself from all sediments and residues, become clear and, in a certain sense, rectified.

He enjoyed comparing the florist's shop to a microcosm, where every class of society could be found: the poor, slum-dwelling plants like the gilliflower - only truly at home on garret window-sills, their roots crammed into old milk tins and clay pots; the pretentious flowers, conventional and stupid, such as roses, which belong in porcelain vases painted by young ladies; and finally the high-born flowers, such as orchids - charming, fastidious, delicate, quivering, living in exile in the palatial hothouses of Paris, princesses of the vegetable kingdom, a race apart from the plants of the street and the bourgeois flowers.

He found himself drawn by a certain pitying fascination towards the lowest class of flowers, exhausted by the foul breath of drains and sinks in the poor quarters of town. At the same time he loathed the bouquets that went with the cream-and-gold drawing-rooms of newly-built homes. But his earlier delight remained for those rare, distinguished plants which had travelled enormous distances and were kept alive by the most careful subterfuge, under false equators maintained by dosed scientific blasts from conservatory stoves.

Yet this definitive choice of hothouse flowers had itself come under the influence of his general ideas. Before, in Paris, a natural inclination towards artifice had led him to spurn the genuine flower for its faithfully executed image, miraculously achieved in rubber and wire, calico, taffeta, paper and velvet.

He had come to possess a fine collection of tropical plants, fashioned by the fingers of remarkable artists who followed nature step by step, creating it anew, taking the flower at birth, bringing it to maturity, tracing it faithfully through to its decline. They managed to note its most infinitesimal nuances, the most fleeting features of its waking or repose. They minutely observed the bearing of the petals, bent by wind or shrivelled by rain. They scattered dew-drops of resin on the corollas; created them full-bloomed and heavy with sap, or elongated and dry, their cupules wrinkled, their calyxes empty and their leaves starting to fall.

This admirable art had long enchanted him; but now he dreamed of another type of flora. After artificial flowers aping real flowers, he wanted real ones that looked like fakes.

He did not have to search long, since his home was in the centre of a prime flower-growing district. He went off at once to browse among the greenhouses of the Avenue de Châtillon and the Aunay valley. He returned exhausted and penniless, astounded by the botanical follies he had seen, thinking only of his purchases, haunted to distraction by memories of the most bizarre and magnificent displays.

Two days later the delivery vans arrived.

List in hand, Des Esseintes read out the roll-call of the plants he had bought, checking them off one by one.

From their carts the gardeners first unloaded a collection of Caladiums with huge heart-shaped leaves on turgid, hirsute stems; all different, yet unmistakably related.

There were some extraordinary creations here: the pinkish Virginale, which looked like a cut-out made of oil-cloth or rubberized English taffeta; the all-white Albane, apparently scissored from the translucent pleura of a cow or a diaphanous pig's bladder; the Madame Mame, which looked exactly like zinc - a parody of embossed green metal flecked with oil paint, splashed with white and red lead. Some, like the Bosphorus, had the feel of heavyweight calico, pebbled with crimson and myrtle-green. Others, like Aurora Borealis, were hung with swollen leaves the colour of raw meat, striated with purple ribs and violet fibrils, oozing blue wine and blood.

Albane and Aurora displayed the plant's extremes of temperament, apoplexy and anaemic chlorosis.

The gardeners carried in more varieties. These had the appearance of artificial skin grooved with false veins; most had the eroded look of syphilis or leprosy, their livid flesh marbled with rashes, damasked with pimply crusts; others were a vivid pink, like wounds that have just closed, or brown as freshly-formed scabs. There were some that seemed blistered by cauterisation, bubbled by burnings; others were hairy, pitted with ulcers and crested with chancres. Then there were some apparently covered in surgical dressings - caked with black mercury, smeared with green belladonna, or dusted with grains of yellow iodine crystals.

Placed side by side, these flowers burst before his vision, even more monstrous than when he had first spotted them in the glazed halls of the hothouses, where they had sat undifferentiated, like patients in a hospital ward.

- Sapristi! he exclaimed in wonder.

A new plant, Alocasia metallica, drove his excitement to new heights. Somewhat similar to the Caladiums, it seemed dipped in green bronze with flashes of silver. It was a masterpiece of artificiality, and looked exactly like a piece of stove pipe cut to the shape of a guardsman's pike.

Next came a bunch of bottle-green rhomboid leaves. In the middle stood a rod with an ace of hearts, shiny as a pepper, trembling on the end; and, as if to confound all botanical expectation, from the centre of this bright vermilion heart sprang a fleshy tassel, cottony, white and yellow - straight in some specimens, corkscrewed in others like a pig's tail.

This was the Anthurium, an aroid recently imported into France from Colombia. In the same consignment came an Amorphophallus from Cochin China, its leaves shaped like fish-slices on long black stems that were scarred and slashed like the limbs of a disfigured negro.

Des Esseintes was exultant.

A new load of monsters emerged from the vans: Echinopsis, with its vile pink flowers like the stumps of amputees poking from cotton-wool wadding; Nidularium, whose sabre-like petals opened to reveal gaping wounds of raw flesh; Tillandsia Lindeni, trailing its notched, grape-red scrapers; Cypripedium, with its complicated, senseless contours, that seemed to have been designed by a demented inventor. The flowers looked like clogs or pots with curled-back human tongues on top, their strings at full stretch, as illustrated in medical texts showing diseases of the mouth and throat. Two little wings, red as boiled sweets, seemed to have been borrowed from a child's windmill to complete this baroque assemblage - half underside of a tongue, the colour of wine-lees and slate, half shiny pill-box lined with viscous, oozing glue.

He could not take his eyes from this improbable Indian orchid. Meanwhile the gardeners were growing bored with his delays. They began reading out the names of the plants from the labels stuck in the pots.

Des Esseintes looked on bewildered as he listened to the repulsive nomenclature: 'Encephalarios horridus' - a gigantic rusty iron artichoke like the spikes placed on château gates to discourage intruders; 'Cocos Micania', a sort of palm, serrated and frail, surrounded by leaves like paddles or oars; 'Zamia Lehmanni', a vast pineapple or monstrous Cheshire cheese with its base stuck in peat and its summit bristling with barbed javelins and savage arrows; 'Cibotium spectabile', outshining its peers with its mad, nightmarish structure, flinging out from its palmate leaves an enormous orang-utang's tail - brown, velvety, and curled at the tip like a bishop's crozier.

But he hardly looked at these. He was waiting impatiently for the plants that really enchanted him, the vegetable ghouls, the carnivores: the Antilles Flytrap with its shaggy limbs secreting a digestive liquid, armed with grilles of downward pointing thorns to imprison invading insects; Drosera, the peat-bog dweller, garnished with glandulous hairs; Sarracena and Cephalothus, whose greedy trumpets are capable of digesting and absorbing whole lumps of meat; finally Nepenthes, its fantastic forms exceeding all known limits of eccentricity.

He turned the pot in his hands, tirelessly fascinated by this quivering floral extravagance. It looked like a rubber-plant with its long, dark, metal-green leaves, but at the end of each dangled a verdant string, an umbilical cord attached to a mottled violet and green urn, a sort of German porcelain pipe, a strange bird's nest swinging softly from side to side, its interior carpeted with hairs.

'That really is special,' murmured Des Esseintes ...

He contemplated the tide of vegetation in his hall. The plants were crowded together, their swords, daggers and lances crossed, forming sheaves of green weapons. Above them, like barbarian pennants, floated *the flowers, their colours dazzling and hard ...*

'These plants are quite staggering,' he said to himself. He took a step back and looked at them en masse. He had achieved his goal. Not one of the plants looked real. Cloth, paper, porcelain and metal seemed to have been lent by man to Nature to help her create monstrosities. When she ran out of manufactured models, she copied the internal membranes of animals, borrowing the garish tints of rotten flesh and the hideous magnificence of gangrene.

It's all due to syphilis, thought Des Esseintes, his eye riveted by the horrible markings of the Caladium which a last beam of daylight was gently caressing. And he suddenly had a vision of humanity endlessly tormented by the virus through the ages. Since the beginning of the world every creature, from father to son, had passed on this everlasting heirloom, the eternal illness that had ravaged man's ancestors and even burrowed into the bones of fossils that were being dug up today!

It had run inexhaustibly through the centuries; even now it lurked, breaking out in niggling pains, disguised as migraines or bronchitis, hysteria or gout. From time to time it leaked to the surface, choosing its victims from the underfed, the ill cared-for, breaking out in gold sovereigns on their skins, ironically ornamenting these poor devils with diadems of sequins, etching them, as a final cruelty, with the images of wealth and well-being!

And now here it was again, in its primary splendour, colouring the leaves of plants!

It's true, thought Des Esseintes, pursuing his original line of reasoning: most of the time Nature is incapable of producing such twisted, unhealthy species unaided. She provides the basic material, the seed and the soil, the nourishing matrix and the elements of the plant, which man then raises, models, paints and sculpts in his own way ... In a few years, man can achieve what Nature, in her laziness, fails to produce over centuries. There's no doubt about it - gardeners are the only true artists these days.

THE FUTURIST GARDEN

Felice Azari, the Italian Futurist, was an anti-gardener of a different kind. He had the same healthy contempt for nature as Huysmans, but he believed in improving it by more drastic means. Here is his manifesto, entitled *Futurist Flora and Plastic Equivalents of Artificial Scents*:

NO MORE NATURAL FLOWERS!

It is time to recognize the decadence of natural flora, which no longer suit our tastes.

Flowers have remained tediously unchanged for thousands of years, appearing in endless, tasteless forms of romantic creation and in the most banal decorative schemes.

Today, apart from a few highly developed and rare tropical species, flowers leave us completely indifferent. In fact they offend our futurist sensibilities with their colours and forms.

Contemporary literature and painting have continued to abuse flowers in the production of trite and insipid images.

The reasons for the decadence of flora in modern aesthetics can be summed up as follows:

1. *The most prized attractions of flowers are delicacy of hue and subtlety of form or colour - qualities which are opposed to our modern taste for synthetic colours and stylised forms.*

2. *Our visual perception of surfaces and volumes has shrunk through the conquest of speed. Flowers are now just tiny spots of colour, like the bibelots, knick-knacks and painted miniatures that once filled our drawing-rooms and have now disappeared.*

3. *Even the scents of flowers have lost the power to stimulate our nostrils, which require ever more violent sensations to set the olfactory nerves on edge. In fact perfumes extracted from flowers, already concentrated to increase their intensity, have today been completely supplanted by the intoxicating synthetic perfumes created by industry.*

4. *Finally, flowers in literature, painting and reality have been used and abused to the point of nausea as symbols, pictures and decorations. Our taste is always searching for new forms through the evolution of fashion, style and art.*

CREATION OF FUTURIST SCULPTURE-FLORA

We have established that the flowers provided by nature are no longer of interest, so as futurists we have started to create sculptural flora to brighten, enliven and adorn our pictures and environments. These are

highly original
absolutely artificial
highly coloured
highly perfumed

and, above all, inexhaustible, thanks to the infinite variety of possibilities.

The futurist painter Depero has already produced examples of these fantastic flowers by going beyond stylization into the realistic construction of flowers that are non-existent in nature.

At this very moment we are continuing our sculptural construction of flowers, colouring them violently and scenting them with ever more powerful perfumes.

Futurist flowers, with their dynamic forms, synthetic colours and unprecedented combinations, constitute one of the most startling manifestations of futurism in the decorative arts.

PLASTIC EQUIVALENTS OF ARTIFICIAL ODOURS

Every natural perfume has its plastic equivalent in a flower. Every species and its scent evoke each other reciprocally through the association of visual and olfactory sensations.

I declare that beyond this associative affinity, produced by habit from the simultaneity of the two sensations, **there exists a link between form, colour and perfume, as there exists a link between music and colour.**

To demonstrate this correspondence, I have created a number of coloured sculptural interpretations of the most fashionable synthetic perfumes of today (Origano, Chypre, Contessa, Azzurra, etc.)

Every one of the intoxicating perfumes created by modern industry for the beauties of Rome, Milan and Paris can have its equivalent floral sculpture.

I have also expanded the field of investigation by making highly expressive chromato-plastic interpretations of some of today's most typical smells (petrol, carbolic acid, chloroform, etc.)

My interpretations are created from a wide variety of materials (silk, velvet, multicoloured cloths woven from metallic threads, cardboard, painted wood, celluloid, tin-foil, etc.)

All artists will now be able to express themselves in these new forms with the most unlimited means.

We are, therefore, opening new fields of research and artistic creation for the modern futurist sensibility, already schooled in the most daring and subtle aesthetic explorations by our symphonic-colouristic concerts and the reading of Marinetti's tactile tables.

F. AZARI, **Futurist**

THE PERSIAN GARDEN

The Persians used to weave carpets depicting gardens. These were laid on cold stone floors in winter, and served to warm both rooms and minds with images of summer days. The famous 'Spring of Khosru' carpet was spread in the audience hall of the palace of Ctesiphon in the 6th century. It showed water channels leading to a central tank - with fishes and birds, footpaths, fruit trees and flowers between the channels. Gold threads stood for gravel, and jewels for the fruit and flowers. The border represented a field, and was stiff with emeralds. The whole thing symbolized the Garden of Eden and the paradise to come.

The 'Spring of Mountcullen' carpet will be equally symbolic. The design depicts the entire estate, including of course our own Gardens of Eden, Eros, Narcosis and Oblivion, and, in one corner, a miniature woven version of the carpet itself. On that miniature version the careful eye will note an even smaller representation of the carpet, with a microscopic Mountcullen estate embroidered with incredible artifice on it - and, as part of that embroidered estate, an even more diminutive likeness of the carpet, and so on down to the level of cells, molecules and fleas.

From the carpet we make our way to the landing stage, and embark for:

THE BLUE GROTTO

As we approach this fairy cavern, the oarsman feathers his blades, and an invisible impulse triggers the revolving stone door. We enter, and the door swings shut with a gurgle behind us. We are in darkness. Now we move on, through dripping, echoing silence, along a flooded tunnel. Ahead is a glimmer of blue light. We glide forward and the light grows faintly redder and brighter. The outlines of mountains become visible. What is this place? It seems a stage-set, a floating opera-house, a dream.

We are inside the Blue Grotto. It's made of cast iron girders coated in canvas and cement. In the main chamber is a lake and waterfall, with a painted backdrop of the Venusberg all ready for a performance of Tannhäuser. Seven furnaces blast heat through underground pipes; a wave machine sends ripples across the lake; two swans float by, and a primitive light show offers a changing spectacle of blue, red, rose, yellow and violet by means of tinted glass wheels rotating slowly in front of arc-lamps. The boat, which looks like a giant upended scallop welded to a Turkish slipper, has a fat pink cupid perched on its curling prow.

Ludwig built the Blue Grotto in the grounds of Schloss Linderhof in 1876-7. This was his routine:

Ludwig enters the grotto accompanied by his valet. Two swans approach, and the king feeds them with delicate morsels of specially baked white bread from a golden basket. Azure light glimmers around the walls, 'ranging from deepest peacock-blue to palest forget-me-not, mingling magically in the lake-waters with the silver shimmer of the shell-canoe'.

The king gives a signal and the valet begins to row. The light darkens to a dull purple glow, like the midnight sun in the arctic, bathing rocks and water in unnatural radiance. Slowly, this changes to the soft rose-pink of dawn. Ludwig sits spellbound on the coral-red cushions of his canoe, watching the show through opera glasses. Green tints now creep into the scene among the forested ravines of the mountains. The sun is rising. A trickle of waters is heard, and suddenly a cascade pours out from the rocky heights, tumbling into the lake and startling the swans into the air. They circle the cavern, their wings catching the golden light. The king is enraptured. The swans settle back onto the waters, and the light turns silvery-white. It is winter, and sunset is near. Gradually, the light subsides in a rainbow of darkening colours. The king awakes, the dream has dissolved...

All this magic took hard work behind the scenes. Theodor Hierneis, whom we last saw trying to sleep under an umbrella in Munich, says that serving dinner in the Blue Grotto was a nightmare. The king never kept regular meal-times. He ordered his food on impulse and expected it to appear - hot, fresh, immaculately presented - within minutes. The kitchen staff had to prepare the food in advance, keep it warm, and - on the word - pack it into baskets and rush it over to the grotto, where it had to be served with the correct china, silver and linen. Space in the grotto was restricted, and only a tiny stove was available for finishing touches. 'But there was no such thing as an impossibility in such matters, and the king's orders had to be obeyed without question.'

Other staff were kept busy there too. There was a 'weary electrician' struggling with state-of-the-art 19th-century dynamos, valets to row the boat, and a gang of workmen stoking the furnaces to keep the temperature at precisely 16° Réaumur. But Ludwig had no interest in any of this. 'I don't want to know how it works,' he said, 'I just want to see the effects.'

Inside the Mountcullen grotto we've pitched a couple of Turkish tents. One contains a model garden made of wax or sweetmeats, of the kind carried by slaves in processions through Constantinople at the time of Murad III (1574-95). These models were a good ten square feet in size and included miniature walks, hills and fruit-trees. We suggest keeping a wax model for everyday use, and knocking up the cake version for birthdays and feasts.

The other tent is furnished with cushions (embroidered gardens), a cabinet of fruit liqueurs (bottled gardens) and a small, very select horticultural library (printed gardens): limited editions of Legeay, Piranesi, Houtin and Lequeu, an anthology of decadent garden verse, and our favourite books about Ludwig: *The Monarch Dines* by Theodor Hierneis, *The Swan King* by Christopher McIntosh, and *The Dream King* by Wilfred Blunt.

A hidden staircase leads to the floor below and the launch-platform for the cable car.

THE CABLE CAR

Before the invention of trains and cars placed speed within reach of the masses, only the rich could afford the erotic thrill of travelling fast enough to kill themselves. Speed in the garden was a French invention. Louis XIV had a 'Roulette' at Marly, a switchback with a gilded toboggan where he took his friends 'to taste the pleasures of speed'. But it was the Russians who really developed the concept. At Oranienbaum near St Petersburg there was a coasting hill 532 metres long.

'It is thus used: a small carriage containing one person, being placed in the centre groove upon the highest point, goes with great rapidity down one hill; the velocity which it acquires in its descent carries it up a second; and it continues to move in a similar manner until it arrives at the bottom of the area, where it rolls for a considerable way.' (William Coxe, 1784).

The starting platform was marked by the blue and white Katalnaya Gorka Pavilion, where you could admire the view and take 'refreshments' (i.e. a stiff drink) before hurtling down the slope. There was a colonnade surrounding the run, with a flat balustraded roof decorated with vases and statues (presumably of friends who had been hurled violently from the carriage and never felt like having another go). Together with the coasting hill at Tsarskoye Selo, this was the prototype of the *montagne russe* and hence of the modern rollercoaster. The injuries it provoked may also have inspired the invention of the *salade russe* - a grisly-looking confection of cold meats, potatoes, gherkins and beetroot suspended in pink mayonnaise - but culinary and gardening histories alike are mysteriously silent on the subject.

Ludwig's speed-fix came from being driven recklessly along snow-covered mountain roads in his royal coach at night. The cable car was a variant, which added the pleasure of flying. It is by far his most impractical design. The car was to hang from a gas balloon 160 feet above the lake of Chiemsee, and float the king from his island castle to the mainland 4,000 feet away at the dreamlike speed of 6.8 miles per hour. But it was never built - the architect decided it was too dangerous. In a storm the cable might break, and then the wind would carry off the car with its royal passenger trapped inside. As Christopher McIntosh remarks, 'The picture of Ludwig making his final farewell in this way is curiously appropriate.'

But Ludwig did not float off across the Alps to Valhalla. Nor did he choose earth or fire as his executioner, although death by avalanche or volcano might equally have been his style. He died by drowning - on the night of June 13, 1886, while out walking with his psychiatrist, Dr Gudden, on the shore of the Starnbergersee. The event remains mysterious. Ludwig had been told only two days before that a commission of alienists thought him insane and unfit to rule; his uncle Luitpold was now Prince Regent. Ludwig had not taken the news well, and seemed to be planning suicide. He was taken to Schloss Berg, where the door-handles had been removed and the windows fitted with bars. He was convinced that his staff were going to poison him. No-one knows what happened on the walk. Did Ludwig plunge into the lake in order to escape or to kill himself? Whichever it was, the doctor tried to stop him, they struggled, and Ludwig (who was much taller and stronger) gave Gudden a black eye. Both men were found drifting face down in the water a couple of hours later. One of the search party was our old friend Hierneis, the cook, who recalled the scene 65 years later:

'Huber suddenly let out a shout and pointed to something white in the water. It was a sight which even now, in my eighty-fourth year, I have never forgotten. There, in his shirt-sleeves, lay the king, his feet in the sand and his lifeless body washed to and fro by the waves.'

Every year on June 13, a group of admirers performs a ritual by the Starnbergersee in honour of Ludwig. Prayers are read, and a wreath is laid on the cross that marks the place where he drowned. We propose a similar event on Lough Doon. Afterwards, the celebrants will retire to the cable car, and, suspended high in candle-light above the gardens, eat again the state banquet served on the day of Ludwig's funeral. The menu is given by the obliging Hierneis:

ROYAL TABLE

Muenchen, 21.6.86

Oxtail soup

Königsee trout
with Bearnaise sauce

Fillets of veal
with stuffed mushrooms

Meat vol-au-vents
à la Richelieu

Chicken breasts
in truffle mayonnaise

King's sorbet

Roast venison with pepper sauce,
salad and fruit compôte

Asparagus with Hollandaise

'Hedgehog' cake with sour cherries

Baked Alaska

L'ETAT

Editors' note: Lucan and Gray's thinking on this part of the garden is summed up in their Note to Conchita Gordon. This includes a copy of Swinburne's poem 'A Forsaken Garden', which may well have suggested the idea of setting a cemetery on the shore of the lake.

The garden they envisage is on a monumental scale, profoundly melancholy in atmosphere, yet with their taste for tricks and illusions in evidence as usual. Ideally this garden was to be viewed at night, by moonlight or during an electric storm. Failing this, say the *Lighting Notes*, "the explosive flashes and livid Pompeiian glow of an erupting artificial volcano would also do the job".

The *Oblivion* file contains two alternative plans for a cemetery, as well as catacombs, a funeral temple, and an Island of the Dead on which various Decadent memorials would be erected. Also on the island is a walled Fatal Garden, thematically linked to the cemetery by the idea of oblivion. The design and planting notes for the Fatal Garden form a substantial body of material on their own, and have therefore been placed in a separate chapter.

Note to Conchita Gordon

Dear Mrs G -

Your garden would not be complete without a cemetery.
It must have urns, statues, ossuaries, catacombs,
rotting sarcophagi, and BONES!
The dead too must have their vegetable plot.
So, next to the cemetery, a poison garden.
Everything here will be beautiful and deadly.
You will have to lock the gates to keep children out.
Priests too. (Or, if they are very nasty, you might lock them in.)
Enemies of the spirit, cabinet ministers, etc.,
are - of course - CORDIALLY WELCOME.

Yrs till Death -

Medlar & Durian.

A FORSAKEN GARDEN

Algernon Charles Swinburne

In a coign of the cliff between lowland and highland,
    At the sea-down's edge between windward and lee,
Walled round with rocks as in inland island,
    The ghost of a garden fronts the sea.
A girdle of brushwood and thorn encloses
    The steep square slope of the blossomless bed
Where the weeds that grew green from the graves of its roses
    Now lie dead.

The fields fall southward, abrupt and broken,
    To the low last edge of the long lone land.
If a step sould sound or a word be spoken,
    Would a ghost not rise at the strange guest's hand?
So long have the grey bare walks lain guestless,
    Through branches and briars if a man make way,
He shall find no life but the sea-wind's, restless
    Night and day.

The dense hard passage is blind and stifled
    That crawls by a track none turn to climb
To the strait waste place that the years have rifled
    Of all but the thorns that are touched not of time.
The thorns he spares when the rose is taken;
    The rocks are left when he wastes the plain.
The wind that wanders, the weeds wind-shaken,
    These remain.

Not a flower to be pressed of the foot that falls not;
    As the heart of a dead man the seed-plots are dry;
From the thicket of thorns whence the nightingale calls not,
    Could she call, there were never a rose to reply.
Over the meadows that blossom and wither
    Rings but the note of a sea-bird's song;
Only the sun and the rain come hither
    All year long.

The sun burns sere and the rain dishevels
　　One gaunt bleak blossom of scentless breath.
Only the wind here hovers and revels
　　In a round where life seems barren as death.
Here there was laughing of old, there was weeping,
　　Haply, of lovers none ever will know,
Whose eyes went seaward a hundred sleeping
　　　　Years ago.

Heart handfast in heart as they stood, 'Look thither,'
　　Did he whisper? 'look forth from the flowers to the sea;
For the foam-flowers endure when the rose-blossoms wither,
　　And men that love lightly may die - but we?'
And the same wind sang and the same waves whitened,
　　And or ever the garden's last petals were shed,
In the lips that had whispered, the eyes that had lightened,
　　　　Love was dead.

Or they loved their life through, and then went whither?
　　And were one to the end - but what end who knows?
Love deep as the seas as a rose must wither,
　　As the rose-red seaweed that mocks the rose.
Shall the dead take thought for the dead to love them?
　　What love was ever as deep as a grave?
They are loveless now as the grass above them
　　　　Or the wave.

All are at one now, roses and lovers,
　　Not known of the cliffs and the fields and the sea.
Not a breath of the time that has been hovers
　　In the air now soft with a summer to be.
Not a breath shall there sweeten the seasons hereafter
　　Of the flowers or the lovers that laugh now or weep,
When as they that are free now of weeping and laughter
　　　　We shall sleep.

Here death may deal not again for ever;
  Here change may come not till all change end.
From the graves they have made they shall rise up never,
  Who have left nought living to ravage and rend.
Earth, stones, and thorns of the wild ground growing,
  While the sun and the rain live, these shall be;
Till a last wind's breath upon all these blowing
  Roll the sea.

Till the slow sea rise and the sheer cliff crumble,
  Till terrace and meadow the deep gulfs drink,
Till the strength of the waves of the high tides humble
  The fields that lessen, the rocks that shrink,
Here now in his triumph where all things falter,
  Stretched out on the spoils that his own hand spread,
As a god self-slain on his own strange altar,
  Death lies dead.

CEMETERY THOUGHTS

We have two suggestions for the cemetery - one English, one French. The English is extremely tight, restrained and correct, hiding its darkness under a bushel. The French speaks for itself.

THE ENGLISH CEMETERY

An early Victorian (strictly, William IV) churchyard. It is taken from *The Suburban Gardener and Villa Companion* by J.C.Loudon (London, 1838). Loudon was a Scots busybody, one of the biggest names in 19th century gardening. As you will see, he was highly practical, brisk and efficient. He thought of absolutely everything, down to the most surreal level of detail. We imagine him as a terrible pain in the neck; his thoroughness, even at this comfortable distance of 160 years, comes over as maddening. We preface the plan with some of Loudon's reflections on 'solemnity of effect'.

Churchyards, like every other description of yard of garden, ought to be laid out, planted and managed, with reference to their use; and the scenery produced should, in its expression and general effect, indicate what that use is, or, at all events, be in accordance with it. A churchyard ought not to be laid out so as to be mistaken for a pleasure-ground, a shrubbery, or a flower-garden; neither, on the other hand, ought it be left in a state of utter neglect, without regular walks, and overgrown with weeds and rank grass. The use of the churchyard is as a place of burial, as an enclosure and protection to the church, as a place sacred to the memory of the dead, as a place of weekly meeting for solemn purposes, and as an approach to the church. All its uses are of a serious and important nature; and it is therefore to be considered as a grave and solemn scene. Now, the question to be solved in laying out a churchyard is, what treatment of the trees, the surface of the ground, the grass, walks, graves, gravestones, and tombs, will be most conducive to solemnity of effect. The expression of the exterior of the church is grave and solemn, by its long-established association with our religious feelings; and it therefore may be considered as having a similar influence on the scenery around. The feeling of solemnity is one more of passive, than of an active, nature: it neither needs to be much cultivated, nor much exercise of the imagination. Strong contrasts are not required to excite this feeling, nor varied and intricate scenery to prolong it. It has its origin in the uses of the place, and will only be interfered with, or weakened, by the introduction of such objects as interfere with these uses. Simplicity, therefore, ought to be a governing principle in every thing relating to churchyards; and, as the appearance of neglect or slovenliness always implies want of respect, order and neatness are next in importance. By order, we mean the avoiding of everything like confusion in the disposition of the trees, or the replacing of the tombs and gravestones; and by neatness, we allude more particularly to keeping the turf short and smooth, the walks firm, even, and free from weeds, the gravestones upright, and the tombs in a state of repair.

Fig 246 is the ground plan of a churchyard laid out agreeably to the foregoing principles: and fig. 247 is an isometrical view, supposing the trees to have been ten or twelve years planted, and some of the gravestones and tombs to have been erected. The churchyard is of small size, and is adapted for an agricultural parish, where the majority of the inhabitants are in moderately good circumstances, and whence it is supposed that the superfluous population will migrate to the towns, and leave the number of permanent inhabitants comparatively stationary. There is only one entrance to the churchyard, at (a), over which there is an archway for the protection of persons waiting during rain or snow. The walk is 8ft. broad, and proceeds direct to the steps (b), which ascend to the platform on which the church stands. The circumferential walk (c) is 6ft. wide, with a border for tombs and gravestones on each side, 12ft. wide. There is also an inner walk (d), of the same width, between which the platform on which the church stands there is another 12ft. border for tombs. The space for graves without marks lies on each side of the walk (e), and is in 14 divisions, with room in each for 24 graves. Each of these divisions is separated by a grass path 2ft. wide. The two surrounding borders, intended for tombs, are planted with trees 20ft. apart. At the angles (ff), these trees are cedars of Lebanon; at the main entrance (gg), they are yew trees; and the remainder of the trees are different species of thorns (Crataegus) (h), and evergreen cypresses (i), alternately; except opposite to the side entrances to the platform, and at the angles adjoining the cedars, where they are the yew trees, marked K. Whatever tree is introduced on one side of the walk, the same sort is also planted on the other; for the sake of preserving uniformity in the perspective. The number of trees wanted for this churchyard will be 8 cedars of Lebanon, 20 yews, 29 cypresses, and 32 plants of Crataegus.

Half the yews may be of the upright Irish variety; but the cypresses should be all of the common upright-growing kind. In many parts of England, and generally in Scotland, the climate is too severe for the cypress; but in all such places the Irish yew, the Oriental arbor vitae, or the Pinus Cembra, may be substituted. The Pinus Cembra, from the slowness of its growth, and its narrow conical form, is admirably adapted for a churchyard tree, and is perhaps, next to the Irish yew, the best of all substitutes for the evergreen cypress. The next best is the upright growing variety of the Oriental arbor vitae. The common holly is also not a bad substitute; and, if a deciduous cypress-like tree were required, we know of none more suitable than the Crataegus Oxyacantha stricta.

The parties wishing to bury in the borders are not to be considered as obliged to erect tombs of any sort, or even to enclose the spot which they have purchased with an iron railing; all that they will be held under obligation to do will be, to confine their operations within the limits of the parallelogram which they may purchase (and which may be either single, as shown in the plan at (t), or double as at (u)), and the four corners

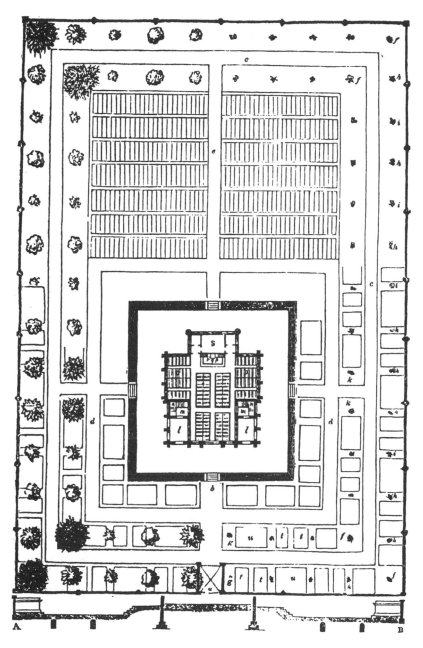

Fig 246

of which will be indicated by four stones let into the soil at the expense of
the parish. *The party purchasing the ground may erect any description
of gravestone, tomb, statue, or monument he chooses within it; or he may
leave it in naked turf, which will be mown or clipped at the expense of the
parish; or he may plant it with shrubs and flowers, in which case, he must
keep it in repair himself. Trees, or shrubs which will grow 15ft. high,
cannot be allowed to be planted in these graves, as they would interfere
with the effect of the cypresses and thorns. We have suggested the idea of
not rendering it compulsory to erect tombs or iron railings, in order that
we may not seem to exclude those who cannot afford the expense of such
memorials, from purchasing a grave to hold in perpetuity. A poor man
may be willing to afford the price of a grave, in order to preserve the
remains of his family from being disturbed; though he might not be able
to afford the farther expense of decorating it, by setting a gravestone, or
erecting a tomb.*

The French Cemetery

Pierre Giraud's design for a Field of Rest (1798-1801), to be built
in Paris either at the Champs-Elysées, or the Buttes-Chaumont, or
Montparnasse. A completely different style, as you can see. The
giant smoking pyramid and sinister masonic air make this the
more obviously decadent choice, but you shouldn't underestimate
the aesthetic power of *deception* in the English cemetery ...

So much for the overall design of the cemetery. (It will be seen,
remember, with a backdrop of the lough). But we must go further,
must we not?

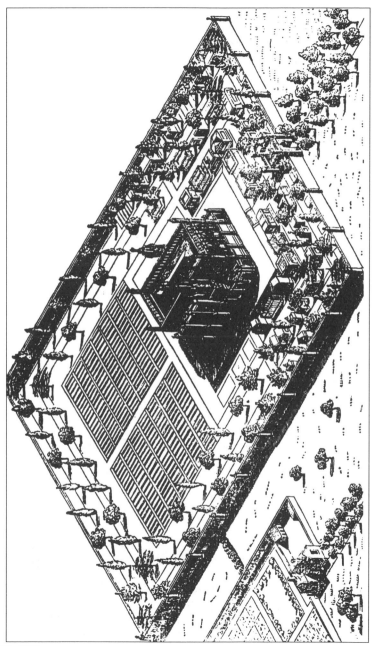

Fig 247

191

For a start, who (or what) is to be buried here?

Well, we could begin with you. And then, perhaps, us. As with the Mogul tomb-gardens in India, build pleasure pavilions for everyday use while we're alive, and turn them into mausolea when we're dead. Supplement these with the wayside gardens created around the resting-places of the Emperor's bier on the way to the capital, and we have a Mogul mortuary microcosm - probably the only one in Ireland.

But that doesn't solve the immediate problem of graves to look at in the short term.

Why not a Decadent Pantheon?

In other words we 'bury' here all our favourite heroes and heroines. It will be a fictional cemetery, packed with cenotaphs, but none the worse for that. Just think of all the glorious names! Baudelaire, de Sade, Huysmans, Beardsley, Poe, Swinburne, Wilde ...

For the church or pyramid in the middle, we have in mind something like the Temple of British Worthies at Stowe. This can be the Temple of British and Irish Unworthies - louts, gluttons, dandies, heretics, pornographers etc.

Inscriptions can be added as time goes on. There's no need to bother with mortal remains. (Grubby business anyway.) For the moment let's get the plot laid out, and a list of suitable inmates.

———

We must consider now how to get in more decadent monuments.

Some should be placed in an underground vault beneath the Temple, possibly spreading in tunnels through the churchyard too. The tunnels will curve so that the visitor is constantly surprised by new sculptures, new wayside mausolea.

The underground railway should pass through for the purposes of touring.

The catacombs of Rome and Paris provide excellent models.

———

We must also dedicate some space to cemetery equipment. Our friend John Claudius Loudon was a great observer of such things. At Calton Hill Graveyard in Edinburgh, he particularly admired 'Lamb's Receiving-Box', designed by a Leith undertaker for maximum graveside convenience. The box was 7 feet long, 4 feet wide, and 32 inches deep, with detachable sides. As the grave was dug it was filled with soil; then, once the coffin was in, one side of the Receiving-Box was removed and the earth spilled straight in on top, without any need for shovelling or mess.

Loudon also admired the gas-lit circular watch-house which commanded a view of the entire cemetery. Such things were a necessity, it seems, because the Scottish medical schools were eager collectors of corpses for anatomical demonstrations. They were known as the Resurrection Men, and various devices were invented to thwart them. Two elegant ones are hollow gateposts in the cemetery entrance - to hide a night-sentry - and the 'mort-safe', a large iron cage, rather like an aviary, that stands over the grave.

Mort safe in the old graveyard of Cathcart, Glasgow

A useful German practice also caught Loudon's eye. In Frankfurt-am-Main, the entrance to the cemetery had two wings. One was the overseer's house, the other a temporary mortuary. The corpses in their coffins were laid here for a few days with strings tied to their fingers, the other ends of which were attached to bells. So if the corpses twitched, the bells would ring. We could install the same system at Mountcullen: a picturesque effect at minimal cost.

No catacomb would be complete without a set of lead-soldering equipment. As it was the practice in certain London cemeteries to bury the dead in sealed lead coffins, there was the danger, the certainty even, of gases building up as putrefaction got under way. As Loudon noted, 'Even in some of the public catacombs of the new London cemeteries explosions have been known to take place, and the undertaker obliged to be sent in order to resolder the coffin; which shows the disgusting nature of this mode of interment, and its danger to the living.' Yes, but (properly handled) what a splendid underground firework display this would make!

———◦◦◦———

To return to the general plan: still more space will be needed, and a more open-air effect. You will now appreciate why we want the cemetery close to the lough. Out of the back wall there should be a gate and a path leading to a jetty with a small boat house. Inside, a Northumbrian skiff or similar narrow craft, together with oars, a chest covered in a white cloth, a wreath, and a tall stately figure in a hooded white cloak. With the aid of these you can row straight into a reconstruction of Arnold Böcklin's *Island of the Dead*. The island is there already. We just need to dress it up a little. Here, hidden by cypresses and steep cliffs, we can really go to town. This is the place for a monument to the Unknown Decadent. And here, walled and gated, lulled by the ocean breakers, let us place the Fatal Garden.

At the landing-stage, we suggest this inscription from Edward Young's *Night Thoughts*:

> This is the Desert, this the Solitude;
> How populous? how vital, is the Grave?
> This is Creation's melancholy Vault,
> The Vale funereal, the sad Cypress gloom;
> The land of Apparitions, empty Shades...

Arnold Böcklin, *Island of the Dead*

Taking into account both the churchyard and the Island of the Dead, there should be plenty of space to create a full-blown Garden of Oblivion, using the best antique models.

We are thinking, for example, of the Marquis de Girardin's garden at Ermenonville, with Jean-Jacques Rousseau buried on an island in the middle of a lake, the *Île des Peupliers*. Or the castle garden at Wörlitz, created for Prince Friedrich Franz of Anhalt-Dessau, with its own replica *Rousseau-Insel* and other eclectic features such as an Iron Bridge, a Pantheon, a Masonic labyrinth, a Gothick house and a Villa Hamilton (named after the diplomat, antiquarian and vulcanologist) perched on a small rocky island under an erupting model of Vesuvius fuelled with fireworks.

The only element that's missing from these examples is a truly foolproof mechanism for defeating Time. Many of these memorial gardens have been destroyed, the shadow of their existence only dimly preserved in engravings and rare books. So for your own mausoleum, we suggest erecting a bridge into the future: leave some money to posterity for its upkeep, with a few conditions attached.

This is how one 18th Century Cornish gentleman handled the matter: John Knill, builder of the Knill Monument above St Ives:

John Knill, a bachelor, and Mayor of St Ives, excavated a hole in the rock at Mount's Bay which he intended to serve as his mausoleum; sadly he died in London and ended up buried in Holborn, the original plan quite forgotten. Knill had a number of little weaknesses which seem to have afforded him great pleasure and offended no one; his predilection for pubs while in London led him to sample four or five every day before invariably dining at Dolly's Chop House. He made provision in his will for a peculiar ceremony to be performed at the monument, and this still continues after 200 years. Every fifth year on 25 July ten girls, each ten years old and dressed in white, climb up to the monument accompanied by two widows, a clergyman, a fiddler, the Mayor of St Ives and the local Customs and Excise man. There they sing the 100th Psalm, after which the girls dance round the monument for a quarter of an hour to the tune of the fiddler, singing an old song which begins 'Shun the barter of the bay, Hasten upward, come away ...' For performing this inexplicable ceremony the young girls, the fiddler and the two widows receive ten shillings each, while the parson, the Mayor and the VAT man get £10 each, which they must use to give a dinner party to which they can invite two friends. The unwavering charms of Dolly's Chop House led Knill to refuse every invitation to dine privately during his lifetime. The presence of the Customs man leads one to speculate that he might have been a smuggler. Joseph Hocking, Cornwall's truly great bad novelist, set The Eye of the Triangle, *one of his more atrocious efforts, at the Knill Monument, and he was as fascinated by the rite as we are... It is merely unfortunate that he [Knill] isn't inside the monument, with the expected bottle of port, waiting for the Day of Judgement and enjoying the virgins' dance.*

(Gwyn Headley & Wim Meulenkamp, *Follies. A Guide to Rogue Architecture in England, Scotland and Wales* (Jonathan Cape, London 1986))

Of course you may object that these and other monuments were created for remembrance - precisely the opposite of our purpose. And of course you would be right. But who remembers these memorials today? And who will ever forget your Garden of Oblivion?

Finally, some black reading:

THE PREMATURE BURIAL
Edgar Allen Poe

For several years I have been subject to attacks of the singular disorder which physicians have agreed to term catalepsy, in default of a more definite title. Although both the immediate and the predisposing causes, and even the actual diagnosis of this disease are still mysterious, its obvious and apparent character is sufficiently well understood. Its variations seem to be chiefly of degree. Sometimes the patient lies, for a day only, or even for a shorter period, in a species of exaggerated lethargy. He is senseless and externally motionless; but the pulsation of the heart is still faintly perceptible; some traces of warmth remain; a slight colour lingers within the centre of the cheek; and, upon application of a mirror to the lips, we can detect a torpid, unequal, and vacillating action of the lungs. Then again the duration of the trance is for weeks - even for months; while the closest scrutiny, and the most rigorous medical tests, fail to establish any material distinction between the state of the sufferer and what we conceive of absolute death. Very usually he is saved from premature interment solely by the knowledge of his friends that he has been previously subject to catalepsy, by the consequent suspicion excited, and, above all, by the non-appearance of decay. The advances of the malady are, luckily, gradual. The first manifestations, although marked, are unequivocal. The fits grow successively more and more distinctive, and endure each for a longer term that the preceding. In this lies the principal security from inhumation. The unfortunate whose *first* attack should be of the extreme character which is occasionally seen, would almost inevitably be consigned alive to the tomb.

My own case differed in no important particular from those mentioned in medical books. Sometimes, without any apparent cause, I sank, little by little, into a condition of semi-syncope, or half swoon; and, in this condition, without pain, without ability to stir, or, strictly speaking, to think, but with a dull lethargic consciousness of life and of the presence of those who surrounded my bed, I remained, until the crisis of the disease restored me, suddenly, to perfect sensation. At other times I was quickly and impetuously smitten. I grew sick, and numb, and chilly, and dizzy, and so fell prostrate at once, Then, for weeks, all was void, and black, and silent, and Nothing became the universe. Total annihilation could be no more. From these latter attacks I awoke, however, with a gradation slow in proportion to the suddenness of the seizure. Just as the day dawns to the friendless and houseless beggar who roams the streets throughout the long desolate winter night - just so tardily - just so wearily - just so cheerily came back the light of the Soul to me.

Apart from the tendency to trance, however, my general health appeared to be good; nor could I perceive that it was at all affected by the one prevalent malady - unless, indeed, an idiosyncrasy in my ordinary *sleep* may be looked upon as superinduced. Upon awakening from slumber, I could never gain, at once, thorough possession of my senses, and always remained, for many minutes, in much bewilderment and perplexity - the mental faculties in general, but the memory in especial, being in a condition of absolute abeyance.

In all that I endured there was no physical suffering, but of moral distress an infinitude. My fancy grew charnel. I talked 'of worms, of tombs, of epitaphs'. I was lost in reveries of death, and the idea of premature burial held continual possession of my brain. The ghastly Danger to which I was subjected haunted me day and night. In the former, the torture of meditation was excessive; in the latter, supreme. When the grim Darkness over spread the Earth, then, with every horror of thought, I shook - shook as the quivering plumes upon the hearse. When Nature could endure wakefulness no longer, it was with struggle that I consented to sleep - for I shuddered to reflect that, upon awaking, I might find myself the tenant of a grave. And when, finally, I sank into slumber, it was only to rush at once into a world of phantasms, above which, with cast, sable, overshadowing wings, hovered, predominant, the one sepulchral Idea.

From the innumerable images of gloom which thus oppressed me in dreams, I select for record but a solitary vision. Methought I was immersed in a cataleptic trance of more than usual duration and profundity. Suddenly there came an icy hand upon my forehead, and am impatient, gibbering voice whispered 'Arise!' within my ear.

I sat erect. The darkness was total. I could not see the figure of him who had aroused me. I could call to mind neither the period at which I had fallen into the trance, not the locality in which I then lay. While I remained motionless, and busied in endeavours to collect my thoughts, the cold hand grasped me fiercely by the wrist, shaking it petulantly, while the gibbering voice said again:

'Arise! did I not bid thee arise?'

'And who,' I demanded, 'art thou?'

'I have no name in the regions which I inhabit,' replied the voice, mournfully; 'I was mortal, but am fiend. I am merciless, but am pitiful. Thou dost feel that I shudder. My teeth chatter as I speak, yet it is not with the chilliness of the night - of the night without end. But this hideousness is insufferable. How canst *thou* tranquilly sleep? I cannot rest for the cry of these great agonies. These sights are more than I can bear. Get thee up! Come with me into the outer Night, and let me unfold to thee the graves. Is not this a spectacle of woe? - Behold!'

I looked; and the unseen figure, which still grasped me by the wrist, had caused to be thrown open the graves of all mankind; and from each issued the faint phosphoric radiance of decay; so that I could see into the innermost recesses, and there view the shrouded bodies in their sad and solemn slumbers with the worm. But alas! the real sleepers were fewer, by many millions, than those who slumbered not at all; and there was a feeble struggling, and there was a general and sad unrest; and from out of the depths of the countless pits there came a melancholy rustling from the garments of the buried. And of those who seemed tranquilly to rest, I saw that a vast number had changed, in a greater or less degree, the rigid and uneasy position in which they had originally been entombed. And the voice again said to me as I gazed:

'Is it not - oh! is it *not* a pitiful sight?' But, before I could find words to reply, the figure had ceased to grasp my wrist, the phosphoric lights expired, and the graves were closed with a sudden violence, while from out them arose a tumult of despairing cries, saying again: 'Is it not - O God! is it not a very pitiful sight?'

Phantasies such as these, presenting themselves at night, extended their terrific influences far into my waking hours. My nerves became thoroughly unstrung, and I fell a prey to perpetual horror. I hesitated to ride, or to walk, or to indulge in any exercise that would carry me from home. In fact, I no longer dared trust myself out of the immediate presence of those who were aware of my proneness to catalepsy, lest, falling into one of my usual fits, I should be buried before my real condition could be ascertained. I doubted the care, the fidelity of my dearest friends. I dreaded that, in some trance of more than customary duration, they might be prevailed upon to regard me as irrecoverable, I even went so far as fear that, as I occasioned much trouble, they might be glad to consider any very protracted attack as sufficient excuse for getting rid of me altogether. It was in vain they endeavoured to reassure me by the most solemn promises. I exacted the most sacred oaths, that under no circumstances they would bury me until decomposition had so materially advanced as to render further preservation impossible. And even then, my mortal terrors would listen to no reason - would accept no consolation. I entered into a series of elaborate precautions. Among other things, I had the family vault so remodelled as to admit of being readily opened from within. The slightest pressure upon a long lever that extended far into the tomb would cause the iron portals to fly back. There were arrangements also for the free admission of air and light, and convenient receptacles for food and water, within immediate reach of the coffin intended for my reception. This coffin was warmly and softly padded, and was provided with a lid, fashioned upon the principle of the vault door, with the addition of springs so contrived that the feeblest movement of the body would be sufficient to set it at liberty. Besides all this, there was suspended from the roof of the tomb, a large bell, the rope of which, it was designed, should extend through a hole in the coffin, and so be fastened to one of the hands of the corpse. But, alas, what avails the vigilance against the Destiny of man? Not even these well contrived securities sufficed to save from the uttermost agonies of living inhumation a wretch to these agonies foredoomed!

There arrived an epoch - as often before there had arrived - in which I found myself emerging from total unconsciousness into the first feeble and indefinite sense of existence. Slowly - with a tortoise graduation - approached the faint grey dawn of the psychal day. A torpid uneasiness. An apathetic endurance of dull pain. No care - no hope - no effort. Then, after a long interval, a ringing in the ears; then, after a lapse still longer, a prickling or tingling sensation in the extremities; then a seemingly eternal period of pleasurable quiescence, during which the awakening feelings are struggling into thought; then a brief re-sinking into nonentity; then a sudden recovery. At length the slight quivering of an eyelid, and immediately thereupon, an electric shock of terror, deadly and indefinite, which sends the blood in torrents from the temples of the heart. And now the first positive effort to think. And now the first endeavour to remember. And now a partial and evanescent success. And now the memory has so far regained its dominion, that in some measure I am cognizant of my state. I feel that I am not awaking from ordinary sleep. I recollect that I have been subject to catalepsy. And now, at last, as if by the rush of an ocean, my shuddering spirit is overwhelmed by the one grim Danger - by the spectral and ever-prevalent idea.

For some minutes after this fancy possessed me, I remained without motion. And why? I could not summon courage to move. I dared not make the effort which was to satisfy me of my fate - and yet there was something at my heart which whispered me it was sure. Despair - such as no other species of wretchedness ever calls into being - despair alone urged me, after long irresolution, to uplift the heavy lids of my eyes. I uplifted them. It was dark - all dark. I knew that the fit was over. I knew that the crisis of my disorder had long passed. I knew that I had now fully recovered the use of my visual faculties - and yet it was dark - all dark - the intense and utter raylessness of the Night that endureth for evermore.

I endeavoured to shriek; and my lips and parched tongue moved convulsively together in the attempt - but no voice issued from the cavernous lungs, which, oppressed as if by the weight of some incumbent mountain, gasped and palpitated, with the heart, at every elaborate and struggling inspiration.

The movement of the jaws, in this effort to cry aloud, showed me that they were bound up, as is usual with the dead. I felt, too, that I lay upon some hard substance; and by something similar my sides were, also, closely compressed. So far, I had not ventured to stir any of my limbs - but now I violently threw up my arms, which had been lying at length, with the wrists crossed. They struck a wooden substance, which extended above my person at an elevation of not more that six inches from my face. I could no longer doubt that I reposed within a coffin at last.

And now, amid all my infinite miseries, came sweetly the cherub Hope - for I though of my precautions. I writhed, and made spasmodic exertions to force open the lid: it would not move. I felt my wrists for the bell-rope: it was not to be found. And now the Comforter fled for ever, and a still sterner Despair reigned triumphant; for I could not help receiving the absence of the paddings which I had so carefully prepared - and then, too, there came suddenly to my nostrils the strong peculiar odour of moist earth. The conclusion was irresistible. I was *not* within the vault. I had fallen into a trance, while absent from home - while among strangers - when, or how, I could not remember - and it was they who had buried me as a dog - nailed up in some common coffin - and thrust, deep, deep, and for ever, into some ordinary and nameless *grave*.

As this awful conviction forced itself, thus, into the innermost chambers of my soul, I once again struggled to cry aloud. And in this second endeavour I succeeded. A long, wild, and continuous shriek, or yell of agony, resounded through the realms of the subterranean Night.

'Hillo! hillo, there!' said a gruff voice, in reply.

'What the devil's the matter now!' said a second.

'Get out o' that!' said a third.

'What do you mean by yowling in that 'ere kind of style, like a cattymount?' said a fourth; and thereupon I was seized and shaken without ceremony, for several minutes, by a junto of very rough-looking individuals. They did not arouse me from my slumber - for I was wide-awake when I screamed - but they restored me to the full possession of my memory.

This adventure occurred near Richmond, in Virginia. Accompanied by a friend, I had proceeded, upon a gunning expedition, some miles down the banks of the James River. Night approached and we were overtaken by a storm. The cabin of a small sloop lying at anchor in the stream, and laden with garden mould, afforded us the only available shelter. We made the best of it, and passed the night on board. I slept in one of the only two berths in the vessel - and the berths of a sloop of sixty or seventy tons need scarcely be described. That which I occupied had no bedding of any kind. Its extreme width was eighteen inches. The distance of its bottom from the deck overhead was precisely the same. I found it a matter of exceeding difficulty to squeeze myself in. Nevertheless, I slept soundly; and the whole of my vision - for it was no dream, and no nightmare - arose naturally from the circumstances of my position - from my ordinary bias of thought - and from the difficulty, to which I have alluded, of collecting my senses, and especially of regaining my memory, for a long time after awakening from slumber. The men who shook me were the crew of the sloop, and some labourers engaged to unload it. From the load itself came the earthy smell. The bandage about the jaws was a silk handkerchief in which I had bound up my head, in default of my customary nightcap.

The tortures endured, however, were indubitably quite equal, for the time, to those of actual sepulture. They were fearfully - they were inconceivably hideous; but out of Evil proceeded Good; for their very excess wrought in my spirit an inevitable revulsion. My soul acquired tone - acquired temper. I went abroad. I took vigorous exercise. I breathed the free air of Heaven. I thought upon other subjects than Death. I discarded my medical books. *Buchan* I burned. I read no *Night Thoughts* - no fustian about churchyards - no bugaboo tales - *such as this*. In short I became a new man, and lived a man's life. From that memorable night, I dismissed for ever my charnel apprehensions, and with them vanished the cataleptic disorder, of which, perhaps, they had been less the consequence than the cause.

There are moments when, even to the sober eye of Reason, the world of our sad Humanity may assume the semblance of a Hell - but the imagination of man is no Carathis, to explore with impunity its every cavern. Alas! the grim legion of sepulchral terrors cannot be regarded as altogether fanciful - but, like the Demons in whose company Afrasiab made his voyage down the Oxus, they must sleep, or they will devour us - they must be suffered to slumber, or we perish.

THE FATAL GARDEN

Editors note: Although Lucan and Gray clearly did a lot of enthusiastic research on poisonous plants, it seems that they were undecided about the design of the garden that was to contain them. Two schemes are described. One is a pastiche of a medieval monastery garden - based on the orchard cemetery at the Abbey of St Gall - with borders laid out in the form of a giant cross. The other is a 'Vitruvian man' in the style of Leonardo, arms and legs outstretched, toes and finger-tips touching the rim of a circle - a humanist's emblem of beauty and perfection.

Together with the planting notes, Lucan and Gray provide a literary piece of a suitably grotesque kind, a short story by the 17th century Japanese eroticist Shomi Yofani. This, they suggest, might be recorded and played by a speaking death's head hologram in an underground grotto, or recited live by a gardener in 16th century apothecary's robes - "black, heavily burned, ragged, and well-infected with mould".

DESIGN FOR THE FATAL GARDEN

In a secret precinct of the Island of the Dead, between high stone walls hung with honeysuckle and wisteria, lies the Fatal Garden. It is fragrant, lush, pregnant with destruction. Its model is the *hortus botanicus* of Dr Rapaccini, Hawthorne's satanic plant-engineer who will sacrifice anything to his all-consuming passion for Science.

We will instruct Ryan to lay out the plants in parterres like human organs, according to which part of the body they affect. Each parterre should be delineated by the traditional (and poisonous) box hedge. Viewed from above the organs will form a human figure. It will be a startling sight. Around the figure, a circular espalier of fruit trees like dancers in a ring, their branches trained, wired, and lopped in severe and perfect geometry.

Depending on the doses, many of the poisonous plants will be medicinal or narcotic. The Ancient Greeks had just one word (φαρμακον = pharmakon) for drugs that kill and drugs that cure and drugs that send you to sleep. Hence there must be three gates.

PORTA SALUTIS - for healing
PORTA INDOLENTIAE - for narcosis
PORTA INFERNORUM - for death

Let the garden form a cross, as at St Gall. A talisman, a symbol of protection and mystical faith.

THE PLANTS

There is a vertiginous choice of poisonous plants - more than a thousand species - many of them to be found in normal, run of the mill gardens of the most depressing kind. Some we have excluded purely out of disgust at this grim association, others we have put in precisely because of it. So, this is just a very small and very personal selection, with one eye to beauty, the other to virulence.

Apple - Only the seeds are poisonous - their bitter taste indicates the presence of amygdalin, which releases hydrocyanic acid into the blood if eaten in big enough quantities. A cupful of apple seeds will do it. Symptoms of posioning are headache, dizziness, salivation, vomiting (with a powerful bitter-almond smell), difficulty in breathing, blackout. The same poison is to be found in **peach, apricot, plum, damson, sloe, bitter almond** and **cherry** kernels - though you would have to crack them open and eat plenty (between 10 and 60 kernels) to feel the effects: the odd glass of sloe gin is quite insufficient.
Still the poison is a silent, lurking presence; we should have at least two of each tree - in a circle around the human figure - a magic ring to warn & guard.

Azalea / Rhododendron - Many species (there are between 500 and 1000) contain poison in their flowers, leaves, seeds and shoots. Honey made from the nectar is bitter and toxic, and affects the bees that make it as well as humans. Pliny, Strabo and Xenophon describe the effects - diarrhoea, vomiting, pain and cramp in the intestines, dizziness and itching.

Beans (French, runner, broad, etc.) - *Phaseolus vulgaris, P. coccineus, Vicia faba.* All beans are poisonous until they're cooked. Raw-food fetishists risk something called 'severe haemorrhagic gastro-enteropathy', which doesn't sound at all pleasant. Broad bean plants have the advantage of turning black and slimy after maturity. A natural Decadent choice for spring & summer planting.

Black bryony - *Tamus communis* - A white-flowered climber, sole British member of the yam family. Black roots and red berries, both poisonous, burn the mouth and blister the skin. Cattle eat it and become addicted, sometimes die.

Box - *Buxus sempervirens* - This fragrant delineator, whose trunk is sliced into fine-grained tablets for the use of wood-engravers, is absolutely *lethal* to pigs. A box meal would not do the human digestion much good either.

Broom - *Cytisus scoparius* - Contains sparteine, which slows down the heart and gradually leads to paralysis.

Buttercup (meadow) - *Ranunculus acris* - Animals are poisoned by buttercups more than humans, but the poison in the sap is a skin irritant of some power. Folk remedies: mix roots with salt to cure plague; hang round neck in a bag to cure lunacy.

Castor oil plant - *Ricinus communis* - Castor oil seeds look pretty and taste like hazelnuts. One of them, if well chewed, is enough to release a lethal dose of the poison ricin. In London a few years ago the Bulgarian journalist Georgy Markov was murdered using a pellet filled with ricin fired from the point of an umbrella into his leg. In the absence of a Bulgarian secret service umbrella , an ethnic necklace may do instead. These are sometimes made from castor oil plant seeds, and the poison, released by boring, leaks out onto the skin causing swelling, irritation, and other allergic reactions. Ricin produces nausea, vomiting, stomach pain, bloody diarrhoea, drowsiness, cyanosis, tenesmus, convulsions, circulatory collapse, necrosis of liver, kidneys, spleen and lymphatic tissue.

Cherry laurel - *Prunus laurocerasus* - A tree with poisonous leaves and fruits that look exactly like cherries. The fruit pulp is fairly harmless, but the stones are full of amygdalin, which they release in bitter fumes when crushed. This is the same poison as in apple pips, which the body (somewhat foolishly in our opinion) converts to cyanide.

Cotoneaster - *Cotoneaster horizontalis, C. racemiflorus, C. zabelii* - These species contain especially high concentrations of cyanide, which was Hermann Goering's chosen *modus morendi*. For the effects of this, see **apple**.

Cowbane - *Cicuta virosa* - (also known as water hemlock). This is one of the most poisonous of all plants. Its roots, with their parsnip-celery scent, are particularly vicious. Merely chewing them brings on burning in the mouth, vomiting and convulsions. They must be grown in water or marshy soil.

Crotalaria - A fine-looking evergreen shrub with big yellow flowers and appallingly dangerous seeds is *Crotalaria agatiflora* (canary-bird bush). Seeds mixed into food cereals led to an epidemic of poisoning in Madhya Pradesh in 1975 (28 deaths).

Cyclamen - The highly poisonous tubers of cyclamen (Rhizoma Cyclaminis) were once used by apothecaries as a purgative. And what a purgative! Effects: convulsions, paralysis, stomach pains, passage to the next world.

Daffodil - *Narcissus pseudonarcissus* - Only the bulbs (sometimes mistaken for onions) are poisonous - inducing diarrhoea, vomiting, dermatitis and violent perspiration.

Dead men's fingers or **hemlock water-dropwort** - *Oenanthe crocata* - It smells and looks like parsley, and is utterly merciless. Its most recent recorded victim was a vegetarian hippie who used the roots in his last salad.

Deadly nightshade - *Atropa belladonna* - Linnaean names are sometimes quite poetic: *Atropa* is from Atropos, the Greek Fate whose shears cut the thread of life. *Belladonna* was added because the juice of the berries was used in medieval Italy to make eyes shine and pupils dilate, so rendering a *donna* more *bella.* The deadly nightshade has sweet black berries, which are eaten without ill effects by pheasants and blackbirds but with very ill effects by humans, who are liable to go red in the face, dry in the mouth, fast in the pulse, wide-eyed, garrulous, frenzied, comatose, and then breathless before giving up the ghost. 2-5 berries can strike down a child, 10-20 an adult. **Woody nightshade** - *Solanum dulcamara* - and **black nightshade** - *Solanum nigrum* - also contain poisons but in lower concentrations.

Delphinium - *Delphinium elatum* is an innocent-looking suburban poisoner which has been bred in several Decadent colour-schemes. Plenty to choose from here: we suggest the varieties Blue Nile, Loch Leven, Lord Butler and Olive Poppleton. They will empurple the garden nicely.

Dieffenbachia - Indigenous in Brazil and the Caribbean, where they grow up to 2 metres high, and used in Europe as house-plants for their pretty white-spotted leaves and unusual tolerance for central heating. The juice squirts people in the face when they try to snap off a leaf or piece of stem, shooting out tiny grooved needles from ampoule-like ejector-cells. These act as miniature injections of poison into the body, with a similar mechanism to snake's fangs. The poison acts on mucous membranes (eyes, mouth and throat) causing burning pain and swelling. On sugar plantations, dieffenbachia was used to torture rebellious slaves and silence troublesome witnesses (swollen tongues made speech impossible). Hence the vernacular name 'dumb cane'.

Dog's mercury - *Mercurialis perennis* - 'There is not a more fatal plant, native of our country, than this,' said Culpeper. A dull shade-loving plant, with small green flowers. No human use has been found for it, so it has been assigned to the canine fraternity. Annual mercury *(M. perennis)* is also nasty. It was a component of medieval emetics and enemas.

Euphorbia - The white latex in the stems is a powerful skin irritant, and causes stomach pain, diarrhoea and vomiting if eaten. The species includes various **spurges** and **poinsettia**. There are only two scientifically-authenticated cases of poinsettia poisoning: a Swiss dachshund that died after eating a poinsettia for lunch, and a 66-year-old man who developed roaring skin-inflammation after cutting and bundling poinsettias bare-chested in his greenhouse all afternoon. (This is giving us grave doubts about the so-called health-giving properties of gardening in the nude).

Foxglove - *Digitalis purpurea* - Two to three leaves is the terminal dose of this pinky-purple, liver-spotted floral radio-mast, though overdosing with the heart drug digitalis has dispatched many a victim too. Acrid leaves & instant vomiting usually save the casual foxglove-eater, but there is a way round this. Here is the curious case-history of an 85 year old man. "Throughout his life the man had generally avoided medical care and relied on home remedies. His wife had regularly concocted herbal teas from leaves found in their backyard without problems for many years. However, on the day of admission his wife had felt ill and he himself had picked some leaves from an unfamiliar plant (later identified as *Digitalis pupurea*). He had made a tea with them and had drunk a cup, even though it had an unusually bitter taste." Despite his age and a lethal level of digitoxin in his blood, the old man was treated in hospital and survived. Another couple, who drank the same brew, did not. Symptoms of digitalis poisoning are dizziness, several days' worth of vomiting, wildly varying heart-rhythms, hallucinations, delirium.

Glory lily - *Gloriosa superba* - Six-petalled, flame-flowered climbing lily of extravagant beauty. The tubers are full of colchicine, one of the grisliest poisons in the vegetable kingdom. See **meadow saffron** for further repulsive details.

Greater celandine - *Chelidonium majus* - An alchemist's favourite: they called it *coeli donum* (gift from the sky) and believed the yellow juice could convert base metals to gold. Another ludicrous use was in folk-medicine, for curing warts and cloudy eyes. Scientific research has shown that it is actually damaging to the eyes, and unusually friendly to warts. Not terribly poisonous - one would need to eat at least half a kilogram of fresh celandine to feel any toxic effects.

Hellebore (black, green, or stinking) - *Helleborus niger* (Christmas rose), *H. viridis, H. foetidus*. One of the oldest chemical weapons. In about 600 BC, according to Pausanias, Solon used hellebore to contaminate the River Pleistus, which provided drinking water for the Cirrhaeans, whose city he was besieging. The Cirrhaeans were all 'seized with obstinate diarrhoea' and Solon captured the city. White hellebore *(Veratrum album)* is a different plant altogether, and far more dangerous (see below).

Hemlock - *Conium maculatum* - Hemlock acts like curare - it starts on the legs, then rises up the body, paralysing and numbing, leaving the mind clear and fully conscious, until it reaches the lungs. At this point breathing stops. Plato describes the process beautifully in *The Death of Socrates.* Apparently the plant smells of mouse-urine when crushed.

Henbane - *Hyoscyamus niger* - This versatile weed has been used 'since time immoral' for hallucinogenic effects, euthanasia, murder, analgesia, and for livening up weak beer. Dosage is crucial. It was used by Dr Crippen to poison his wife. It might also be the 'cursed hebenon' in this famous Shakespearean assassination:

Sleeping within my orchard,
My custom always of the afternoon,
Upon my secure hour thy uncle stole,
With juice of cursed hebenon in a vial,
And in the porches of my ears did pour

The leperous distilment; whose effect
Holds such an enmity with blood of man
That swift as quicksilver it courses through
The natural gates and alleys of the body;
And with a natural vigour it doth posset
And curd, like eager droppings into milk,
The thin and wholesome blood. So did it mine;
And a most instant tetter barked about,
Most lazar-like, with vile and loathsome crust,
All my smooth body.
Thus was I, sleeping, by a brother's hand
Of life, of crown, of queen, at once dispatch'd;
Cut off even in the blossoms of my sin,
Unhous'led, disappointed, unanel'd;
No reck'ning made, but sent to my account
With all my imperfections on my head.
O, horrible! O, horrible! most horrible!

(*Hamlet* I.v)

Holly - *Ilex aquifolium* - Two or more berries of this prickly Christmas accessory will bring on vomiting, diarrhoea and stomach-ache.

Honeysuckle - *Lonicera periclymenum* - Evergreen perfumed climber with poison berries, which we propose draping profusely around the walls.

Laburnum or **golden chain** - *Laburnum anagyroides* - Smart but suburban tree, with niagarous ejaculations of yellow flowers. The seeds are the nasty bit. Particularly dangerous for children, who are mysteriously drawn to them. Vomiting is the usual result.

Larkspur - *Consolida regalis, C. ambigua* - A tall, handsome, wicked plant with spikes of purple flowers that contain deadly alkaloids similar to aconitine (see **monkshood**).

Lords and ladies (or **cuckoo-pint**) - *Arum maculatum* - This is a double murderer - it has poisonous bright red berries and a deathtrap for insects in its hood. The erect brown cudgel of its spadix smells putrid and attracts flies. They crawl in for a sniff and are imprisoned by downward-pointing hairs. Their only hope of escape is if the spadix dies first.

Lupin - *Lupinus* - The contents of a couple of seed-pods should be enough to make even a gladiator lose his breakfast. If not, convulsions, restlessness, death, etc will soon follow. A purple-blue variety, highly suitable for the Decadent garden, is 'Thundercloud'.

Mandrake - *Mandragora officinarum* - This is described in the Royal Horticultural Society *Gardener's Encyclopaedia* as a 'rosetted, fleshy-rooted perennial with coarse, wavy-edged leaves.' To us it looks more like a mutant cauliflower dipped in a bucket of yacht varnish. A very strange-looking plant indeed. The forked root is uncannily humanoid, and was said to cry out when pulled from the ground. Much used in black magic, poetry, folklore, etc. Same family (Solanaceae) as **potato, aubergine, tomato, paprika, tobacco** and **deadly nightshade**.

Meadow saffron - *Colchicum autumnale* - This is a particularly vicious plant, known as 'vegetable arsenic'. Its poisonous ingredient, colchicine, only becomes active after absorption inside the body - i.e. when it's too late to sluice or vomit it out. Symptoms are too disgusting and horrible to describe, but they include the usual eruptions from stomach and intestines with the addition of blood. Used for suicide and murders, and to adulterate hard drugs. In low doses it's supposed to help treat gout.

Mezereon or **spurge olive**- *Daphne mezereum* - What a pretty arsenal of horrors this ornamental bush holds in store. Springtime brings out its gorgeous, perfumed, cardinal-purple flowers before its leaves, but both are poisonous enough to kill even in small quantities. (So are the fruit, seeds and bark.) The main poisons present, daphnetoxin and mezerein, cause burning in the mouth, headache and stomach-pains, swollen lips and face, hoarseness, salivation, difficulty in swallowing, disorientation, twitching, fearfulness, convulsions and bloody diarrhoea. Professional beggars found the juice useful for blistering the skin in grotesque ways. A study by Schildknecht et al has established the useful fact that the 'mouse-ear inflammation unit' of mezerein is 0.2 mg per ear.

Monkshood or **helmet flower** - *Aconitum napellus* - Leaves, flowers and seeds are all poisonous, so this tall, purple-blossomed terminator well deserves its reputation of 'most poisonous plant in Europe.' Only its Indian cousin, *Aconitum ferox*, outvenoms it. A favourite murder poison since antiquity, just 3-6 mg of aconitine (or a few leaves) will do the business. Accidental poisonings have occurred from confusing the root with horse-radish, and from using the root as a narcotic. Aconitine can also be absorbed through the skin, so even handling the plant can be dangerous. Symptoms appear within minutes, and include burning and tingling in the mouth, fingers and toes, then sweating, numbness, freezing cold, violent vomiting, diarrhoea, paralysis, extreme pain and blindness. Death is caused by paralysis of the lungs or heart failure, but the mind remains fully conscious until the end.

Mullein (great, dark, white, moth) - *Verbascum thapsus, V. nigrum, V. lychnitis, V. blattaria* - Tall, spiky plants, usually with silver-furred leaves and yellow or white flowers in a knobbled inverted ice-cream cone at the top. Nasty to taste, poisonous in large quantities, the leaves of great mullein are sometimes used in herbal cigarettes.

Oleander - *Nerium oleander* - Although the pink-flowered mediterranean oleander is poisonous, and mentioned as such by Theophrastus, Galen and Pliny, the yellow oleander *(Thevetia peruviana)* is much more dangerous. 8-10 seeds are fatal, and a favourite source of poison for murders in India.

Philodendron - Another poisonous houseplant, which is fatally attractive to cats for some reason. People who come into contact with philodendron regularly get dermatitis, skin eruptions, etc.

Poppy - *Papaver somniferum* - A slow killer, which can take years or hours according to the dose. Used medicinally for at least two millennia, its latex is the source of opium, morphine, codeine, and noscapine. Poisoning is caused by eating the seed-heads or boiling them up to make tea. Also by overdosing with morphine. Symptoms of poisoning are a narcotic state, muscular relaxation, extremely slow breathing (2-4 breaths per minute), and the pupils of the eyes shrinking to pinpoints. Low oxygen supply to the tissues makes them cyanotic. Eventually breathing stops altogether.

Potato - *Solanum tuberosum* - Here's a sly operator. The edible tubers are hidden under the ground, while the poisonous parts - stems, leaves, fruits and flowers - luxuriate on top. The solanine poison is also present in the tuber but in harmless amounts (7mg per 100g). That is until they start to sprout, when it suddenly increases to critical levels (35mg per 100g). In a sprouting potato, eyes, skin, shoots and green parts are the nasty bits, and cooking has no effect (baked in their skins is the most dangerous way to eat them). Possible effects of solanine poisoning are exhaustion, vomiting, headache, stomach pain, diarrhoea, fever, apathy, hallucinations, agoraphobia and restlessness.

Privet - *Ligustrum vulgare* - The shiny black poisonous berries grow in late summer. There's some doubt about whether they are lethal or just violently emetic. The flowers are white and fragrant, the seeds purple. If you prefer vile-smelling flowers, plant *Ligustrum ovalifolium.*

Saffron crocus - *Crocus sativus* - Harmless in tiny quantities as saffron - the dried stigma of the flower - but 5-10 grams (about £70 worth) is a lethal dose. Mix with **meadow saffron** for a truly vicious crocus display.

Sumach - some varieties provide low-grade but reliable aggression: poison oak *(Toxicodendron quercifolium)*, western poison oak *(T. diversilobium)*, poison ivy *(T. radicans)*, and poison sumach *(T. vernix).*

Thorn-apple (Jimsonweed) - *Datura stramonium* - Many intoxicating properties, much used in black magic, love-potions, and horse-trading, where a couple of rolled up leaves stuck in the posterior orifice of a jaded beast would give it a lively look. Hallucinogenic effects make it a favourite with do-it-yourself drug addicts too. They have been found wandering naked in the fields, or swimming in ponds in search of red-eyed dolphins. One patient "held conversations with a man in a suit whom only he could see, and felt that he was being followed by black and red knee-high spiders". The effects of overdosing are the same as those of deadly nightshade, though the sedative action is stronger. Other *Datura* species, e.g. *D. candida* (**angel's trumpet**) and *D. suaveolens* have similar properties, smell glorious, and must certainly have a place in the poison garden.

Tobacco - *Nicotiana tabacum* - Fragrant-blooming companion of the good life and its destroyer - 'they that like not tobacco and small boys are fools' (Marlowe). 40-60g is the lethal dose. 'Nicotine acts on the vegetative ganglia initially as a stimulant (increase in blood pressure and gastro-intestinal tone, etc.) and subsequently as a blocker (convulsions, respiratory paralysis). It acts extremely rapidly after being absorbed through the skin, through inhalation, or orally. Taking a concentrated solution can lead to death within a few minutes.' A curious variation on the 60-a-day habit is the case of the tobacco smuggler who wrapped the leaves around his body to get them through customs, and died - the plant has hairs on the leaves that secrete the poison into the skin. Nicotine is also a great garden insecticide: inhaling the spray may wipe out the gardener too. Effects: headache, dizziness, vomiting, diarrhoea, cold sweats, racing pulse, convulsions, blackout, cardiac arrest. Huichol Indians in Mexico use a related tobacco (*Nicotiana rustica*) for ceremonial hallucinations, while Europeans, North Americans, etc, use *N. tabacum* in a number of interesting rituals including those associated with food, courtship, rites of passage, angst, and sex.

Toothwort - *Lathraea squamaria* - also known as 'corpse flower' - This is not actually poisonous, but you would never believe it, so disgusting does it look. We could place it in the eye section, since this is the organ it most offends.

Tulip - *Tulipa gesneriana* - Well-known among gardeners for producing 'tulip finger' (brittle nails and swollen, itching, inflamed skin) from irritating secretions from their bulbs. The variety 'Rose Copeland' is a particularly rich source of tulip finger. Eating tulip bulbs instead of onions doesn't seem to be too dangerous, provided you keep consumption down to five per day.

White hellebore - *Veratrum album* - The roots are sometimes mistaken by amateur herbalists for valerian or gentian, with grim consequences: sneezing, convulsions, numbness, feelings of cold, violent diarrhoea, difficulty in breathing, coma, and then the end. 1 or 2 grams of dried root is lethal.

Wild rosemary - *Ledum palustre* - The Vikings used the shoots and leaves to crank up the octane of their beer. It also cranked them up to amazing acts of recklessness, and has been proposed as an explanation of their 'berserker' culture. The plant contains an essential oil that produces both narcotic and intoxicating effects: excitement and convulsions, followed by paralysis, loss of balance and prolonged sleep. It grows well on peaty soil.

Wisteria - *Wisteria sinensis* - Bark, roots, and especially the seeds are poisonous. We could plant this right round the garden wall, alternating with honeysuckle, glory-lilies, black bryony and arching cotoneaster.

Yellow iris - *Iris pseudacorus.* Ditch and river plant, mud lover, causes violent stomach upsets when eaten.

Yew - *Taxus baccata* - a cemetery and topiary favourite, the classic 'tree of death', popular in the ancient world for murder and suicide. With poisonous seeds and leaves, it has also been accused of emitting venomous gases, but this is almost certainly untrue since it is stated as a fact in the newspapers. Symptoms of poisoning: dizziness, nausea, stomach pain, dilated pupils, crimson lips, shallow breathing, rapid heartbeats, coma. Later the pulse slows, blood pressure falls and respiratory paralysis ushers in the undertaker and his mate. An alternative is Japanese yew, *Taxus cuspidata*, which is even more poisonous.

Tennyson wrote a creepy poem to the yew which we might get Ryan to chisel for us on a tombstone at its foot:

> Old Yew, which graspest at the stones
> > That name the under-lying dead,
> > Thy fibres net the dreamless head;
> Thy roots are wrapt about the bones.

> The seasons bring the flower again,
> > And bring the firstling to the flock;
> > And in the dusk of thee, the clock
> Beats out the little lives of men.

> O not for thee the glow, the bloom,
> > Who changest not in any gale!
> > Nor branding summer suns avail
> To touch thy thousand years of gloom.

> And gazing on thee, sullen tree,
> > Sick for thy stubborn hardihood,
> > I seem to fail from out my blood,
> And grow incorporate into thee.

THE PLANTING SCHEME

This is how we might distribute the plants in our Vitruvian man:
Head: meadow saffron, rhododendron, thorn-apple, wild rosemary
Mouth: cowbane, deadly nightshade, dieffenbachia, mezereon
Eyes: corpse flower, dieffenbachia, monkshood, poppy
Throat: arum, black hellebore, mistletoe
Lungs: fool's parsley, hemlock, monkshood, poppy, yew

Heart: broom, cowbane, foxglove, tobacco
Arms and legs: azalea, cyclamen, hemlock, white hellebore
Hands: buttercup, tulip,
Stomach: beans, cowbane, euphorbia, holly, laburnum, yellow iris
Kidneys: castor oil plant
Liver: bog asphodel, crotalaria

ALL COMRADE-LOVERS DIE BY HARA-KIRI
SHOMI YOFANI

The fairest plants and trees meet their death because of the marvel of their flowers. And it is the same with humanity; many men perish because they are too beautiful.

There was a page named Ukyo-Itami who served a Lord at Yedo. He was cultured and elegant and so extremely beautiful that he troubled the eyes of those who looked at him. His master had another page named Uneme Mokawa, eighteen years of age, who also had great beauty and a countenance full of graces. Ukyo was so smitten with this other as almost to lose his senses, so moved was he by his virile loveliness. He suffered to such an extent from his love that he fell ill and had to take to his bed, where he sighed and moaned his unheard love in solitude. But he was very popular, and many people had pity in him and came to see him in his illness to care for him and console him.

One day his fellow-pages came to visit him and among them was his beloved Uneme. At the sight of him, Ukyo betrayed by his expression the sentiments which he felt for him, and the pages then guessed the secret of his illness. Samanosuke Shiga, another page who was Uneme's lover, was also present and was much moved at seeing the suffering of poor Ukyo. He stayed with the invalid when the other went away, knelt down beside him and whispered: 'I am sure, dear Ukyo, that there is a grief in your soul. Open your heart to me who am your friend and love you very much. Do not keep any secret from me. If you love any of the pages who were here just now, tell me frankly. I shall do my best to help you, Ukyo.' But the bashful Ukyo could not open his sick heart to him. He

223

simply said: 'You are wrong, my Samanosuke, you are mistaken about me.'

And since Samanosuke insisted, he pretended to be asleep. Samanosuke went away.

They caused two high priests to pray for Ukyo's recovery, and after they had prayed without ceasing for two days and two nights Ukyo seemed better. Then Samanosuke again went secretly to Ukyo and said:

'Dear friend, write him a love letter. I will give it to him without fail and he shall at once send you a kind answer. I know whom you love so desperately, and you need not consider me in your passion. He and I are lovers, but I am quite ready to satisfy your desire because of our long and sincere friendship, Ukyo'

Then Ukyo took courage and wrote a letter with trembling hand and entrusted it to Samanosuke. When Samanosuke reached the palace he met Uneme, who was looking in silence at the flowers in the garden. Uneme saw him and said:

'Dear friend, I have been very busy every evening amusing my Lord with Nô plays, and this evening I have only come out for a few moments to breathe a little air. I have read my master the ancient classical poem "Seuin Kokin" and was alone and without a friend except for the silent cherry blooms. I am very lonely.' And he looked tenderly at Samanosuke.

'Here is another silent flower, Uneme,' said Samanosuke, and held out the letter to him.

Uneme smiled at him and said, 'This letter cannot be for me, dear friend.'

He went behind some thick trees to read it. He was touched by the letter and kindly replied to Samanosuke: 'I cannot remain unmoved if he suffers so much for me.'

When Ukyo received Uneme's answer, he was filled with joy and quickly recovered his health. And the three men loved each other with a loyal and harmonious love.

Now it happened that their master took into his service a new courtier named Shyuzen Hosono. This man was rough, evil, and of a hasty temper; he had no finesse or elegance; he was continually boasting of his exploits and no one liked him. When he saw Ukyo he fell in love with him; but he had not the delicacy to make his love known to him in some charming letter: he had not sufficiently good taste for that. He pursued Ukyo with smiles and tears whenever he saw him alone in the palace or the garden. But Ukyo despised him.

The Lord had a servant with head shaven, whose duty it was to take care of the utensils belonging to the tea ritual. He was named Shyusai Tushiki, and he had become an intimate friend of Shyuzen; so he undertook to convey a message from him to Ukyo. Accordingly he said one day to Ukyo: 'I pray you to give Shyuzen a kind answer. He loves you passionately.'
And he gave him Shyuzen's letter.

But Ukyo threw the letter away and said: 'It is not your business to carry love-letters. Attend to your duty of keeping the master's house clean for the tea matters.' And he went away.

Shyuzen and Shyusai were consumed with rage. They determined to kill Ukyo that same night and then to run away. They could not endure the insult and humiliation which Ukyo had inflicted upon them and made ready for their vicious deed. But Ukyo was warned of their plot and decided to kill them both before they could attack him. He thought of speaking to Uneme about it, but, on reflection told himself that it was unworthy of a samurai to speak about his business to his lover with the sole object of obtaining his help. Besides, he did not want to make Uneme his accomplice. So he decided to execute his plan by himself.

It was the month of May and very wet. It rained heavily on that night. It was the seventeenth day of the moon in the seventeenth year of Kanyei (A.D. 1641). All the samurai of the guard were in a state of deep fatigue and were sleeping. Ukyo put on a thin silk garment as white as snow with a splendid skirt. He perfumed himself more than ordinarily so as to be pure, for he had determined to die after having killed his two enemies. He put two swords in the girdle which encircled his hips, and crossed through the halls of the palace. Since he was in the habit of doing this every evening, the guards let him pass without questioning.

Shyuzen was on guard that night in one of the rooms. He was leaning against a screen pictured with hawks, and was looking at his fan. Ukyo rushed upon him and thrust his sword deep into his right shoulder as far as his breast. But Shyuzen was a brave and strong man. With his left hand he seized his own sword and defended himself bravely. Yet he was losing blood and getting weak and finally he fell, cursing Ukyo. Ukyo finished him with two more sword thrusts; then he went in search of Shyusai.

But the guards had been aroused by the noise of the struggle and had lit lamps in the rooms. They arrested Ukyo and their captain led him before the Lord who was much disturbed and very angry. He spoke harshly to Ukyo and said to him: 'What reason had you for killing Shyuzen? You deserve punishment for having thus troubled my palace in the night with your crime. Confess your reason for having killed him.'

But Ukyo kept silent. He was brought before the Chief Judge, Tonomo Tokumatsu, who examined him; and Ukyo confessed. When the Lord was informed of this, he grew calm and ordered Ukyo to be kept in a room in the palace, where he was treated with respect.

Shyuzen's father was one of the Lord's hereditary courtiers. He was so outraged by the crime committed against his son that he swore to die by hara-kiri on the same spot where his son had fallen. His mother also was a favourite of the Princess, the Lord's wife. She used to take part in the Princess's poetical gatherings. All night, with bare feet, she wept and mourned her son's death. She besought the Princess to punish the murderer, saying: 'If the Lord pardons the murderer, there is no law and no justice in the world.'

Accordingly the Lord grudgingly resolved to condemn Ukyo to die by hara-kiri. Shyusai, who had carried the message to Shyuzen, contrived his own death also.

Uneme had at that time received leave of absence from his master to visit his mother at Kanagawa, and did not know that Ukyo had been condemned to death. But Samanosuke wrote to him to say that Ukyo was to kill himself next morning at the Keiyoji temple at Asakusa. Uneme sent Samanosuke his thanks, and hastened at daybreak to the temple without even taking time to bid his mother farewell. As he stood in the chief entrance to the temple, which was in the form of a low tower, several people started talking noisily about hara-kiri. They said: 'Early this morning a young samurai is coming here to kill himself. They say that he is very beautiful. Even an ugly son is dear to his parents.

The father and mother of this young samurai will be smitten with despair at realising that so accomplished a son must die. Surely it is a pity to kill such a splendid young man.'

Uneme could hardly restrain his tears on hearing these people. The temple quickly filled and he hid himself behind a door and waited for the arrival of his darling Ukyo.

Shortly after, a fine new litter was seen to approach, borne by several men, surrounded by guards. It stopped opposite the door and Ukyo descended from it with the utmost calmness. He was wearing a white silk garment embroidered with autumn flowers, having pale blue facings and a skirt. He stopped for a moment and looked about him. On the tombs were some thousands of wooden tablets bearing the names of those who were buried there. Among them rose a wild cherry tree with white blossom on the upper branches only. Ukyo looked at the pale, fading flowers and softly murmured an old Chinese poem:

> *The flowers wait for next Spring,*
> *Trusting that the same hands shall caress them.*
> *But men's hearts will no longer be the same,*
> *And you will only know that everything changes,*
> *O poor lovers.*

The seat destined for the hara-kiri had been placed in the garden of the temple. Ukyo calmly seated himself on the gold-bordered mats and summoned his attendant whose duty it was to cut off the condemned man's head to shorten his suffering after he had manipulated the dagger in his belly.

This attendant's name was Kajuyu Kitji Kawa, and he was a courtier of the same Lord. Ukyo cut off his wonderful locks of his hair, put them in a white paper and gave them to Kajuyu, praying him to send them to his venerable mother at Horikawa in Kyoto as a keepsake. The priest then began to pray for the salvation of Ukyo's soul.

Ukyo said: 'Beauty in this world cannot endure for long. I am glad to die while I am young and beautiful, and before my countenance fades like a flower.' Then he took a green paper from his sleeve and wrote his farewell poem upon it. This was his poem:

I loved the beauty of flowers in springtime;
In autumn the glory of the moon
Was my delight;
But now that I am looking upon death face to face,
These joys are vanishing;
They were all dream.

Then he thrust the knife into his belly, and Kajuyu at once struck off his head from behind. At that moment Uneme ran to the mats and cried: 'Finish me also,' and pierced himself. Kajuyu struck off his head. Ukyo was sixteen years old and Uneme was eighteen. The tombs of these two young men remained for a long time in the temple, and Ukyo's farewell poem was inscribed in their joint stones. On the seventeenth day after their death, Samanosuke also died by hara-kiri, leaving a letter to say that he could not survive his lovers' death. Such is the tragedy of these young men who died for love.

GARDENS OF THE MIND

By this stage, we are finding it increasingly difficult to avoid the conclusion that it is the spaces of imaginary gardens which attract us most. Despite our prodigious research, our elaborate plans, the detailed specifications, the careful supervision of construction, there is a sense in which for both of us - and perhaps for all truly Decadent gardeners - no garden which exists in the real world could possibly live up to the sorts of gardens which can be created in the mind. This may be at the root of our (qualified) admiration for such men as Bernard Palissy. So, after sifting through our design notes, we have made a selection of some of the imaginary gardens which have excited and inspired us. We begin with *Sept jardins fantastiques* by André Pieyre de Mandiargues.

SEVEN FANTASY GARDENS

I

Through the first garden, the channelled water flows with no purpose other than to justify the presence of a bridge, under the roof of an ancient Roman railway station. There gapes the nakedness of a girl who is still ill-at-ease with the weight and swing of her breasts.

'Love.' This word is uttered by a barefoot woman who handles a grape while dipping her toes in the water... 'Do you want me to love you now?'

'Now? No,' replies the young girl, lips parted. 'When love was over, you'd go away and I'd be left with nothing but the sound of the water...'

The third woman paddles in the water and her naked rear silently echoes a peacock's crest and the coil of a serpent.

II

At the foot of the primordial tree, the boughs of the second garden form a rustic bed. Here recline three nudes, more ample than nature herself. Four of their six arms are lost to view. As two hands, both equally tender, join together, these arms form a yoke within which the mask of death and the head of philosophy overlap in such a way that the gaze of Plato or Aristotle plunges into the empty eye-sockets of the Grim Reaper and the perpetual serpent stretches out along the rump of a sphinx.

III

The third garden - Italianate - is a Tivoli fallen from the sky, a Villa d'Este raised from the sea. On each terrace of a verdant theatre eleven monstrous beauties appear. They are more gracious than real girls, more generous than created women, and they realise full well that the irresistible attraction of their breasts and thighs will lure young suitors whose bony remains will be incorporated into the configuration of the place, behind the blue pond, where they will bathe, after they have gobbled up the eyes of their last lover. They are the hybrid creatures of some vegetable world or animal kingdom which only ever existed in the fecund day-dreams of some painter-poet.

IV

At the fourth spot, I see one who sharpens her claws.
They grew out of her frantic desire to be a naked beast
And to only ever walk on all-fours.
She wants her rear-end to contain her whole being
And to proffer it as she purrs out her name, Leonie.
Lucinda is the name of the other who lies
Outstretched, gently fingering her tender boredom.
The garden has adorned her hair with premature fruits
Ripened by the light of a cold pleasure.

V

On top of a small neo-Roman temple, in which the venerated deity is more likely to be Venus than Vesta, two horses, who could only be mares, with blond curly manes and bright eyes, have leapt out of the marble and the acanthus at the side of Evelyne. She sits on the facade, quite naked. While looking away, she holds out a fruit the attractions of which are slight in comparison to those exerted by her breasts. I can feel her nipples, like a gaze, bearing down on me joyously as I write ... Loving Evelyne... Loving her breasts, her thighs, her mares; three sets of unabashed charms, brazen and exalted against the deep blue sky above the fifth garden...

VI

Here daylight has sunk behind dark trunks and gloomy columns. The bird's silent flight merges with the darkness. The calyxes of enormous *belles-de-nuit* blossom everywhere behind the nakedness of the great nonchalant beauty. Her rump is rounded like a bare mountain. Some serpent shows an interest, certainly, but not that monstrous being which lurks behind a column like the manifestation of an idea of prehistory in the empty head of her who has stripped off before lying down. The day slips away but summer weighs heavily. At the base of this sixth garden, the faces of fifteen young victims are surrounded by as many coils of a long double reptile. The heads and the tails of this creature are lost at the edge of our vision. Waste no pity on them!

VII

Certainly there are good reasons why a skin-coloured skull is to be found at the centre of the seventh garden. A pond of greenish liquid as thick as mercury is where this head bone floats. And equally good reasons why she who pretends to be bathing there leans on it and does not wet her hands as she dallies with the little waves of clear light. A girl, disrobed, sits astride the bony back of a sort of river horse. It turns its head in order to avoid seeing its companion whom it might have loved in a former garden, before seeking, in the features of the carnal skull, the form of its final moments . Isn't it the name of Pompeii, or its echo, which will be snuffed out under the shelter of parasol pines? What do we know, other than that the only inhabitants of the fabulous gardens of Yamashita are heat, silence, non-communication, the nakedness of the woman, the serpent and death?

Editors' note: The translation of *Sept jardins fantastiques* was done by Durian Gray. Another of their favourite gardens was that imagined by Aubrey Beardsley in his fantasy tale *Under the Hill*, being ' The story of Venus and Tannhaüser in which is set forth an exact account of the manner of state held by Madam Venus, goddess and meretrix, under the famous Horselberg and counting the adventures of Tannhaüser in that place, his repentance, his journeying to Rome and return to the loving mountain'.

The following is a description of the gates of the garden of Venus, just before he enters the *Mons Veneris*.

The place where he stood waved drowsily with strange flowers, heavy with perfume, dripping with odours. Gloomy and nameless weeds not to be found in Mentzelius. Huge moths so richly winged they must have banqueted upon tapestries and royal stuffs, slept on the pillars that flanked either side of the gateway, and the eyes of all the moths remained open and were burning and bursting with a mesh of veins. The pillars were fashioned in some pale stone and rose up like hymns in praise of Venus, for, from cap to base each one was carved with loving sculptures showing such cunning invention and such a curious knowledge that Tannhaüser lingered not a little in reviewing them.

In order to welcome the knight Tannhäuser, Venus lays on a sumptuous feast for him, in equally sumptuous surroundings.

The orange-trees and myrtles looped with vermilion sashes, stood in frail porcelain pots and the rose-trees were wound and twisted with superb invention over trellis and standard. Upon one side of the terrace, a long gilded stage for the comediams was curtained off with Pagonian tapestries and in front of it the music stands were placed. The tables arranged between the fountain and the flight of steps to the sixth terrace were all circular, covered with white damask, and strewn with irises, roses, kingcups, columbines, daffodils, carnations and lilies.

The following morning, the two go for a drive around the grounds of the Venusberg.

The drive proved interesting and various, and Tannhaüser was quite delighted with almost everything he saw.

And who is not pleased when on either side of him rich lawns are spread with lovely frocks and white limbs, and upon flower beds the dearest ladies are implicated in a glory of underclothing, - when he can see in the deep cool shadow of the trees warm boys entwined, here at the base, there in the branch - when in the fountain's wave love holds his court and the insistent water burrows in every delicious crease and crevice?

A pretty sight too was little Rosalie perched like a postilion upon the painted phallus of the god of all gardens. Her eyes were closed and she was smiling as the carriage passed.

The landscape grew rather mysterious. The park no longer troubled and adorned with figures was full of grey echoes and mysterious sounds, the leaves whispered a little sadly and there was a grotto that murmured like the voice that haunts the silence of a deserted oracle. Tannhaüser became a little triste. In the distance through the trees gleamed a still argent lake - a reticent romantic water that must have held the subtlest fish that ever were. Around its marge the terrs and flags and fleurs de luce were unbreakably asleep.

The Chevalier fell into a strange mood as he looked at the lake. It seemed to him that the thing would speak, reveal some curious secret, say some beautiful word ...

... Then he wondered what there might be upon the other side; other gardens, other gods? A thousand drowsy fancies passed though his brain. Sometimes the lake took fantastic shapes or grew to twenty times its size or shrunk into a miniature of itself without ever once losing its unruffled calm, its deathly reserve. When the water increased, the Chevalier was very frightened for he thought how huge the frogs must have become. He thought of their big eyes and monstrous wet feet, but when the water lessened he laughed to himself whilst thinking how tiny the frogs must have grown. He thought of their dwindling legs that must look thinner than spiders' and of their dwindling croaking that never could be heard. Perhaps the lake was only painted after all.

A story by Matteo Bandello, an early 16th century Italian writer, tells of Cassandra, a beautiful young woman who is hired out to lovers by her parents. Then Francesco, a Dominican friar living outside the order and tutor to the grandsons of the Doge of Venice, comes to an arrangement with the parents; he will provide for them lavishly but in return he wants exclusive rights to Cassandra. This is agreed upon. However, a little later the friar is outbid by a Venetian gentleman. Cassandra becomes his mistress and they plot to rid themselves of the troublesome friar. Warned of this by a maidservant, Francesco waits for the plotters. In the ensuing fight, he stabs his rival on the bedroom balcony then mutilates Cassandra. Three days later she dies of her wounds.

There is a theory that this story is based on fact and that the friar was none other than Francesco Colonna, a Dominican from Venice and author of the *Hypnerotomachia Poliphili*, one of the most famous Italian Renaissance texts. The *Hypnerotomachia*, published in 1499, tells of a dream journey undertaken by Poliphilus in pursuit of his beloved Polia. In a surrealistic landscape, he comes across five nymphs who sport with him and take him to their queen, Eleuterilida (Daughter of Freedom) who entertains him with, among other things, a danced game of chess. He is then entrusted to the care of two nymphs, Thelemia (Wish) and Logistica (Reason) who show him around the gardens of their queen. First they visit a glass garden, then a water labyrinth (see pages 83-85), then a garden of silk and precious stones.

Let vs goe a little while to an other garden no lesse pleasant ioyning to the glasse garden, vppon the right side of the Pallas: and when wee were come in thither, I was amazed with excessiue wondering, to see the curiousnesse of the worke, as vneasie to report as vncredibel to beleeue: aequiuolent with that of glasse, wyth lyke disposition of benches or bankes; theyr lyppes set out with coronishing and golden ground worke, and such trees, but that the boxes and Cyprus trees, were all silke, sauing the bodies and greater branches, or the strength of the armes: the rest, as the leaues, flowers, and outermost rynde, was of fine silke, wanting no store of Pearles to beautifie the same: and the perfect fine collour, smelling as the glasse flowers before mentioned, and alike that they about compassing walles, of meruailous and incredibel sumpteousness, were all couered ouer with

a crusting of Pearle, close ioyned and set together: and towardes the toppe,
there sprouted out greene yuie, the leaues thickning and blusing out from
the Pearles, with the stringes and veines of golde, running vppe in diuers
places betwixt the Pearles, in a most rare and curius sort, as if it had beene
very growing yuie, with berries of precious stones sette in the stalkes in
little bunches: and in the bushes were Ringe-doues of silke, as if they beene
feeding of the berries, all along the sides of the square plotted garden
walles: ouer the which, in master-like and requisite order, stretched out
the beame and Zophor of golde.

The plaine smooth of the settles, where-vpon the boxe trees stoode,
couered ouer with Histories of Loue and venerie, in a worke of silke and
threddes of golde and siluer, in suche a perfect proportioned ymaginarie
and counterfaiting as none may goe beyonde. The ground of the leuell
garden was of leaues, grasse, and flowers of silke, like a farie sweete
meddoe: in the midst whereof, there was a large and goodly Arbour, made
with golde wyer, and ouerspread with roses of the lyke worke, more
beautifull to the eye, than if they have been growing roses, vunder which
couering and within which Arbour about the sides, were seates of red
Diaspre, & all the round pauement of a yellow Diaspre, according to the
largenes of the place, with dyuers colloured spottings, confusedly agreeing

*together in pleasant adulterated vniting, and so cleere and shining, that
to euery object was it selfe gaine represented. Vnder the which Arbour,
the fayre and pleasant Thelemia, solaciously sitting downe, tooke her Lute
which she carryed with her, and with a heauenly melodie and vn-hearde
sweetenesse, she began to sing in the commendation and delightes of her
Queene.*

THE DOMAIN OF ARNHEIM

Editor's note: The following extract comes from the pen of Edgar
Allen Poe, a writer much admired by the Decadents. It would be
interesting to know how much Gray and Lucan's thinking about
gardens was inspired by this tale. In *The Domain of Arnheim*, the
narrator tells the story of his friend, Mr Ellison. Ellison, although
wealthy in his own right, had come into an inheritance, to the tune
of four hundred and fifty millions dollars. Ellison was 'in the
widest and noblest sense, a poet' whose inclination was towards
'novel forms of beauty'. In fact he believed that the 'sole legitimate
field for the poetic exercise lies in the creation of novel moods of
purely *physical* loveliness'. It therefore followed that he should be
attracted to landscape gardening. In fact, this seemed to him a
perfect and unjustly neglected arena for poetic expression.

Over several pages, the gardener/poet explains the theory
behind his project. In choosing between the natural and the
artificial approach to gardening, Ellison comes down clearly on
the side of the artificial. 'The original beauty is never so great as
that which may be introduced' and 'a mixture of pure art in a
garden scene adds to it a great beauty.' In fact, the sort of garden
Ellison is after exists somewhere between the human and the
divine. 'Let us imagine a landscape whose combined vastness and
definitiveness - whose united beauty, magnificence, and
strangeness shall convey the idea of care, or culture on the part of
human beings superior, yet akin to humanity.' In other words,
Ellison's ideal is a garden that could have been built by angels.
After the theory came the practice -

Mr. Ellison's first step regarded, of course, the choice of locality; and scarcely had he commenced thinking on this point, when the luxuriant nature of the Pacific Islands arrested his attention. In fact, he had made up his mind for a voyage to the South Seas, when a night's reflection induced him to abandon the idea. "Were I misanthropic," he said "such a locale would suit me. The thoroughness of its insulation and seclusion, and the difficulty of ingress and egress, would in such case be the charm of charms; but as yet I am not Timon. I wish the composure but not the depression of solitude. There must remain with me a certain control over the extent and duration of my repose. There will be frequent hours in which I shall need, too, the sympathy of the poetic in what I have done. Let me seek, then, a spot not far from a populous city - whose vicinity also will best enable me to execute my plans."

In search of a suitable place so situated, Ellison travelled for several years, and I was permitted to accompany him. A thousand spots with which I was enraptured he rejected without hesitation, for reasons which satisfied me, in the end, that he was right.

* * *

It was not until towards the close of the fourth year of our search that we found a locality with which Ellison professed himself satisfied. It is, of course, needless to say where was the locality. The late death of my friend, in causing his domain to be thrown open to certain classes of visitors, has given to Arnheim a species of secret and subdued if not solemn celebrity, similar in kind, although infinitely superior in degree, to that which so long distinguished Fonthill.

The usual approach to Arnheim was by the river. The visitor left the city in the early morning. During the forenoon he passed between shores of a tranquil and domestic beauty, on which grazed innumerable sheep, their white fleeces spotting the vivid green of rolling meadows. By degrees the idea of cultivation subsided into that of merely pastoral care. This slowly became merged in a sense of retirement - this again in a consciousness of solitude. As the evening approached, the channel grew more narrow; the banks more and more precipitous; and these later were clothed in richer, more profuse, and more sombre foliage. The water increased in transparency. The stream took a thousand turns, so that at no moment could its gleaming surface be seen for a greater distance than a furlong. At every instant the vessel seemed imprisoned within an enchanted circle, having insuperable and impenetrable walls of foliage, a roof of ultra-marine satin, and no floor - the keel balancing itself with admirable nicety on that of a phantom bark which, by some accident having been turned upside down, floated in constant company with the substantial one, for the purpose of sustaining it ...

The walls of the ravine (through which the clear water still tranquilly flowed) arose to an elevation of a hundred and occasionally of a hundred and fifty feet, and inclined so much towards each other as, in a great measure, to shut out the light of day; while the long plume-like moss which depended densely from the intertwining shrubberies overhead, gave the whole chasm an air of funeral gloom. The windings became more frequent and intricate, and seemed often as if returning in upon themselves, so that the voyager had long lost all idea of direction. He was, moreover, enwrapt in an exquisite sense of the strange. The thought of nature still remained, but her character seemed to have undergone modification; there was a weird symmetry, a thrilling uniformity, a wizard propriety in these her works. Not a dead branch - not a withered leaf - not a stray pebble - not a patch of the brown earth was anywhere visible. The crystal water welled up against the clean granite, on the unblemished moss, with a sharpness of outline that delighted while it bewildered the eye.

Having threaded the mazes of this channel for some hours, the gloom deepening every moment, a sharp and unexpected turn of the vessel brought it suddenly, as if dropped from heaven, into a circular basin of very considerable extent when compared with the width of the gorge. It was about two hundred yards in diameter, and girt in at all points but one - that immediately fronting the vessel as it entered - by hills equal in general height to the walls of the chasm, although of a thoroughly different character. Their sides sloped from the water's edge at an angle of some forty-five degrees, and they were clothed from base to summit - not a perceptible point escaping - in a drapery of the most gorgeous flower-blossoms; scarcely a green leaf being visible among the sea of odorous and fluctuating color. This basin was of great depth, but so transparent was the water that the bottom, which seemed to consist of a thick mass of small round alabaster pebbles, was distinctly visible by glimpses - that is to say, whenever the eye could permit itself not to see, far down in the inverted heaven, the duplicate blooming of the hills. On these latter there were no trees, nor even shrubs of any size. The impressions wrought on the observer were those of richness, voluptuousness and a miraculous extremeness of culture that suggested dreams of a new race of fairies, laborious, tasteful, magnificent, and fastidious; but as the eye traced upwards the myriad-tinted slope, from its sharp junction with the water to its vague termination amid the folds of over-hanging cloud, it became, indeed, difficult not to fancy a panoramic cataract of rubies, sapphires, opals and golden onyxes, rolling silently out of the sky.

The visitor, shooting suddenly into this bay from out of the gloom of the ravine, is delighted but astounded by the full orb of the declining sun, which he had supposed to be already far below the horizon, but which now confronts him, and forms the sole termination of the otherwise limitless vista seen through another chasm-like rift in the hills.

But here the voyager quits the vessel which has borne him so far, and descends into a light canoe of ivory, stained with arabesque devices in vivid scarlet, both within and without. The poop and beak of this boat arise high above the water, with sharp points, so that the general form is that of an irregular crescent. It lies on the surface of the bay with the proud grace of a swan. On its ermined floor reposes a single feathery paddle of satin-wood; but no oarsman or attendant is to be seen. The guest is bidden to be of good cheer - that the fates will take care of him. The larger vessel disappears, and he is left alone in the canoe, which lies apparently motionless in the middle of the lake. While he considers what course to pursue, however, he becomes aware of a gentle movement in the fairy bark. It slowly swings itself around until its prow points towards the sun. It advances with a gentle but gradual accelerated velocity, while the slight ripples it creates seem to break about the ivory sides in divinest melody - seem to offer the only possible explanation of the soothing yet melancholy music for whose unseen origin the bewildered voyager looks around him in vain.

The canoe steadily proceeds, and the rocky gate of the vista is approached, so that its depths can be more distinctly seen. To the right arise a chain of lofty hills rudely and luxuriantly wooded. It is observed, however, that the trait of exquisite cleanness where the bank dips into the water, still prevails. There is not one token of the usual river debris. To the left the character of the scene is softer and more obviously artificial. Here the bank slopes upwards from the stream in a very gentle ascent, forming a broad sward of grass of a texture resembling nothing so much as velvet, and of a brilliancy of green which would bear comparison with the tint of the purest emerald. This plateau varies in width from ten to three hundred yards; reaching from the river bank to a wall, fifty feet high, which extends, in an infinity of curves, but following the general direction of the river, until lost in the distance to the westwards. This wall is one continuous rock, and has been formed by cutting perpendicularly the once rugged precipice of the stream's southern bank; but no trace of the labor has been suffered to remain. The chiselled stone has the hue of ages and is profusely overhung and overspread with the ivy, the coral honeysuckle, the eglantine, and the clematis. The uniformity of the top and bottom lines of the wall is fully relieved by occasional trees of gigantic height, growing singly or in small groups, both along the plateau and in the domain behind the wall, but in close proximity to it; so that frequent limbs (of black walnut especially) reach over and dip their pendent extremities into the water. Farther back within the domain, the vision is impeded by an impenetrable screen of foliage.

These things are observed during the canoe's gradual approach to what I have called the fate of the vista. On drawing nearer to this, however, its chasm-like appearance vanishes; a new outlet from the bay is discovered to the left - in which direction the wall is also seen to sweep, still following the general course of the stream. Down this new opening the eye cannot penetrate very far, for the stream, accompanied by the wall, still bends to the left, until both are swallowed up by the leaves.

The boat, nevertheless, glides magically into the winding channel... Lofty hills, rising occasionally into mountains, and covered with vegetation in wild luxuriance, still shut in the scene.

Floating gently onwards, but with a velocity slightly augmented, the voyager, after many short turns, finds his progress apparently barred by a gigantic gate or rather door of burnished gold, elaborately carved and fretted, and reflecting the direct rays of the now fast-sinking sun with an effulgence that seems to wreath the whole surrounding forest in flames. This gate is inserted in the lofty wall; which here appears to cross the river at right angles. In a few moments, however, it is seen that the main body of the water still sweeps in a gentle and extensive curve to the left, the wall following it as before, while a stream of considerable volume, diverging from the principal one, makes its way, with a slight ripple, under the door, and is thus hidden from sight. The canoe falls into the lesser channel and approaches the gate. Its ponderous wings are slowly and musically expanded. The boat glides between them, and commences a rapid descent into a vast amphitheatre entirely begirt with purple *mountains, whose bases are laved by a gleaming river throughout the full extent of their circuit. Meantime the whole Paradise of Arnheim bursts upon the view. There is a gush of entrancing melody, there is an oppressive sense of strange sweet odor; - there is a dream-like intermingling to the eye of tall slender Eastern trees - bosky shrubberies - flocks of golden and crimson birds - lily-fringed lakes - meadows of violets, tulips, poppies, hyacinths and tuberoses - long intertangled lines of silver streamlets - and, upspringing confusedly from amid all, a mass of semi-Gothic, semi-Saracenic architecture, sustaining itself as if by miracle in mid air; glittering in the red sunlight with a hundred oriels, minarets, and pinnacles; and seeming the phantom handiwork, conjointly, of the Slyphs, of the Fairies, of the Genii, and of the Gnomes.*

THE AUTHORS

By the time their *Decadent Cookbook* was published in 1995, Medlar Lucan and Durian Gray had vanished into mysterious exile. They reappeared in Ireland, where their labours as garden-designers for Mrs Conchita Gordon have borne fruit in their second book, *The Decadent Gardener*. Mrs Gordon has described them as 'a very odd couple indeed'. They have described themselves as 'collectors, aesthetes, gastronomes, scene-painters, lovers, exhibitionists, and jewelled worshippers at the Temple of Extreme' - a list to which must now be added, albeit cautiously, the term 'gardeners'. Since writing *The Decadent Gardener* they have once again disappeared, leaving no clues as to their whereabouts - only a faint odour of cigar-smoke, eau de vétyver, and bruised orchids.

THE EDITORS

ALEX MARTIN

Alex Martin has published four children's novels and is the editor (with Robert Hill) of the four-volume Prentice Hall *Introductions to Modern English Literature*. His novel *The General Interruptor* introduced the world to Victor Ubriakov's lost imaginary masterpiece *La Cuisine érotique* (St Petersburg, 1888).

JEROME FLETCHER

Jerome Fletcher, former real tennis professional and elver catcher, is the author of two children's novels - *Alfreda Abbot's Lost Voice* and *Escape from the Temple of Laughter* - and a book of poems - *A Gerbil in the Hoover*. He teaches and translates French and Spanish, works with Big Wheel - a Theatre-in-Education group - and collaborates with an installation artist on a large-scale museum project entitled *Divers Memories*. At present he is working on a second book of children's poems - *The Broken Joke* - and a third novel - *Mr Fish and the Ship of Fools*. He is also co-authoring two film scripts.

FRANÇOIS HOUTIN

Having started his career as a designer of real gardens, François Houtin decided in true Decadent spirit that the realm of the imaginary was more appealing. He has built a major reputation with his drawings and engravings of imaginary gardens which have been exhibited in Paris, Brussels, Rome, Hamburg, Saarbrücken, Geneva and New York. He was awarded the Prix de Gravure Lacourière in 1981 and the Prix Gravure Florence Gould in 1986. His engravings have also been published in a series of limited-edition books (*Vie Folle, Folle Vie, Débile*, 1976; *Désirs, Délices, Délires*, and *Jardins*, 1978; *Topiaire*, 1979; *La fille de Rappaccini*, 1980; *Cinq Jardins, Cinq Sens*, 1982; *Fantaisies Romaines*, 1985; *Les Quatre Éléments ou la Fête à Versailles*, 1988). In Britain, François Houtin's works can be seen at the Francis Kyle Gallery in London.

The works by François Houtin reproduced here are:

Acknowledgments

The editors would like to thank the following for their kind help: Julian Bingley, Anna Braioni, Gianna Braioni, Barrie Bullen, Roderick Conway Morris, Christine Donougher, Gregory Dowling, the Fondazione Benetton, Robert Hill, François Houtin, Nicola Kennedy, Francis Kyle, Dr. David Lambert of the Garden History Society, Donna Leon, William and Ione Martin, Oxford University Botanical Gardens, Horti Praefectus, Katinka Pree, Vera Ryhajlo, Robert Stoney, Clova Stuart-Hamilton, and Roma Tearne, Timothy Walker, Charlotte Ward-Perkins.

They would like to express their particulat thanks to Pierre Higonnet of the Galleria del Leone, Venice, and to Galerie Michèle Broutta, Paris, for introducing them to the works of François Houtin.

The editors would also like to thank Gwyn Headley for permission to quote from *Follies, A Guide to Rogue Architecture in England, Scotland and Wales* by Gwyn Headley & Wim Meulenkamp (Jonathan Cape, London 1986); and Éditions Gallimard, Paris, for permission to reproduce *Sept jardins fantastiques* by André Pieyre de Mandiargues.

THE DECADENT COOKBOOK
by Lucan Medlar & Durian Gray
edited by Alex Martin & Jerome Fletcher

BOOK OF THE YEAR CHOICE FOR:
Nigella Lawson in *The Times*
& John Bayley in *The Standard.*

"There should be something here to delight and offend everyone: the recipes for cooking with endangered species looking particularly tasty. Mouthwatering."

Phil Baker in The Sunday Times.

" The putative authors are Medlar Lucan and Durian Gray, a bit of a tip-off: the medlar is a small, brown fruit, eaten when decayed; the durian fruit tastes goods but smells like sewage. These two coves left editors Alex Martin and Jerome Fletcher to tidy up this compendium of hideous repasts, taboo-busting banquets, and surprisingly sensible fare, accompanied by passages from decadent literature: menus courtesy of the Marquis de Sade, J.K.Huysmans, King George IV, the Grand Inquisitor and other gluttons."

The Independent on Sunday

"Not just fun but useful, containing workable recipes for Panda Paw Casserole, Cat in Tomato Sauce, and Dog à la Beti ("prior to being killed, the dog should be tied to a post for a day and hit with smallsticks, to shift the fat in the adipose tissue"), myriad blood sausages recipes, a recipe for aye-aye, of which some 20 remain in the wild, and stories by Louis de Bernières, Huysmans, inevitably, and Charles Lamb on sucking pig. Not, as you will have gathered, for the squeamish."

Nicholas Lezard in The Guardian

"Fancy boiled ostrich? Cat in tomato sauce? Or virgin's breasts? The droll compilers trawl ancient Rome and other OTT times for kitchen oddities, mixed with literary off-cuts and pungent commentary. Delia Smith it ain't".

New Statesman & Society

"a fabulous and shocking assemblage."
Christopher Hirst in The Independent

"I point blank refuse to eat Virgin's Breasts"
Sean Hughes in the Observer

"If meat is the hard-core of food-as-sex, *The Decadent Cookbook* is a walk on the wild side, a book for those who scorn not only the Prohibitions of Leviticus but also the dictates of common sense, good health and kindness to animals."
John Ryle's City of Words Column in The Guardian

"Get these Decadent boys out of my kitchen."
Katie Puckrick on Granada Television's Pyjama Party

"A scholarly work, cleverly disguised as a very amusing read, from Medlar Lucan and Durian Gray. 223 pages of about every kind of weird or simply repugnant food from the Romans to the 19th Century, with intriguing recipes for boiled ostrich, roast testicles, boneless frog soup and other obscure delicacies. There's even a whole section on cooking with blood. The perfect gift for posh friends: it is the kind of book they always have in their loo."
Attitude Magazine

"Forget Prue Leith and Delia Smith, the cookery manual that every Venue reader needs is *The Decadent Cookbook*. If your palate is a little jaded, if you thought you'd tried everything, then this is the book to make your smart dinner parties go bang (and several yechs!). The pseudonymous authors have trawled through the world's great works of history and literature to assemble a truly sumptuous feast of decadent dishes and ghastly gastronomy."
Eugene Byrne in Venue

"An extravagant , shameless and highly entertaining book that could change the course of contemporary cuisine."
The International Cookbook Review

£8.99 ISBN 1 873982 22 4